sam sykes · selina espiritu · sarah stern

BRAVE CHEF BRIANNA ™

D0601091

kaboom!™

ROSS RICHIE .... CEO & Founder
MATT GAGNON .... Editor-in-Chief
FILIP SABLIK .... President of Publishing & Marketing
STEPHEN CHRISTY .... President of Development
LANCE KREITER .... VP of Licensing & Merchandising
PHIL BARBARO .... VP of Finance
ARUNE SINGH .... VP of Marketing
BRYCE CARLSON .... Managing Editor
MEL CAYLO .... Marketing Manager
SCOTT NEWMAN .... Production Design Manager
KATE HENNING .... Operations Manager

SIERRA HAHN .... Senior Editor
DAFNA PLEBAN .... Editor, Talent Development
SHANNON WATTERS .... Editor
ERIC HARBURN .... Editor
WHITNEY LEOPARD .... Editor
JASMINE AMIRI .... Editor
CHRIS ROSA .... Associate Editor
ALEX GALER .... Associate Editor
CAMERON CHITTOCK .... Associate Editor
MATTHEW LEVINE .... Assistant Editor
SOPHIE PHILIPS-ROBERTS .... Assistant Editor

JILLIAN CRAB .... Production Designer
MICHELLE ANKLEY .... Production Designer
KARA LEOPARD .... Production Designer
GRACE PARK .... Production Design Assistant
ELIZABETH LOUGHRIDGE .... Accounting Coordinator
STEPHANIE HOCUTT .... Social Media Coordinator
JOSÉ MEZA .... Event Coordinator
HOLLY AITCHISON .... Operations Assistant
MEGAN CHRISTOPHER .... Operations Assistant
MORGAN PERRY .... Direct Market Reprsentative

WWW.BOOM-STUDIOS.COM

BRAVE CHEF BRIANNA, December 2017. Published by KaBOOM!, a division of Boom Entertainment, Inc. Brave Chef Brianna is ™ & © 2017 Sam Sykes. Originally published in single magazine form as BRAVE CHEF BRIANNA No. 1-4. ™ & © 2017 Sam Sykes. All rights reserved. KaBOOM!™ and the KaBOOM! logo are trademarks of Boom Entertainment, Inc, registered in various countries and categories. All characters, events, and institutions depicted herein are fictional. Any similarity between any of the names, characters, persons, events, and/or institutions in this publication to actual names, characters, and persons, whether living or dead, events, and/or institutions is unintended and purely coincidental. KaBOOM! does not read or accept unsolicited submissions of ideas, stories, or artwork.

BOOM! Studios, 5670 Wilshire Boulevard, Suite 450, Los Angeles, CA 90036-5679. Printed in China. First Printing.

ISBN: 978-1-68415-050-2, eISBN: 978-1-61398-727-8

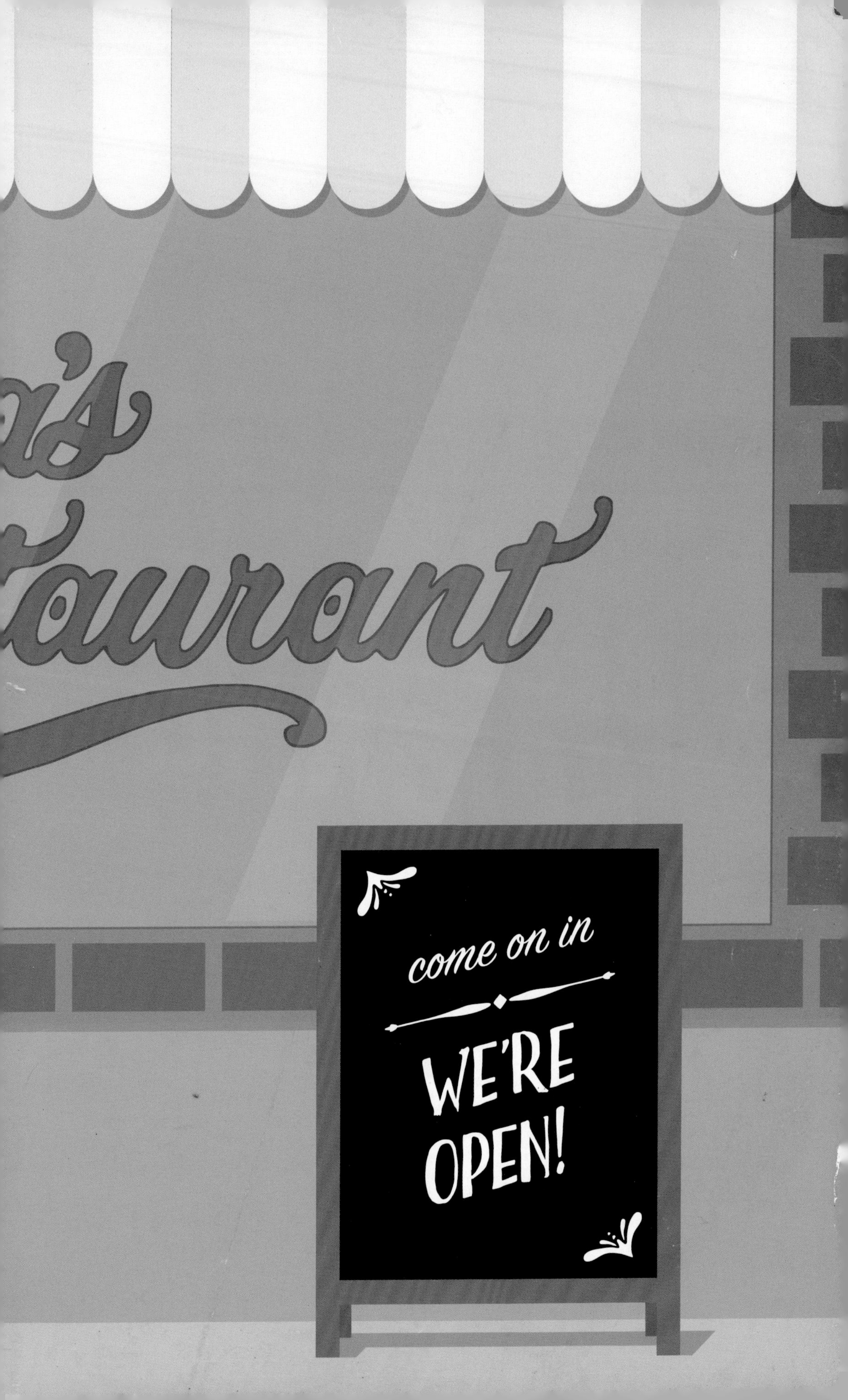
come on in
WE'RE
OPEN!

BRAVE CHEF BRIANNA™

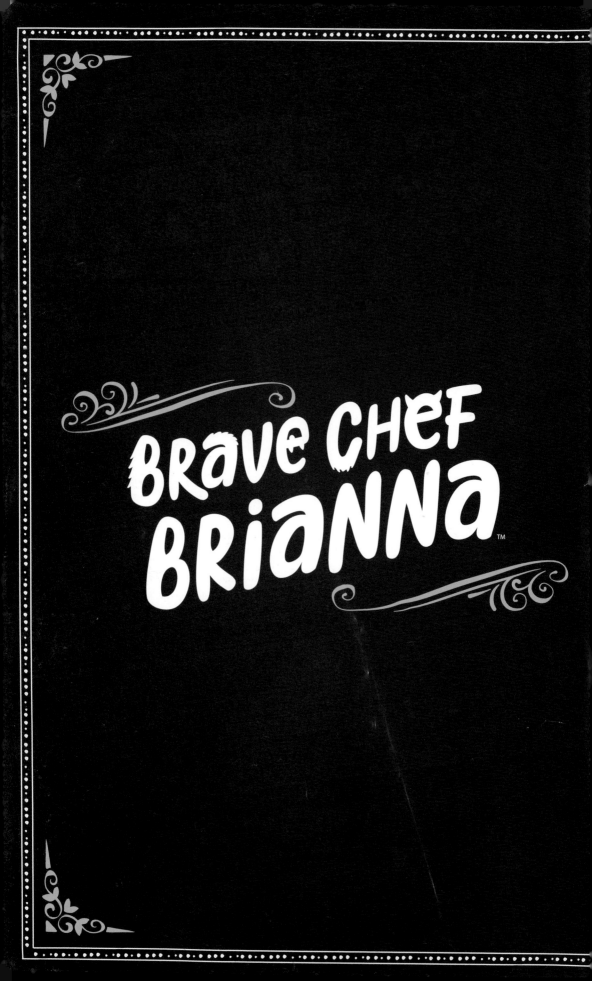

created & written by
SAM SYKES

illustrated by
SELINA ESPIRITU

colored by
SARAH STERN

lettered by
JIM CAMPBELL

cover by
BRIDGET UNDERWOOD

recipes by
STEPHANIE GOLDFARB

designer
JILLIAN CRAB

editor
JASMINE AMIRI

Daily Specials

BRAZILIAN CHEESE WAFFLE BREAKFAST SANDWICHES

BÁNH XÈO - SAVORY VIETNAMESE CRÊPES

BUFFALO CHICKEN TATER TOT CASSEROLE

CALAMARI SUSHI

chapter
ONE

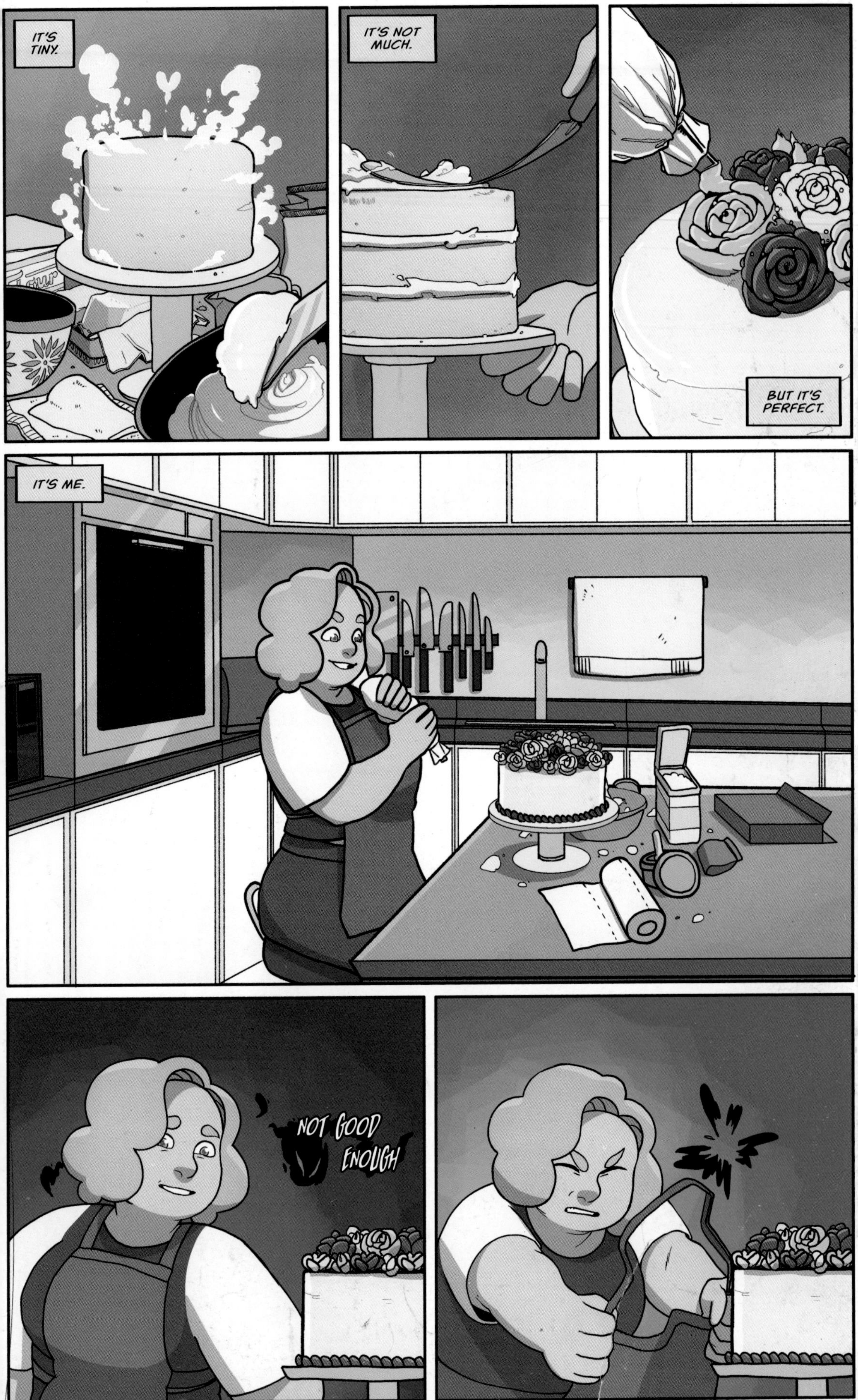
IT'S TINY.
IT'S NOT MUCH.
BUT IT'S PERFECT.
IT'S ME.
NOT GOOD ENOUGH

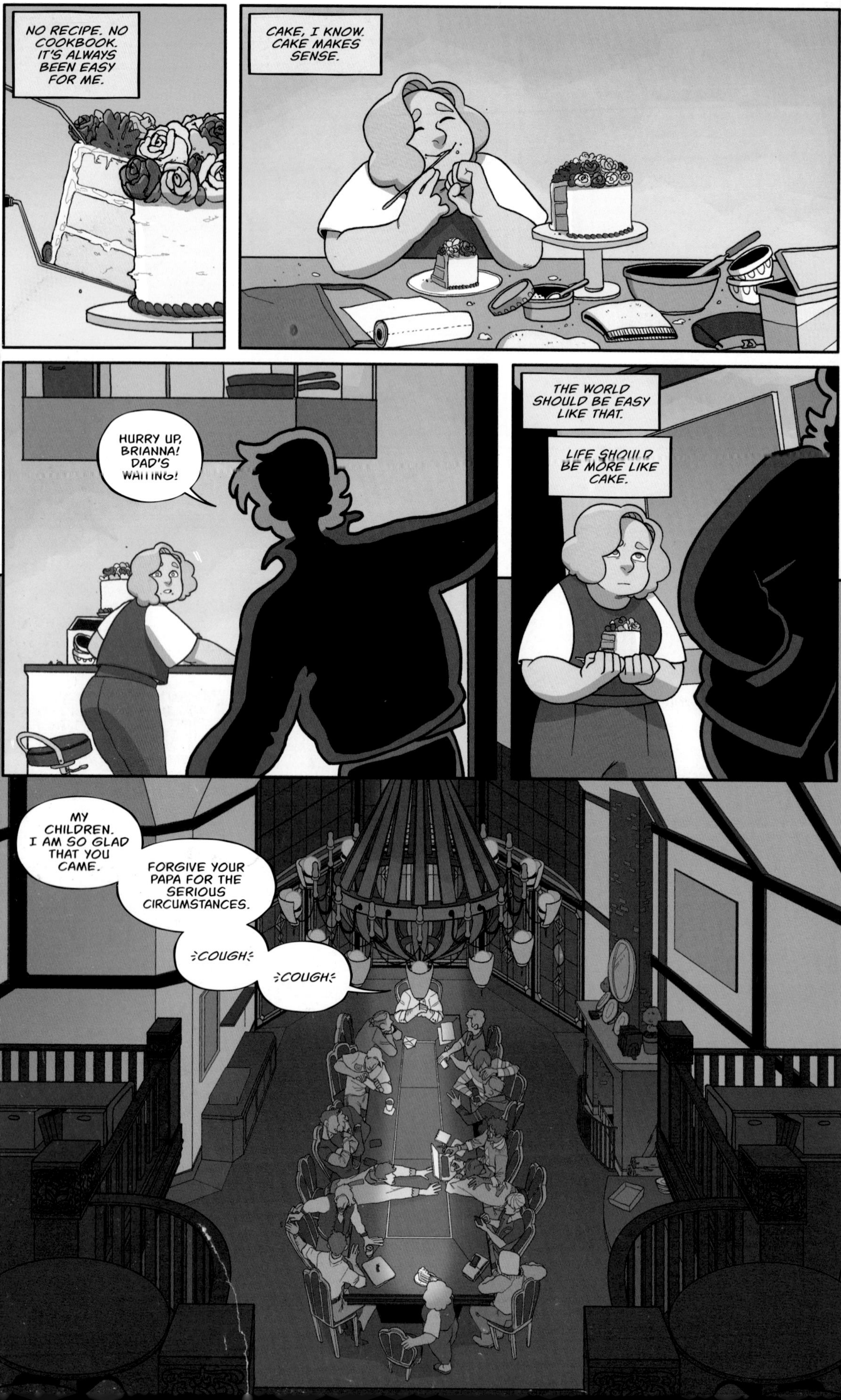
NO RECIPE. NO COOKBOOK. IT'S ALWAYS BEEN EASY FOR ME.
CAKE, I KNOW. CAKE MAKES SENSE.
HURRY UP, BRIANNA! DAD'S WAITING!
THE WORLD SHOULD BE EASY LIKE THAT.
LIFE SHOULD BE MORE LIKE CAKE.
MY CHILDREN. I AM SO GLAD THAT YOU CAME.
FORGIVE YOUR PAPA FOR THE SERIOUS CIRCUMSTANCES.
COUGH
COUGH

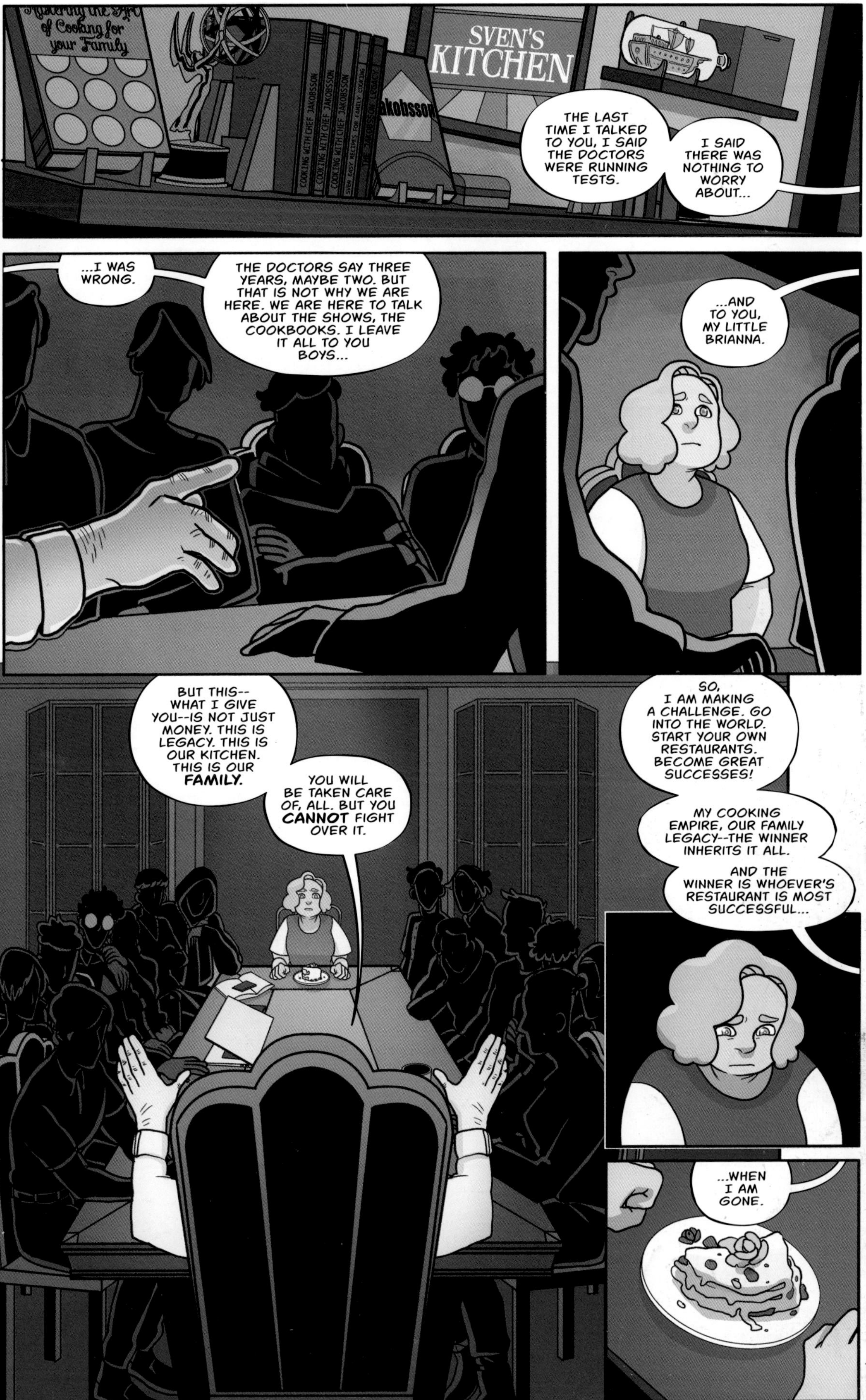
of Cooking for your Family
COOKING WITH CHEF JAKOBSSON
COOKING WITH CHEF JAKOBSSON
COOKING WITH CHEF JAKOBSSON
SVEN EASY RECIPES FOR FAMILY COOKING
THE JAKOBSSON LEGACY
SVEN'S KITCHEN
THE LAST TIME I TALKED TO YOU, I SAID THE DOCTORS WERE RUNNING TESTS.
I SAID THERE WAS NOTHING TO WORRY ABOUT...
...I WAS WRONG.
THE DOCTORS SAY THREE YEARS, MAYBE TWO. BUT THAT IS NOT WHY WE ARE HERE. WE ARE HERE TO TALK ABOUT THE SHOWS, THE COOKBOOKS. I LEAVE IT ALL TO YOU BOYS...
...AND TO YOU, MY LITTLE BRIANNA.
BUT THIS--WHAT I GIVE YOU--IS NOT JUST MONEY. THIS IS LEGACY. THIS IS OUR KITCHEN. THIS IS OUR **FAMILY.**
YOU WILL BE TAKEN CARE OF, ALL. BUT YOU **CANNOT** FIGHT OVER IT.
SO, I AM MAKING A CHALLENGE. GO INTO THE WORLD. START YOUR OWN RESTAURANTS. BECOME GREAT SUCCESSES!
MY COOKING EMPIRE, OUR FAMILY LEGACY--THE WINNER INHERITS IT ALL.
AND THE WINNER IS WHOEVER'S RESTAURANT IS MOST SUCCESSFUL...
...WHEN I AM GONE.

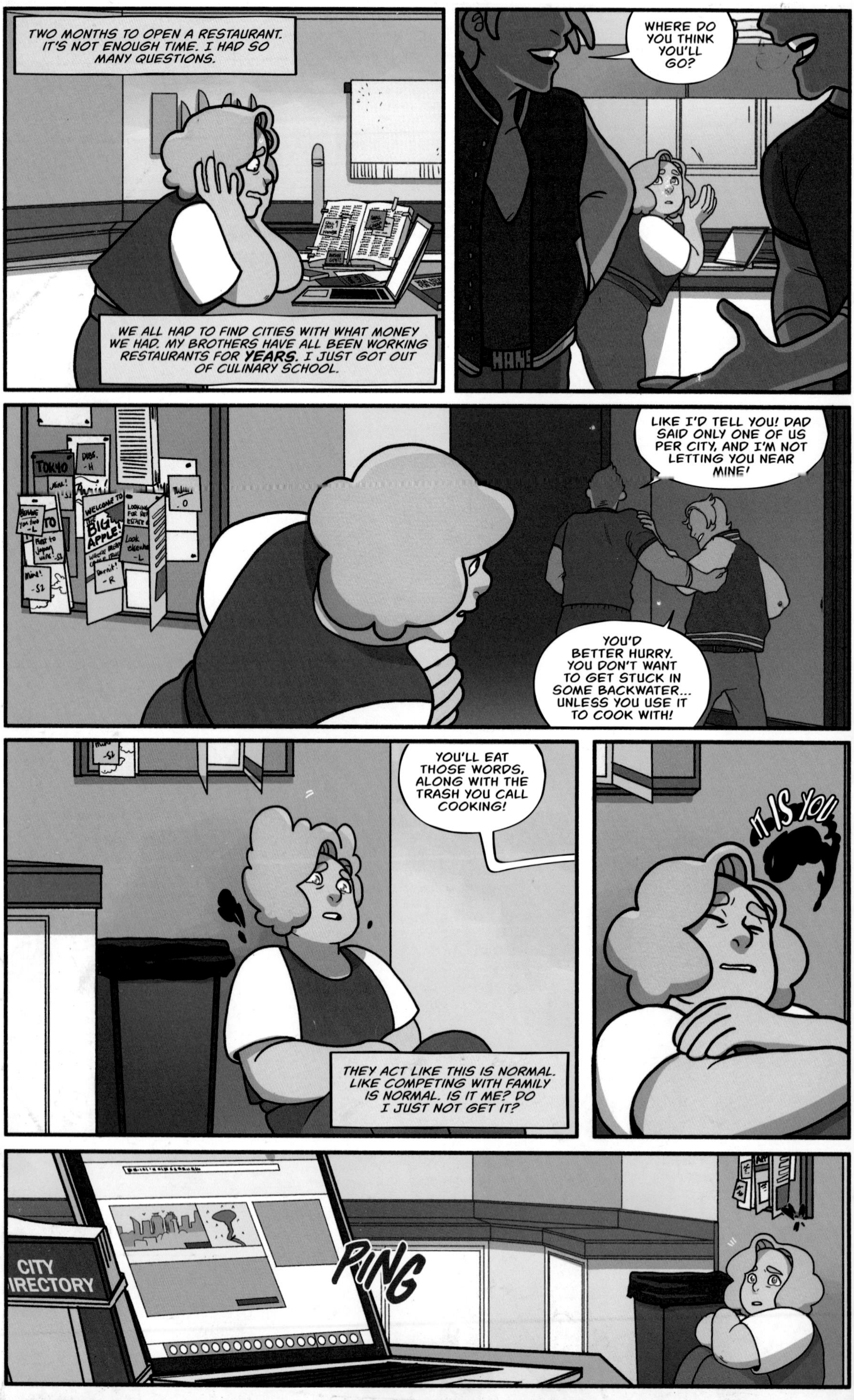
TWO MONTHS TO OPEN A RESTAURANT. IT'S NOT ENOUGH TIME. I HAD SO MANY QUESTIONS.
WE ALL HAD TO FIND CITIES WITH WHAT MONEY WE HAD. MY BROTHERS HAVE ALL BEEN WORKING RESTAURANTS FOR **YEARS.** I JUST GOT OUT OF CULINARY SCHOOL.
WHERE DO YOU THINK YOU'LL GO?
TOKYO
BIG APPLE!
LIKE I'D TELL YOU! DAD SAID ONLY ONE OF US PER CITY, AND I'M NOT LETTING YOU NEAR MINE!
YOU'D BETTER HURRY. YOU DON'T WANT TO GET STUCK IN SOME BACKWATER... UNLESS YOU USE IT TO COOK WITH!
YOU'LL EAT THOSE WORDS, ALONG WITH THE TRASH YOU CALL COOKING!
THEY ACT LIKE THIS IS NORMAL. LIKE COMPETING WITH FAMILY IS NORMAL. IS IT ME? DO I JUST NOT GET IT?
IT IS YOU
CITY DIRECTORY
PING

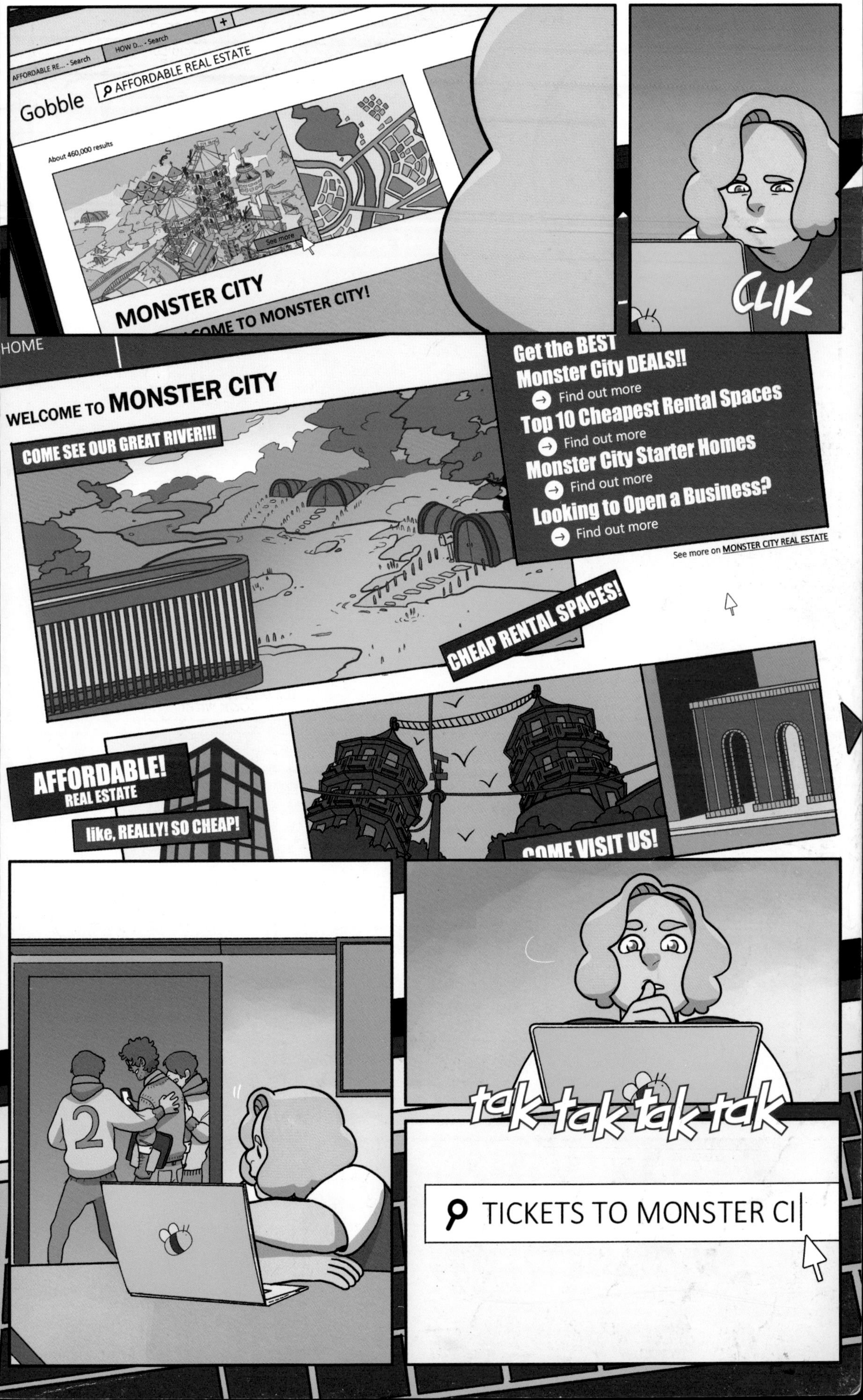
AFFORDABLE RE... - Search
HOW D... - Search
Gobble
AFFORDABLE REAL ESTATE
About 460,000 results
See more
MONSTER CITY
WELCOME TO MONSTER CITY!
CLIK
HOME
WELCOME TO MONSTER CITY
COME SEE OUR GREAT RIVER!!!
Get the BEST
Monster City DEALS!!
Find out more
Top 10 Cheapest Rental Spaces
Find out more
Monster City Starter Homes
Find out more
Looking to Open a Business?
Find out more
See more on MONSTER CITY REAL ESTATE
CHEAP RENTAL SPACES!
AFFORDABLE!
REAL ESTATE
like, REALLY! SO CHEAP!
COME VISIT US!
tak tak tak tak
TICKETS TO MONSTER CI

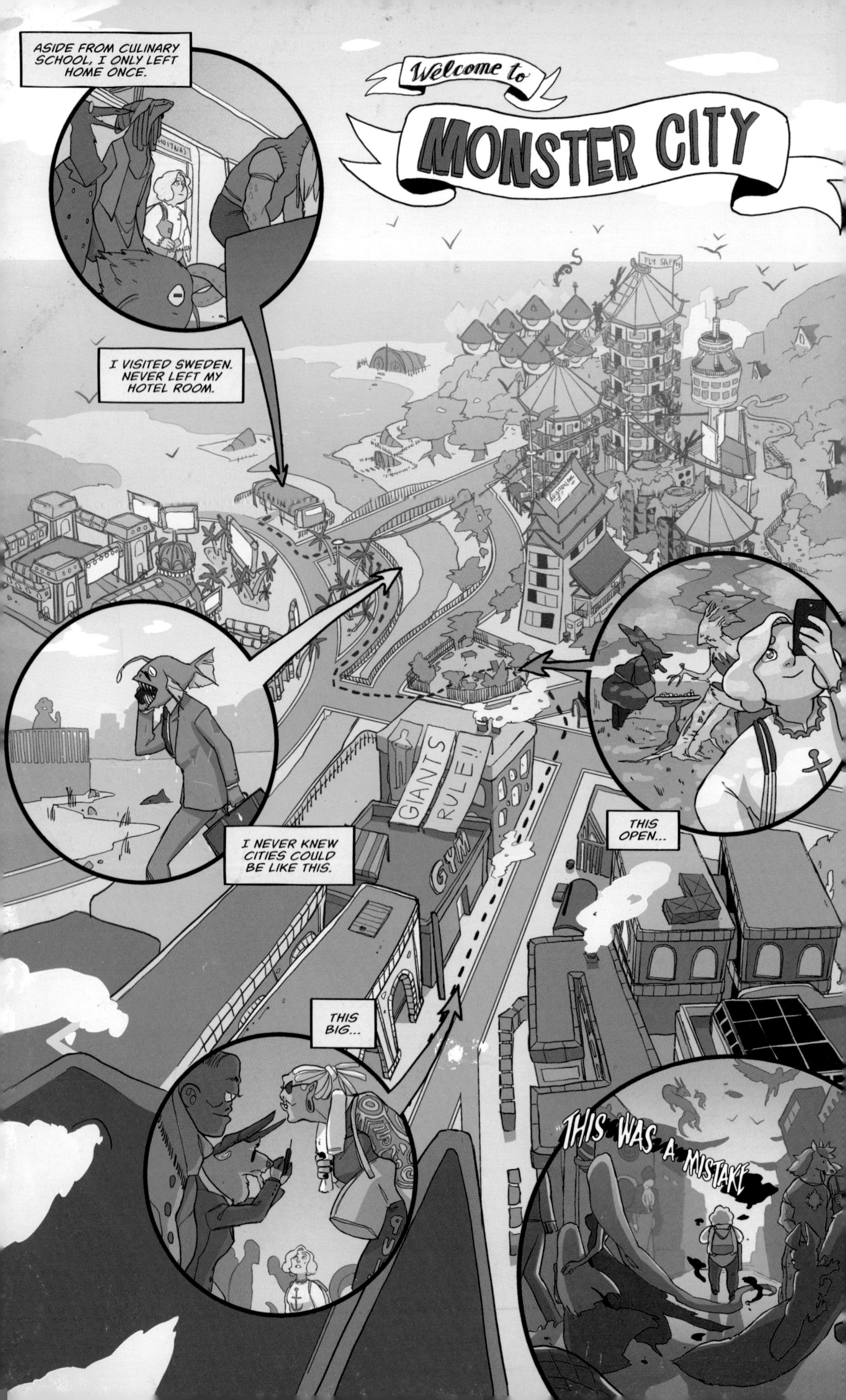
ASIDE FROM CULINARY SCHOOL, I ONLY LEFT HOME ONCE.
Welcome to
MONSTER CITY
I VISITED SWEDEN. NEVER LEFT MY HOTEL ROOM.
I NEVER KNEW CITIES COULD BE LIKE THIS.
GIANTS RULE!!
GYM
THIS OPEN...
THIS BIG...
THIS WAS A MISTAKE

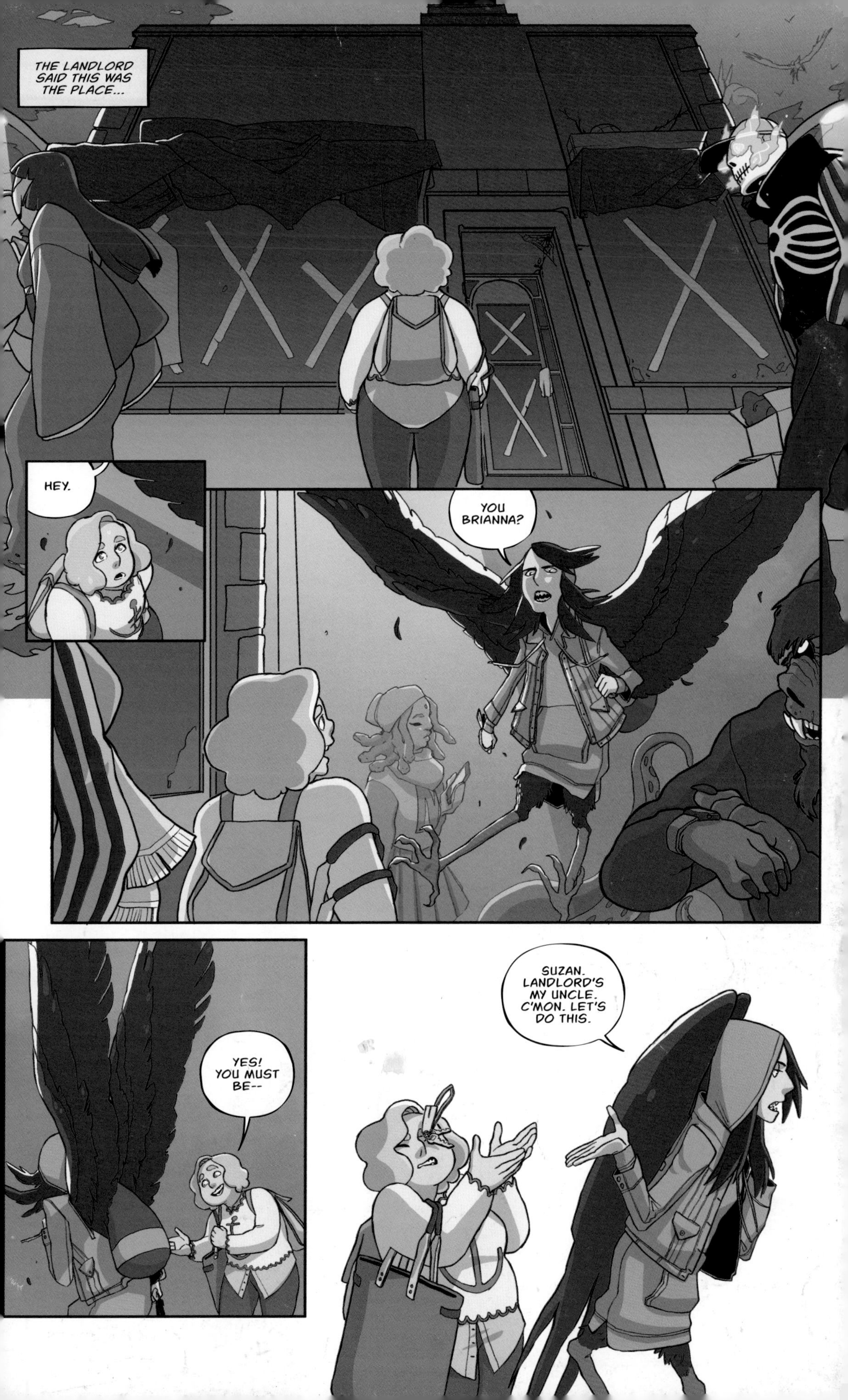
THE LANDLORD SAID THIS WAS THE PLACE...
HEY.
YOU BRIANNA?
YES! YOU MUST BE--
SUZAN. LANDLORD'S MY UNCLE. C'MON. LET'S DO THIS.

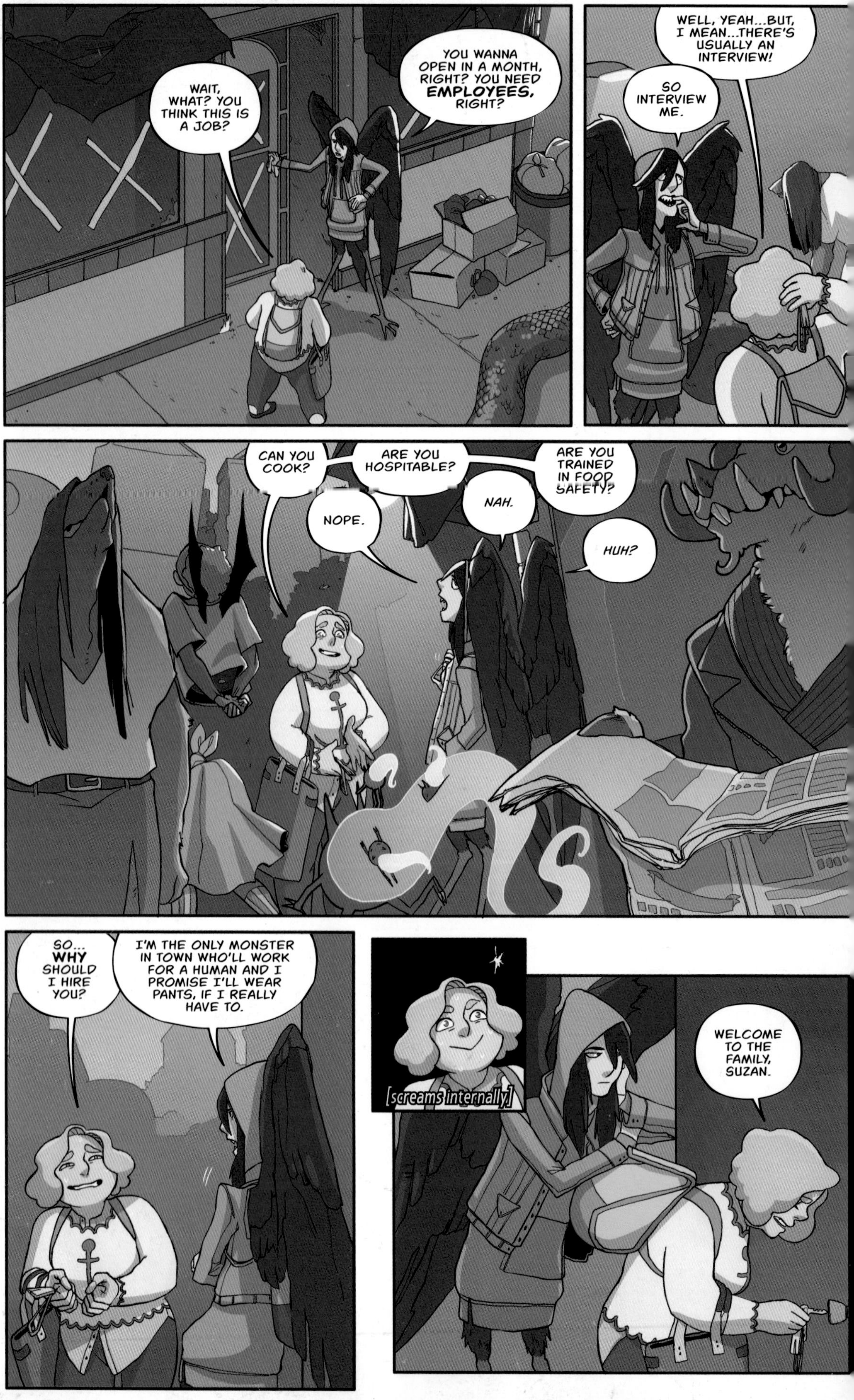
WAIT, WHAT? YOU THINK THIS IS A JOB?
YOU WANNA OPEN IN A MONTH, RIGHT? YOU NEED **EMPLOYEES,** RIGHT?
WELL, YEAH...BUT, I MEAN...THERE'S USUALLY AN INTERVIEW!
SO INTERVIEW ME.
CAN YOU COOK?
NOPE.
ARE YOU HOSPITABLE?
NAH.
ARE YOU TRAINED IN FOOD SAFETY?
HUH?
SO... **WHY** SHOULD I HIRE YOU?
I'M THE ONLY MONSTER IN TOWN WHO'LL WORK FOR A HUMAN AND I PROMISE I'LL WEAR PANTS, IF I REALLY HAVE TO.
[screams internally]
WELCOME TO THE FAMILY, SUZAN.

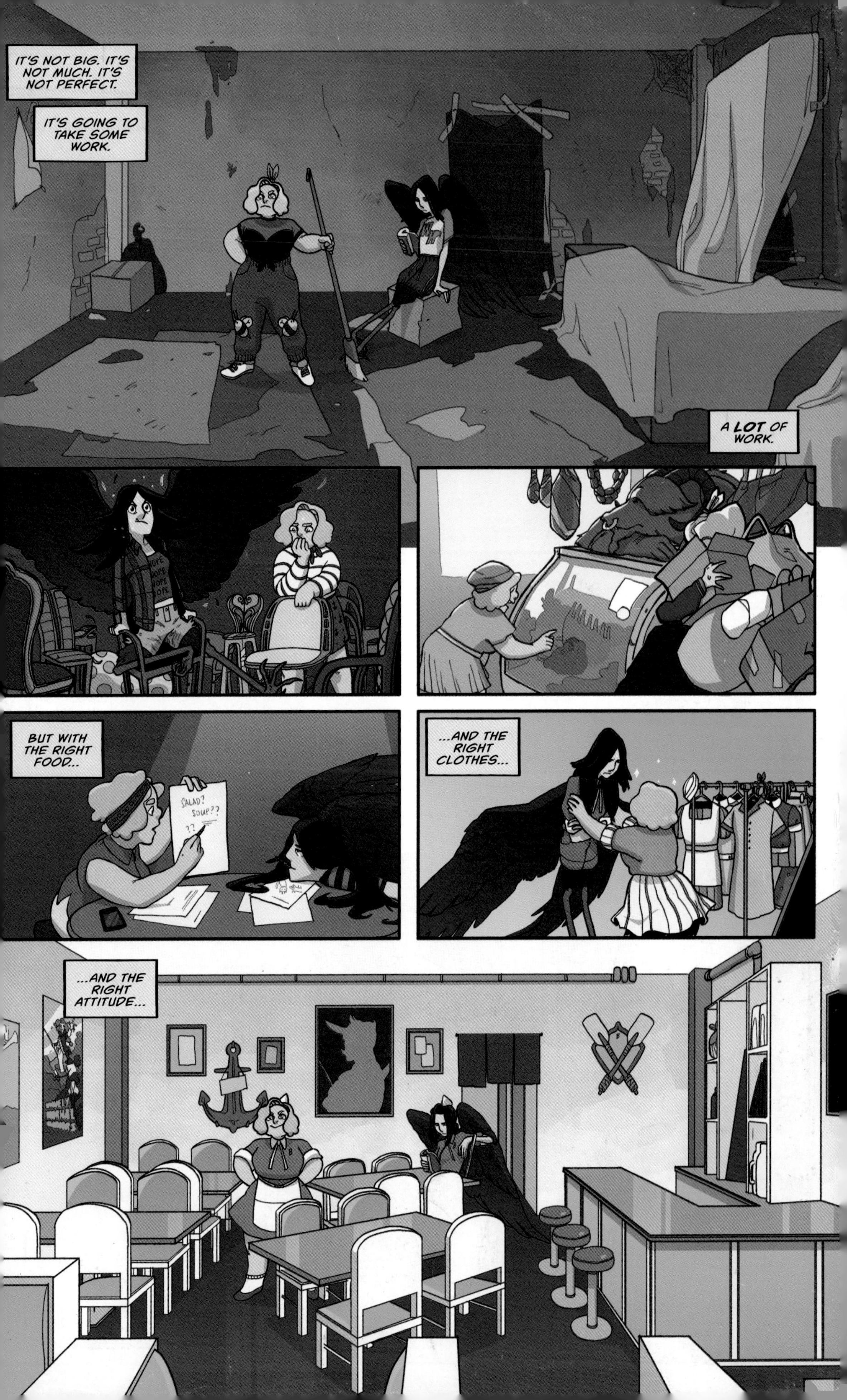
IT'S NOT BIG. IT'S NOT MUCH. IT'S NOT PERFECT.
IT'S GOING TO TAKE SOME WORK.
A LOT OF WORK.
NOPE NOPE NOPE NOPE
BUT WITH THE RIGHT FOOD...
SALAD? SOUP?? ??
...AND THE RIGHT CLOTHES...
...AND THE RIGHT ATTITUDE...

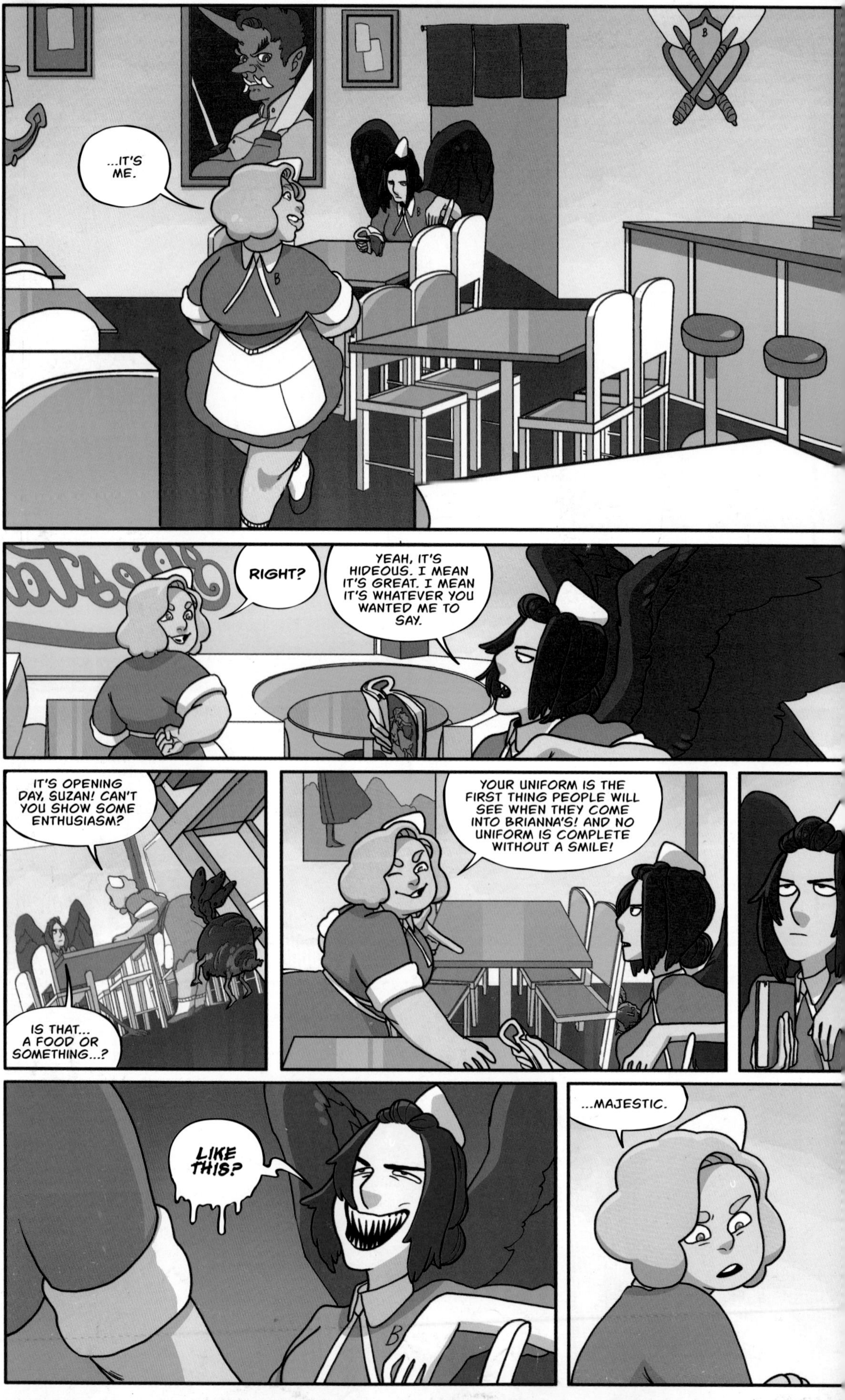
...IT'S ME.
RIGHT?
YEAH, IT'S HIDEOUS. I MEAN IT'S GREAT. I MEAN IT'S WHATEVER YOU WANTED ME TO SAY.
IT'S OPENING DAY, SUZAN! CAN'T YOU SHOW SOME ENTHUSIASM?
IS THAT... A FOOD OR SOMETHING...?
YOUR UNIFORM IS THE FIRST THING PEOPLE WILL SEE WHEN THEY COME INTO BRIANNA'S! AND NO UNIFORM IS COMPLETE WITHOUT A SMILE!
LIKE THIS?
...MAJESTIC.

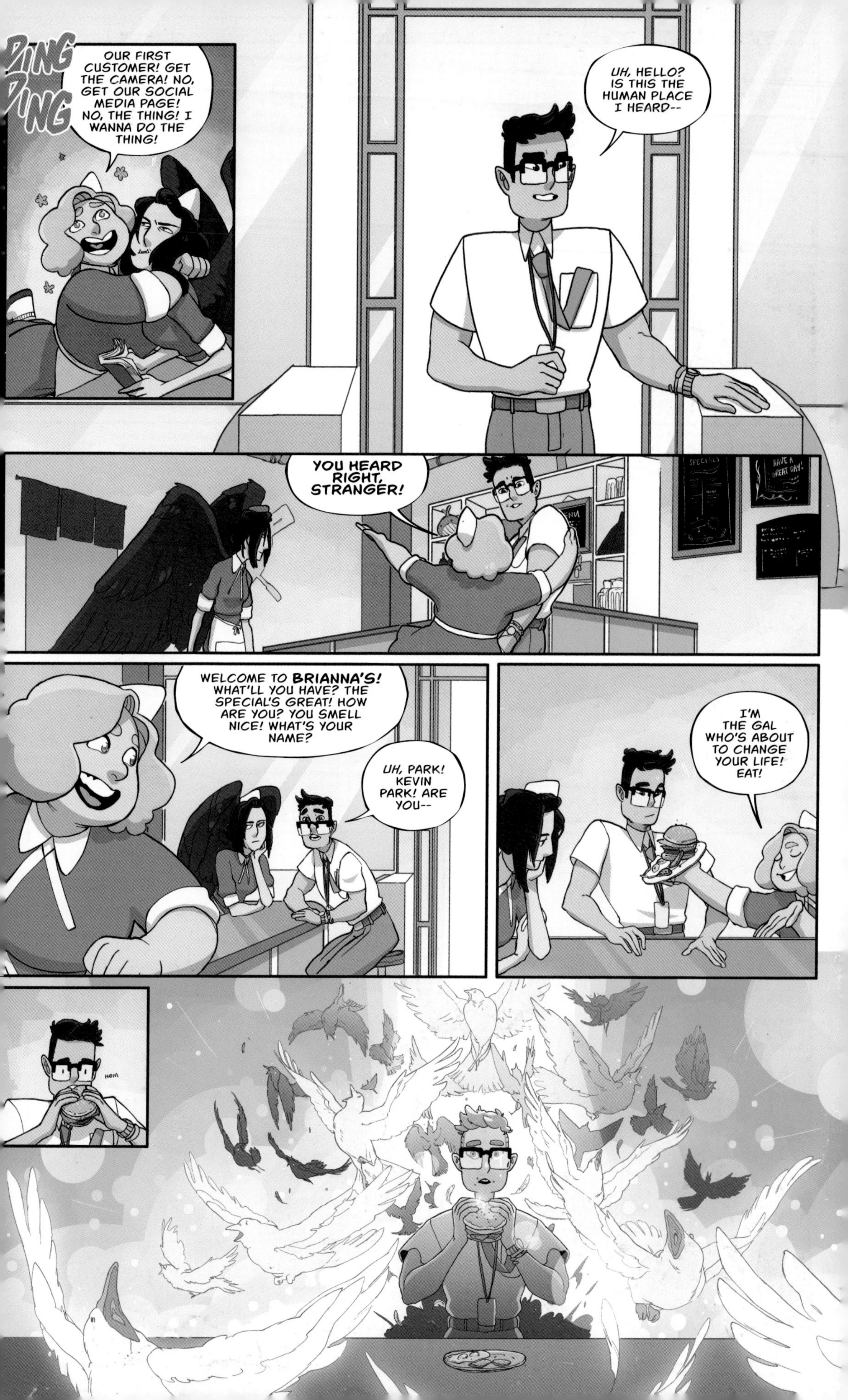
DING DING
OUR FIRST CUSTOMER! GET THE CAMERA! NO, GET OUR SOCIAL MEDIA PAGE! NO, THE THING! I WANNA DO THE THING!
UH, HELLO? IS THIS THE HUMAN PLACE I HEARD--
YOU HEARD RIGHT, STRANGER!
WELCOME TO BRIANNA'S! WHAT'LL YOU HAVE? THE SPECIAL'S GREAT! HOW ARE YOU? YOU SMELL NICE! WHAT'S YOUR NAME?
UH, PARK! KEVIN PARK! ARE YOU--
I'M THE GAL WHO'S ABOUT TO CHANGE YOUR LIFE! EAT!
NOM

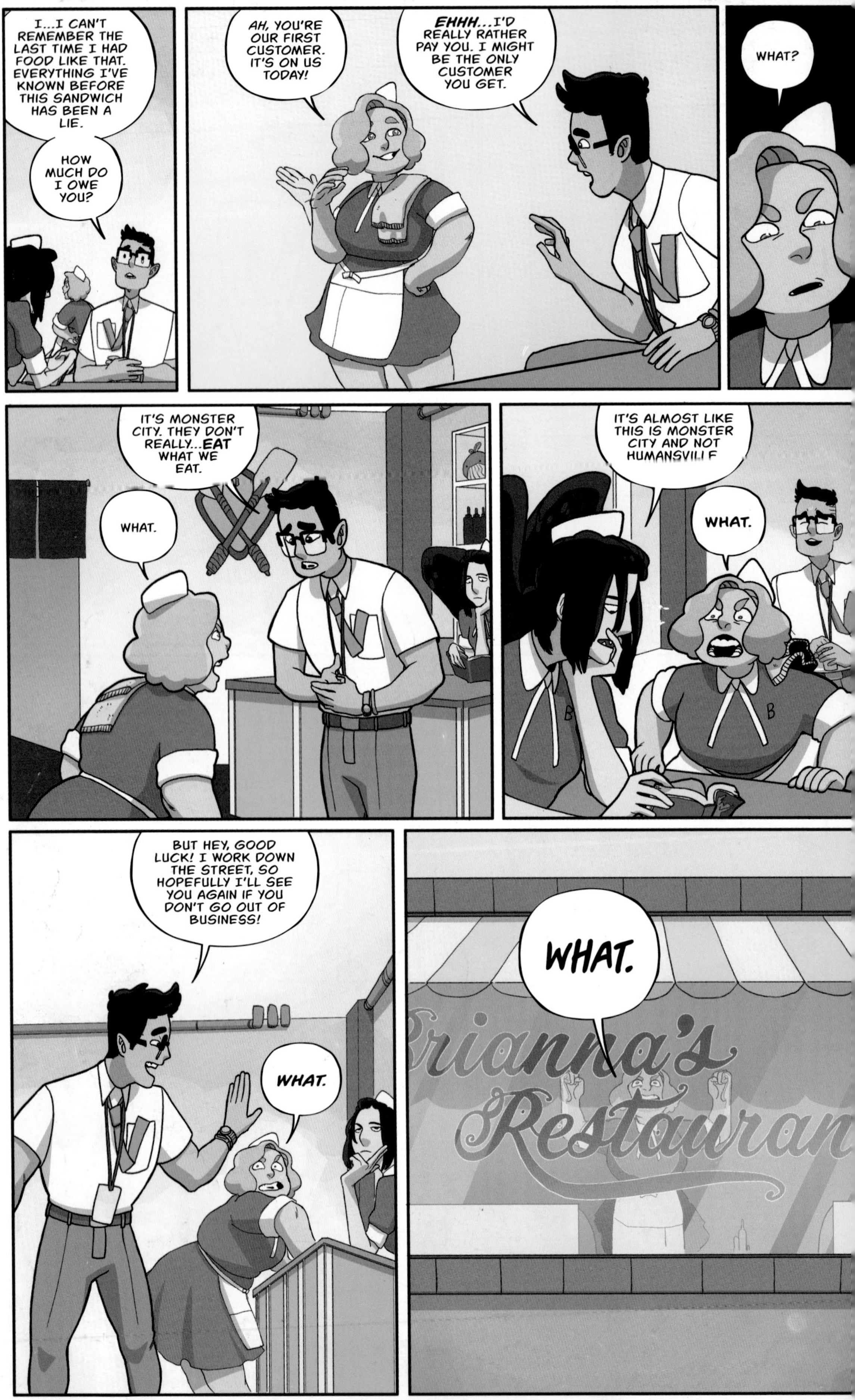
I...I CAN'T REMEMBER THE LAST TIME I HAD FOOD LIKE THAT. EVERYTHING I'VE KNOWN BEFORE THIS SANDWICH HAS BEEN A LIE.
HOW MUCH DO I OWE YOU?
AH, YOU'RE OUR FIRST CUSTOMER. IT'S ON US TODAY!
EHHH...I'D REALLY RATHER PAY YOU. I MIGHT BE THE ONLY CUSTOMER YOU GET.
WHAT?
IT'S MONSTER CITY. THEY DON'T REALLY...EAT WHAT WE EAT.
WHAT.
IT'S ALMOST LIKE THIS IS MONSTER CITY AND NOT HUMANSVILLE.
WHAT.
BUT HEY, GOOD LUCK! I WORK DOWN THE STREET, SO HOPEFULLY I'LL SEE YOU AGAIN IF YOU DON'T GO OUT OF BUSINESS!
WHAT.
WHAT.
Restauran

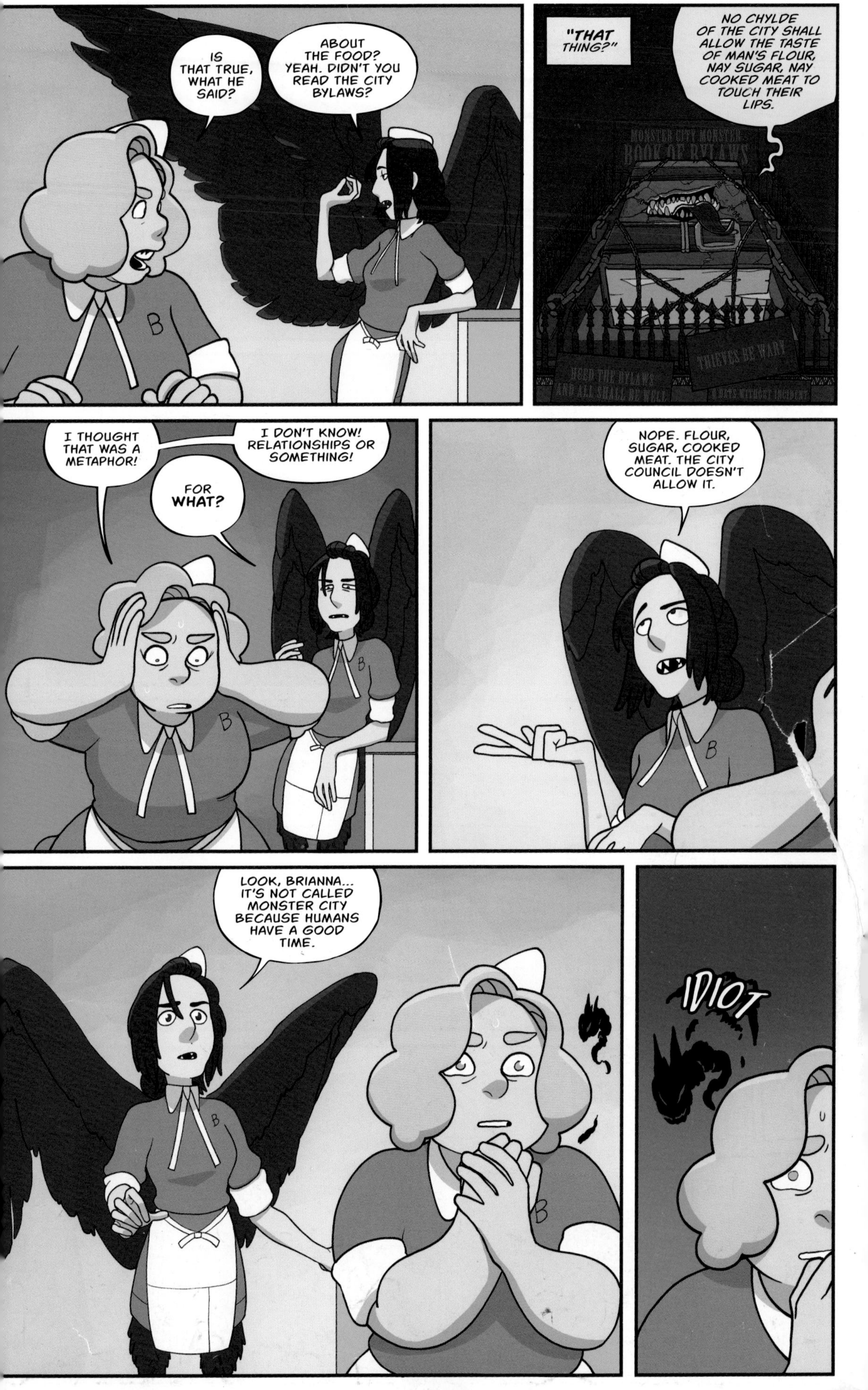
IS THAT TRUE, WHAT HE SAID?
ABOUT THE FOOD? YEAH. DIDN'T YOU READ THE CITY BYLAWS?
"THAT THING?"
NO CHYLDE OF THE CITY SHALL ALLOW THE TASTE OF MAN'S FLOUR, NAY SUGAR, NAY COOKED MEAT TO TOUCH THEIR LIPS.
MONSTER CITY MONSTER BOOK OF BYLAWS
HEED THE BYLAWS AND ALL SHALL BE WELL
THIEVES BE WARY
0 DAYS WITHOUT INCIDENT
I THOUGHT THAT WAS A METAPHOR!
FOR WHAT?
I DON'T KNOW! RELATIONSHIPS OR SOMETHING!
NOPE. FLOUR, SUGAR, COOKED MEAT. THE CITY COUNCIL DOESN'T ALLOW IT.
LOOK, BRIANNA... IT'S NOT CALLED MONSTER CITY BECAUSE HUMANS HAVE A GOOD TIME.
IDIOT

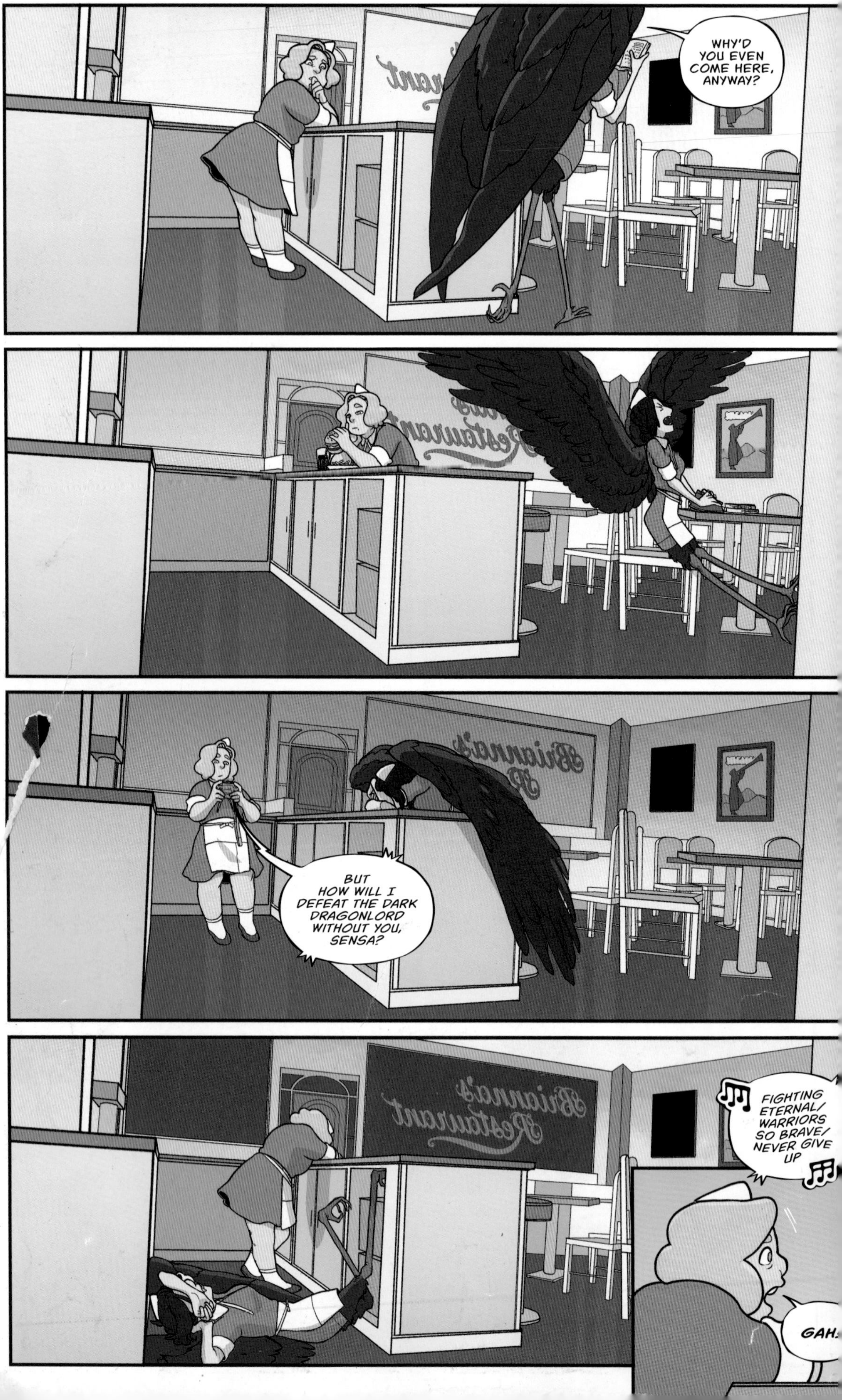
WHY'D YOU EVEN COME HERE, ANYWAY?
BUT HOW WILL I DEFEAT THE DARK DRAGONLORD WITHOUT YOU, SENSA?
FIGHTING ETERNAL/ WARRIORS SO BRAVE/ NEVER GIVE UP
GAH!

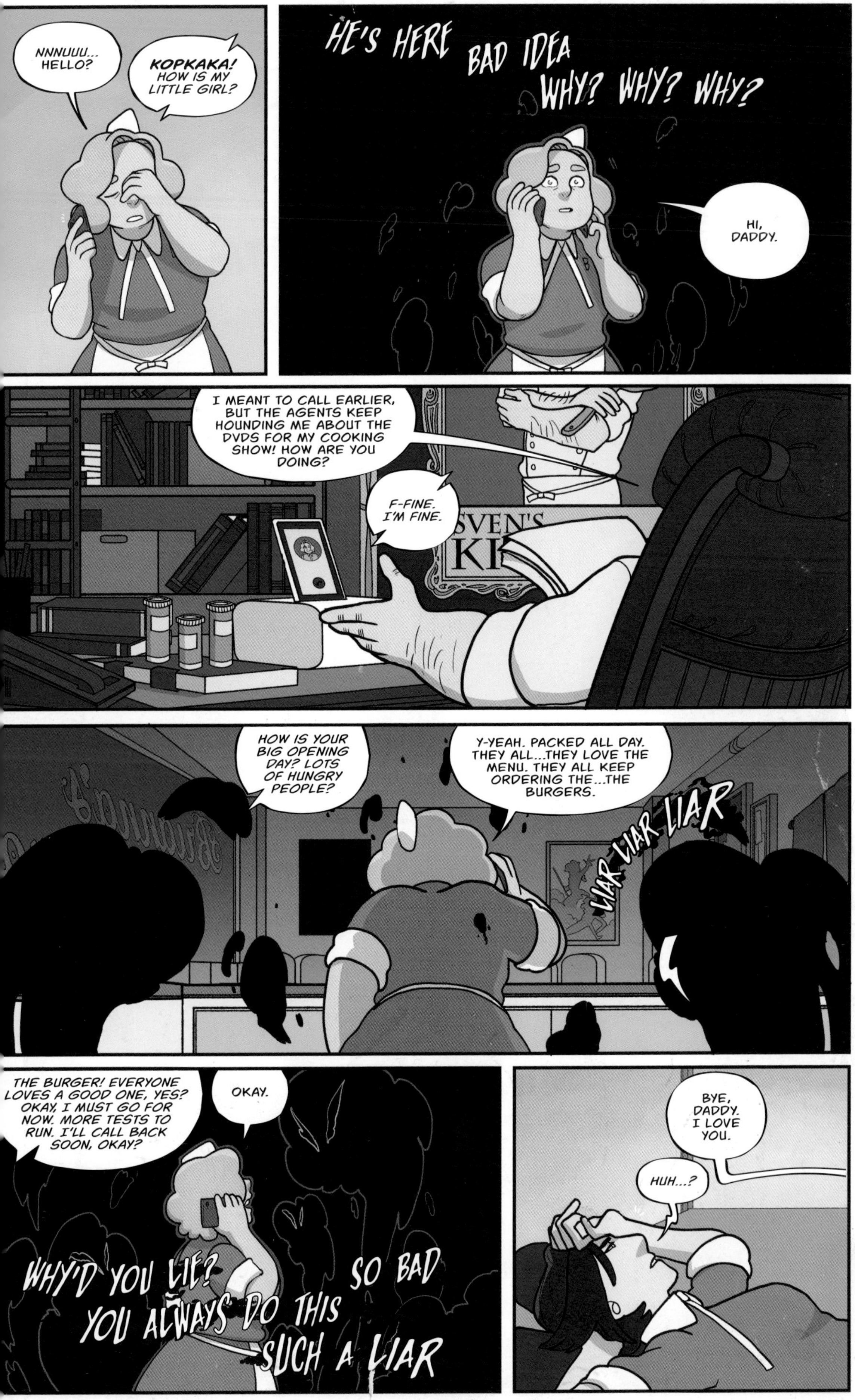
NNNUUU... HELLO?
KOPKAKA! HOW IS MY LITTLE GIRL?
HE'S HERE
BAD IDEA
WHY? WHY? WHY?
HI, DADDY.
I MEANT TO CALL EARLIER, BUT THE AGENTS KEEP HOUNDING ME ABOUT THE DVDS FOR MY COOKING SHOW! HOW ARE YOU DOING?
F-FINE. I'M FINE.
SVEN'S KI
HOW IS YOUR BIG OPENING DAY? LOTS OF HUNGRY PEOPLE?
Y-YEAH. PACKED ALL DAY. THEY ALL...THEY LOVE THE MENU. THEY ALL KEEP ORDERING THE...THE BURGERS.
LIAR LIAR LIAR LIAR
THE BURGER! EVERYONE LOVES A GOOD ONE, YES? OKAY, I MUST GO FOR NOW. MORE TESTS TO RUN. I'LL CALL BACK SOON, OKAY?
OKAY.
WHY'D YOU LIE?
SO BAD
YOU ALWAYS DO THIS
SUCH A LIAR
BYE, DADDY. I LOVE YOU.
HUH...?

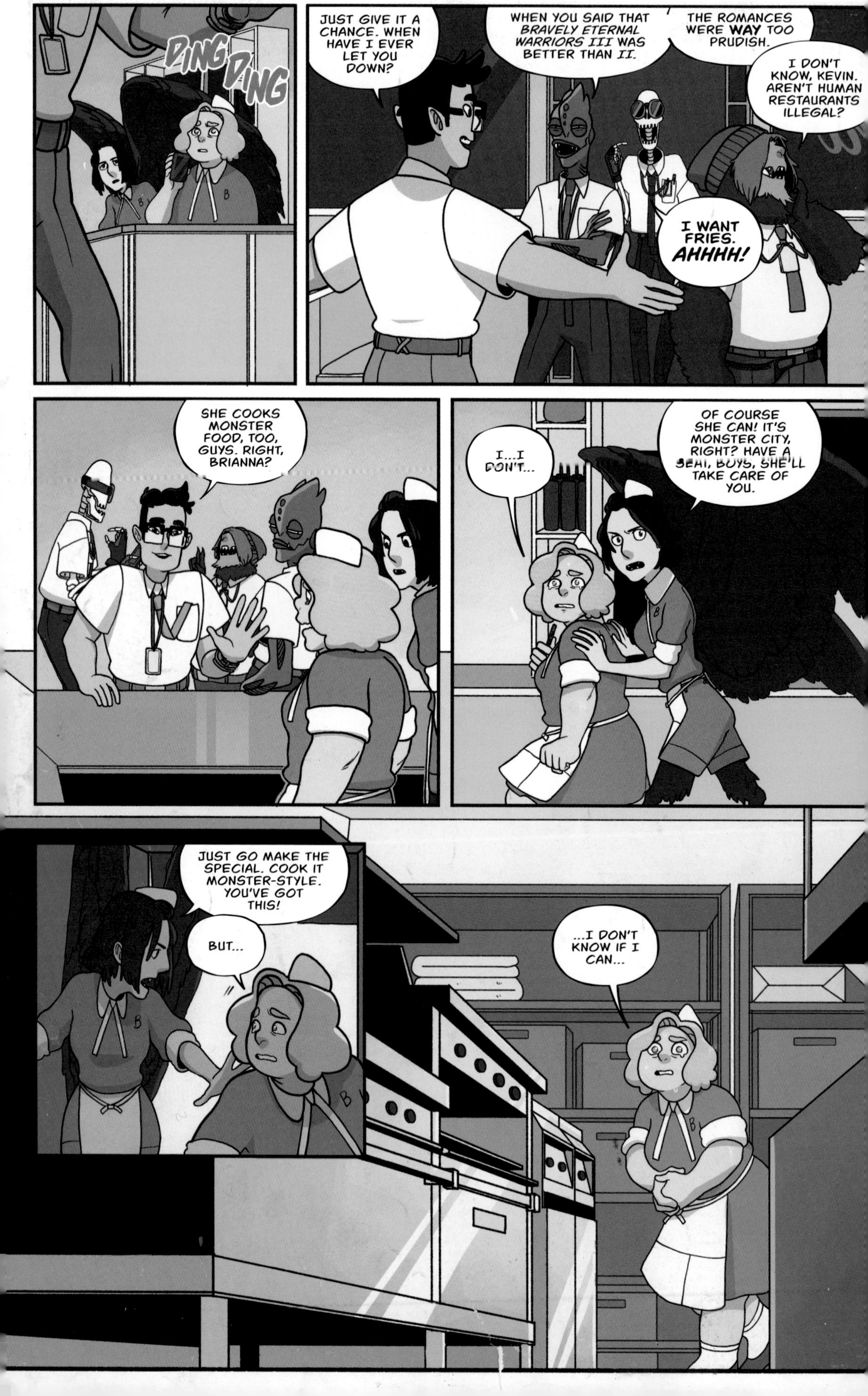
DING DING
JUST GIVE IT A CHANCE. WHEN HAVE I EVER LET YOU DOWN?
WHEN YOU SAID THAT *BRAVELY ETERNAL WARRIORS III* WAS BETTER THAN *II*.
THE ROMANCES WERE **WAY** TOO PRUDISH.
I DON'T KNOW, KEVIN. AREN'T HUMAN RESTAURANTS ILLEGAL?
I WANT FRIES. **AHHHH!**
SHE COOKS MONSTER FOOD, TOO, GUYS. RIGHT, BRIANNA?
I...I DON'T...
OF COURSE SHE CAN! IT'S MONSTER CITY, RIGHT? HAVE A SEAT, BOYS, SHE'LL TAKE CARE OF YOU.
JUST GO MAKE THE SPECIAL. COOK IT MONSTER-STYLE. YOU'VE GOT THIS!
BUT...
...I DON'T KNOW IF I CAN...

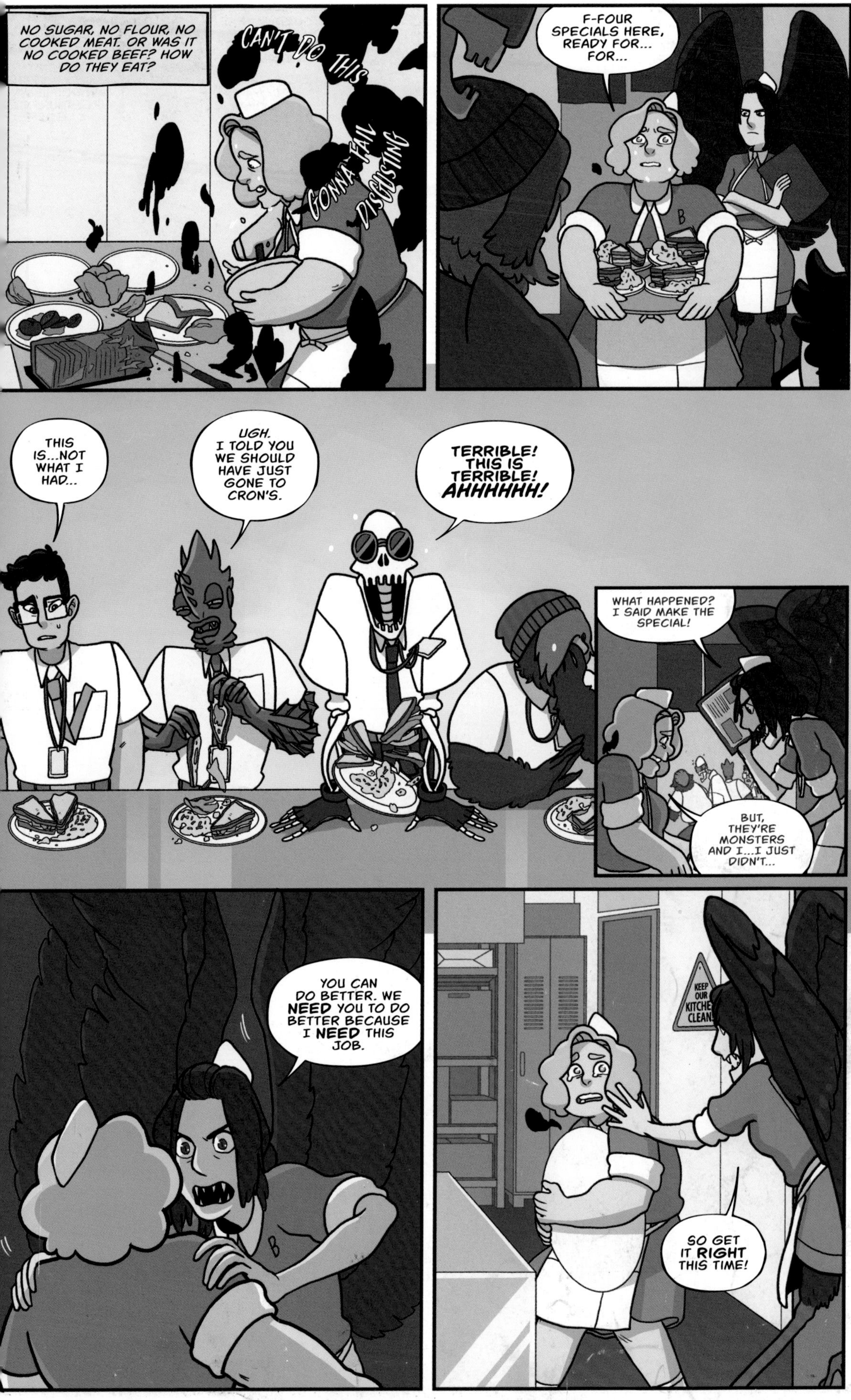
NO SUGAR, NO FLOUR, NO COOKED MEAT. OR WAS IT NO COOKED BEEF? HOW DO THEY EAT?
CAN'T DO THIS
GONNA FAIL
DISGUSTING
F-FOUR SPECIALS HERE, READY FOR... FOR...
THIS IS...NOT WHAT I HAD...
UGH. I TOLD YOU WE SHOULD HAVE JUST GONE TO CRON'S.
TERRIBLE! THIS IS TERRIBLE! AHHHHHH!
WHAT HAPPENED? I SAID MAKE THE SPECIAL!
BUT, THEY'RE MONSTERS AND I...I JUST DIDN'T...
YOU CAN DO BETTER. WE NEED YOU TO DO BETTER BECAUSE I NEED THIS JOB.
KEEP OUR KITCHE CLEAN
SO GET IT RIGHT THIS TIME!

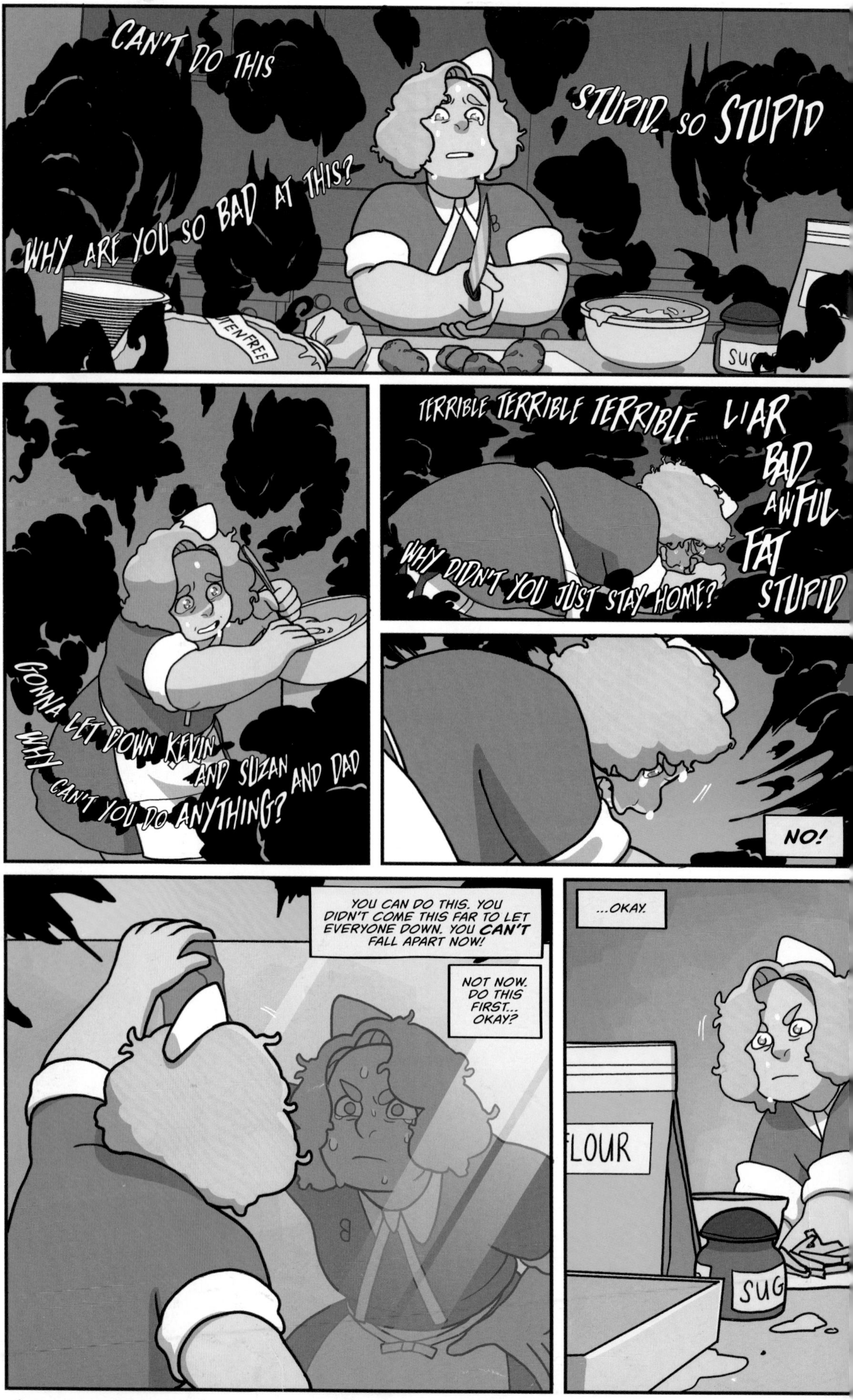

CAN'T DO THIS
STUPID. SO STUPID
WHY ARE YOU SO BAD AT THIS?
TERRIBLE TERRIBLE TERRIBLE
LIAR
BAD
AWFUL
FAT
STUPID
WHY DIDN'T YOU JUST STAY HOME?
GONNA LET DOWN KEVIN
AND SUZAN
AND DAD
WHY CAN'T YOU DO ANYTHING?
NO!
YOU CAN DO THIS. YOU DIDN'T COME THIS FAR TO LET EVERYONE DOWN. YOU **CAN'T** FALL APART NOW!
NOT NOW. DO THIS FIRST... OKAY?
...OKAY.
FLOUR
SUG

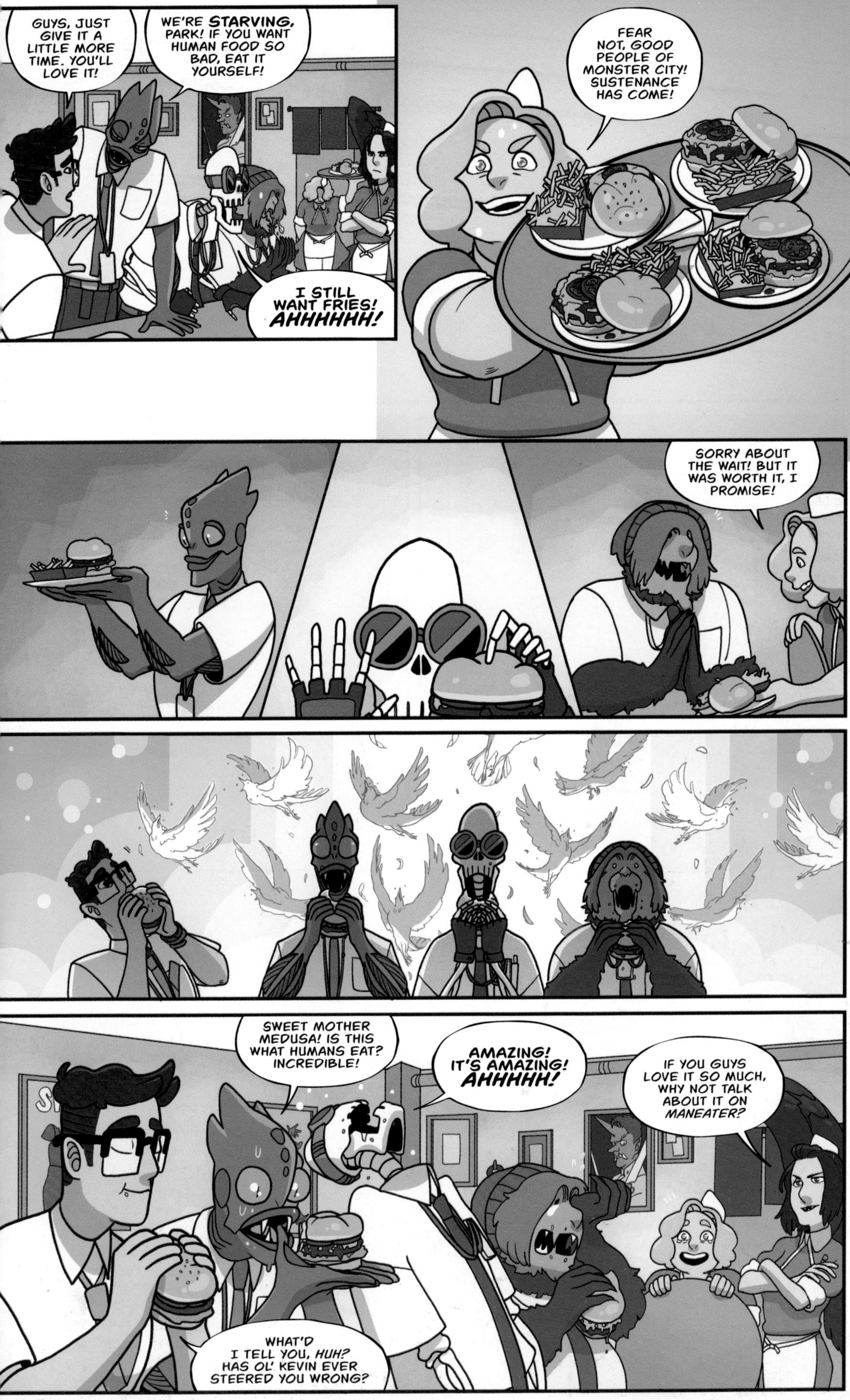
GUYS, JUST GIVE IT A LITTLE MORE TIME. YOU'LL LOVE IT!
WE'RE **STARVING,** PARK! IF YOU WANT HUMAN FOOD SO BAD, EAT IT YOURSELF!
I STILL WANT FRIES! ***AHHHHHH!***
FEAR NOT, GOOD PEOPLE OF MONSTER CITY! SUSTENANCE HAS COME!
SORRY ABOUT THE WAIT! BUT IT WAS WORTH IT, I PROMISE!
SWEET MOTHER MEDUSA! IS THIS WHAT HUMANS EAT? INCREDIBLE!
AMAZING! IT'S AMAZING! *AHHHHH!*
IF YOU GUYS LOVE IT SO MUCH, WHY NOT TALK ABOUT IT ON *MANEATER?*
WHAT'D I TELL YOU, *HUH?* HAS OL' KEVIN EVER STEERED YOU WRONG?

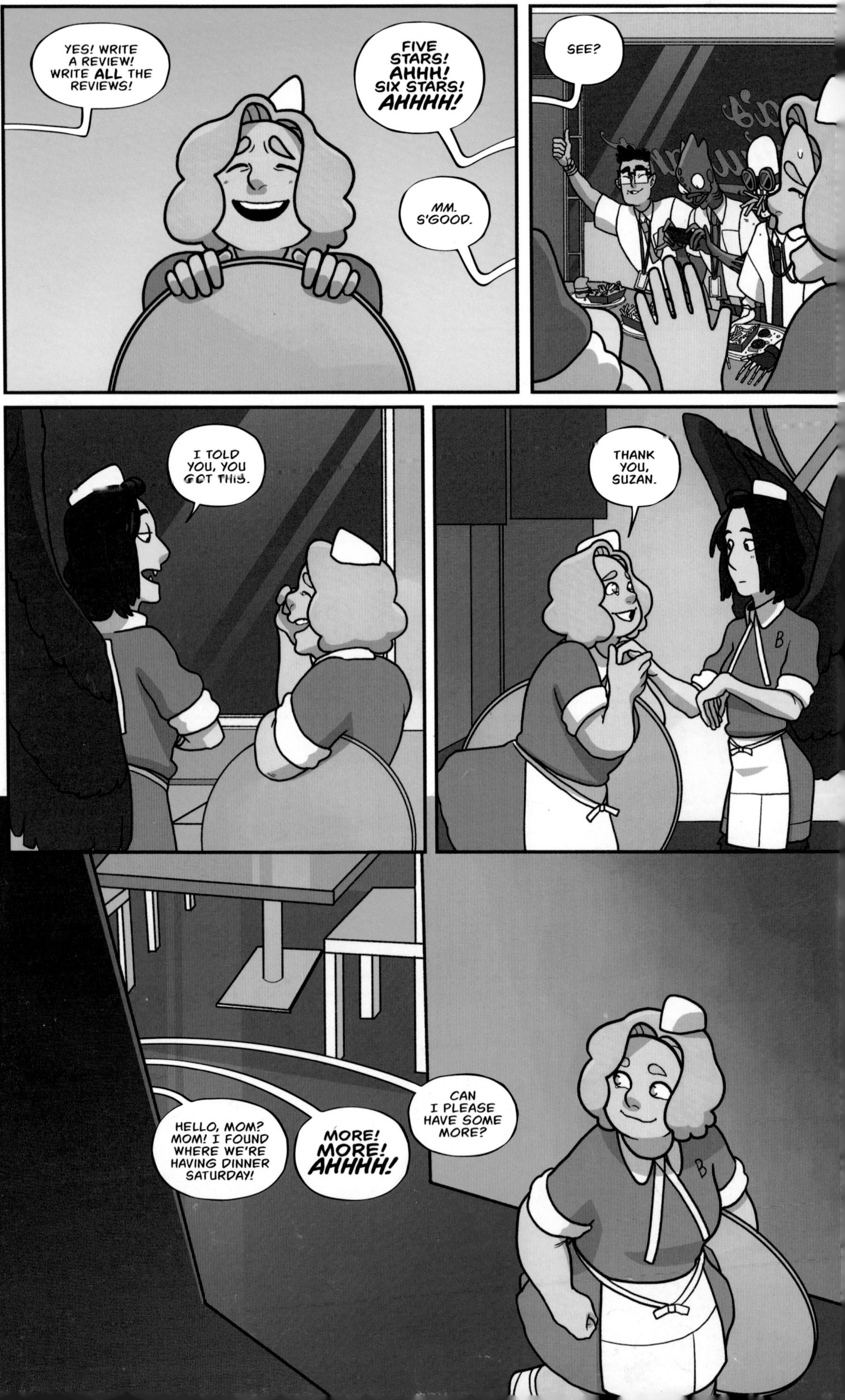
YES! WRITE A REVIEW! WRITE ALL THE REVIEWS!
FIVE STARS! AHHH! SIX STARS! AHHHH!
MM. S'GOOD.
SEE?
I TOLD YOU, YOU GOT THIS.
THANK YOU, SUZAN.
HELLO, MOM? MOM! I FOUND WHERE WE'RE HAVING DINNER SATURDAY!
MORE! MORE! AHHHH!
CAN I PLEASE HAVE SOME MORE?

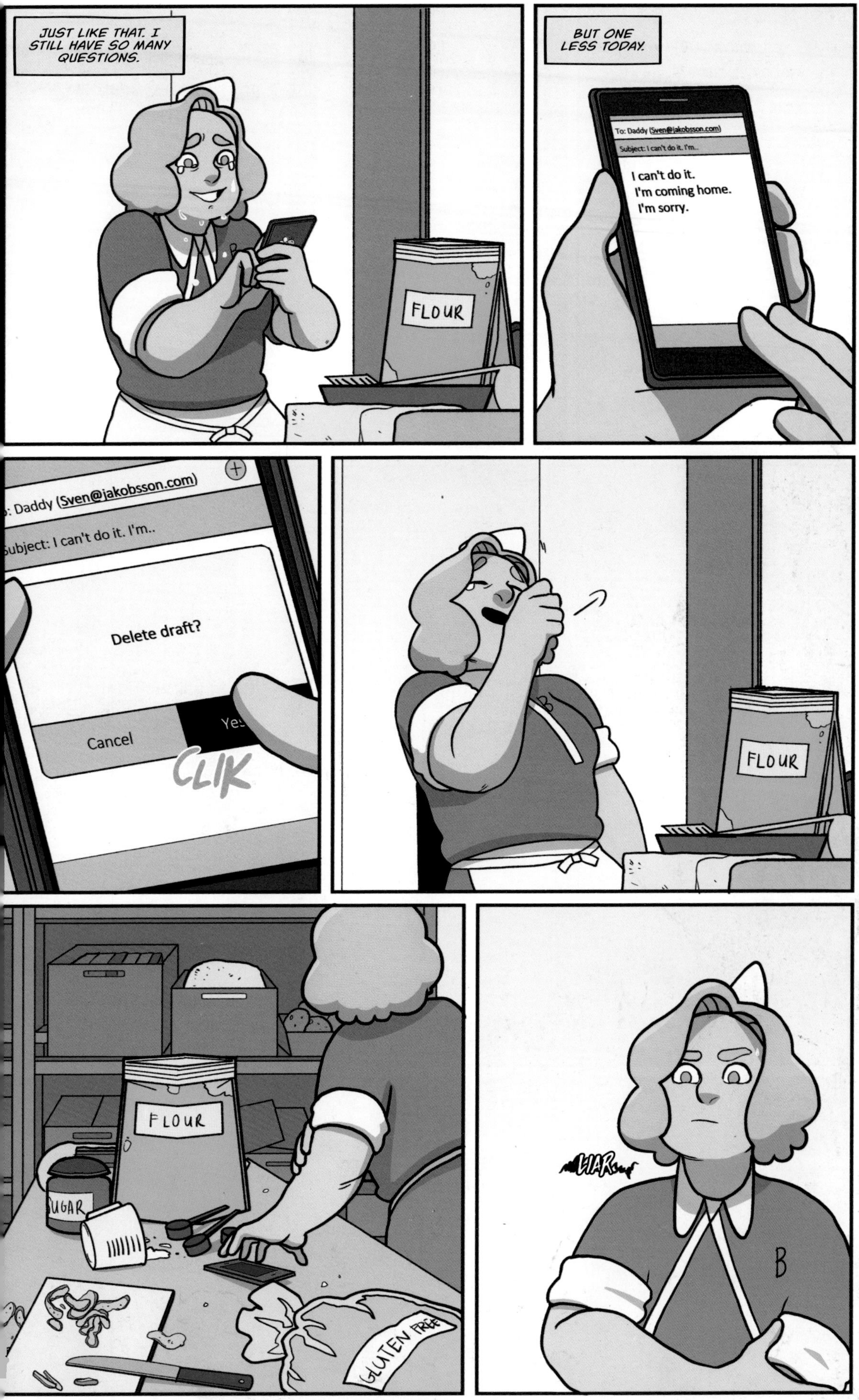
JUST LIKE THAT. I STILL HAVE SO MANY QUESTIONS.
FLOUR
BUT ONE LESS TODAY.
To: Daddy (Sven@jakobsson.com)
Subject: I can't do it. I'm..
I can't do it.
I'm coming home.
I'm sorry.
Delete draft?
Cancel
CLIK
FLOUR
FLOUR
SUGAR
GLUTEN FREE
LIAR
B

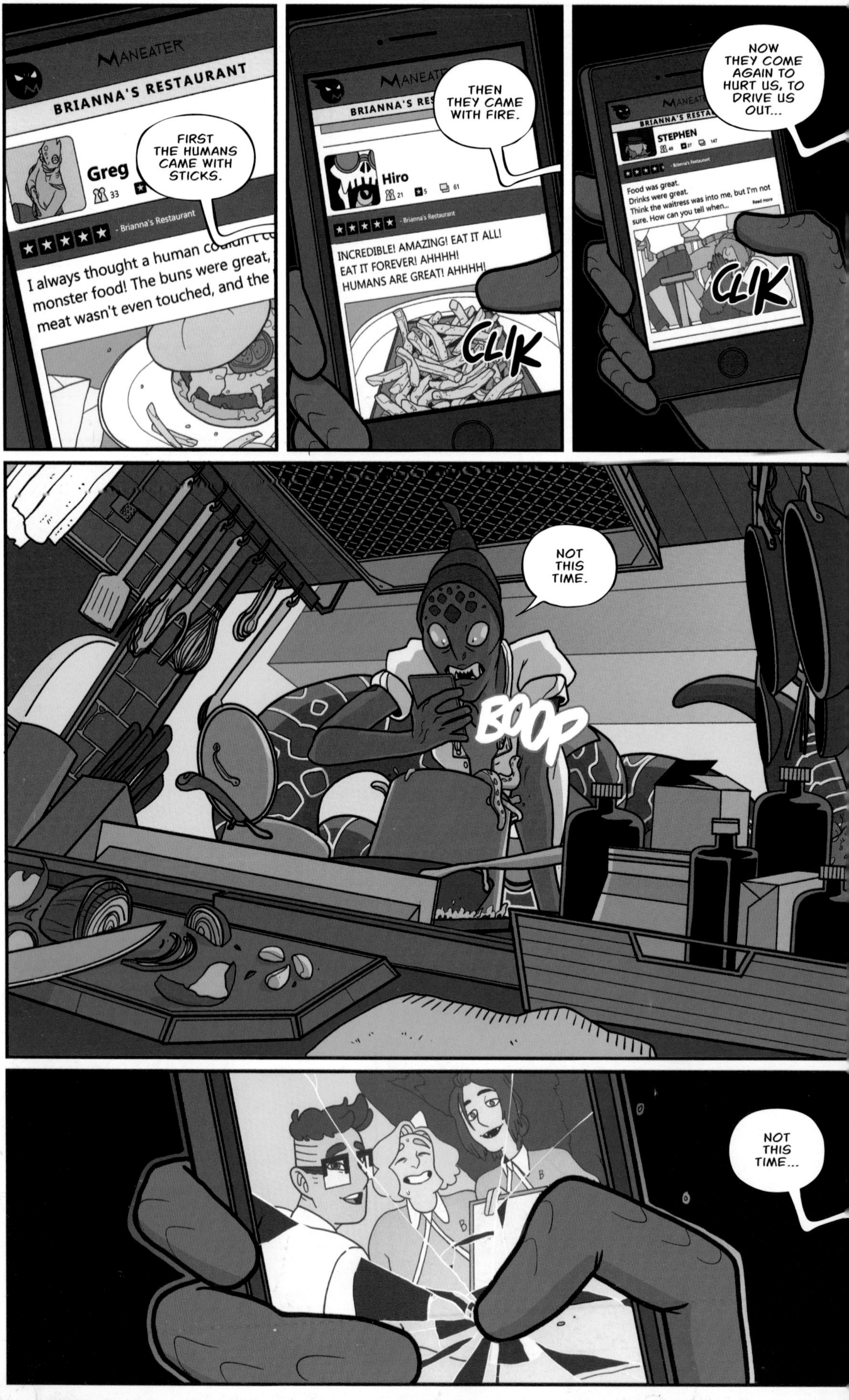
MANEATER
BRIANNA'S RESTAURANT
Greg
33
- Brianna's Restaurant
I always thought a human
monster food! The buns were great,
meat wasn't even touched, and the
FIRST THE HUMANS CAME WITH STICKS.
MANEATER
BRIANNA'S RES
Hiro
21 5 61
- Brianna's Restaurant
INCREDIBLE! AMAZING! EAT IT ALL!
EAT IT FOREVER! AHHHH!
HUMANS ARE GREAT! AHHHH!
THEN THEY CAME WITH FIRE.
CLIK
MANEATER
BRIANNA'S RESTAUR
STEPHEN
48 27 147
- Brianna's Restaurant
Food was great.
Drinks were great.
Think the waitress was into me, but I'm not sure. How can you tell when...
Read more
NOW THEY COME AGAIN TO HURT US, TO DRIVE US OUT...
CLIK
NOT THIS TIME.
BOOP
NOT THIS TIME...

chapter
TWO

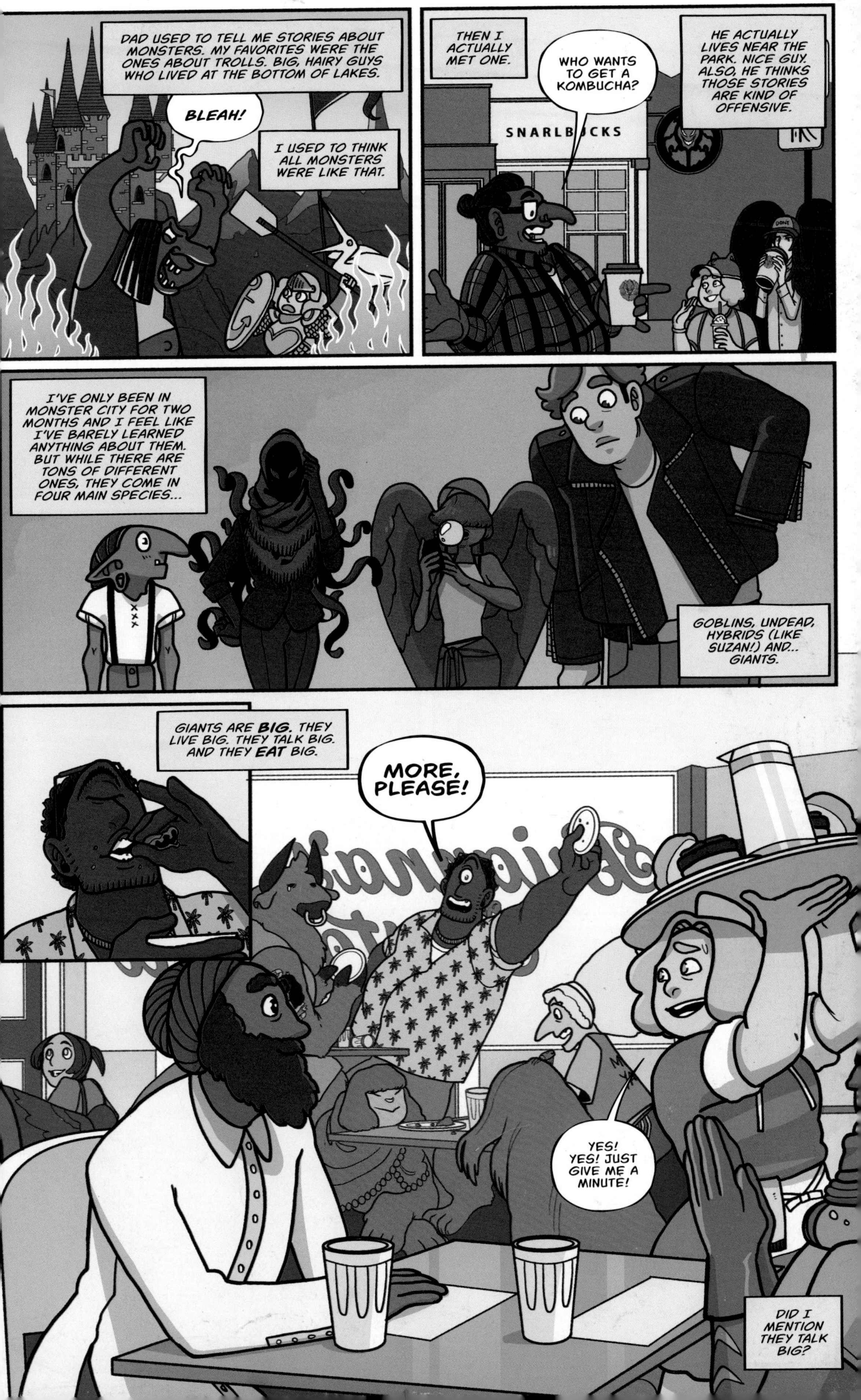
DAD USED TO TELL ME STORIES ABOUT MONSTERS. MY FAVORITES WERE THE ONES ABOUT TROLLS. BIG, HAIRY GUYS WHO LIVED AT THE BOTTOM OF LAKES.
BLEAH!
I USED TO THINK ALL MONSTERS WERE LIKE THAT.
THEN I ACTUALLY MET ONE.
WHO WANTS TO GET A KOMBUCHA?
SNARLB CKS
HE ACTUALLY LIVES NEAR THE PARK. NICE GUY. ALSO, HE THINKS THOSE STORIES ARE KIND OF OFFENSIVE.
I'VE ONLY BEEN IN MONSTER CITY FOR TWO MONTHS AND I FEEL LIKE I'VE BARELY LEARNED ANYTHING ABOUT THEM. BUT WHILE THERE ARE TONS OF DIFFERENT ONES, THEY COME IN FOUR MAIN SPECIES...
GOBLINS, UNDEAD, HYBRIDS (LIKE SUZAN!) AND... GIANTS.
GIANTS ARE BIG. THEY LIVE BIG. THEY TALK BIG. AND THEY EAT BIG.
MORE, PLEASE!
YES! YES! JUST GIVE ME A MINUTE!
DID I MENTION THEY TALK BIG?

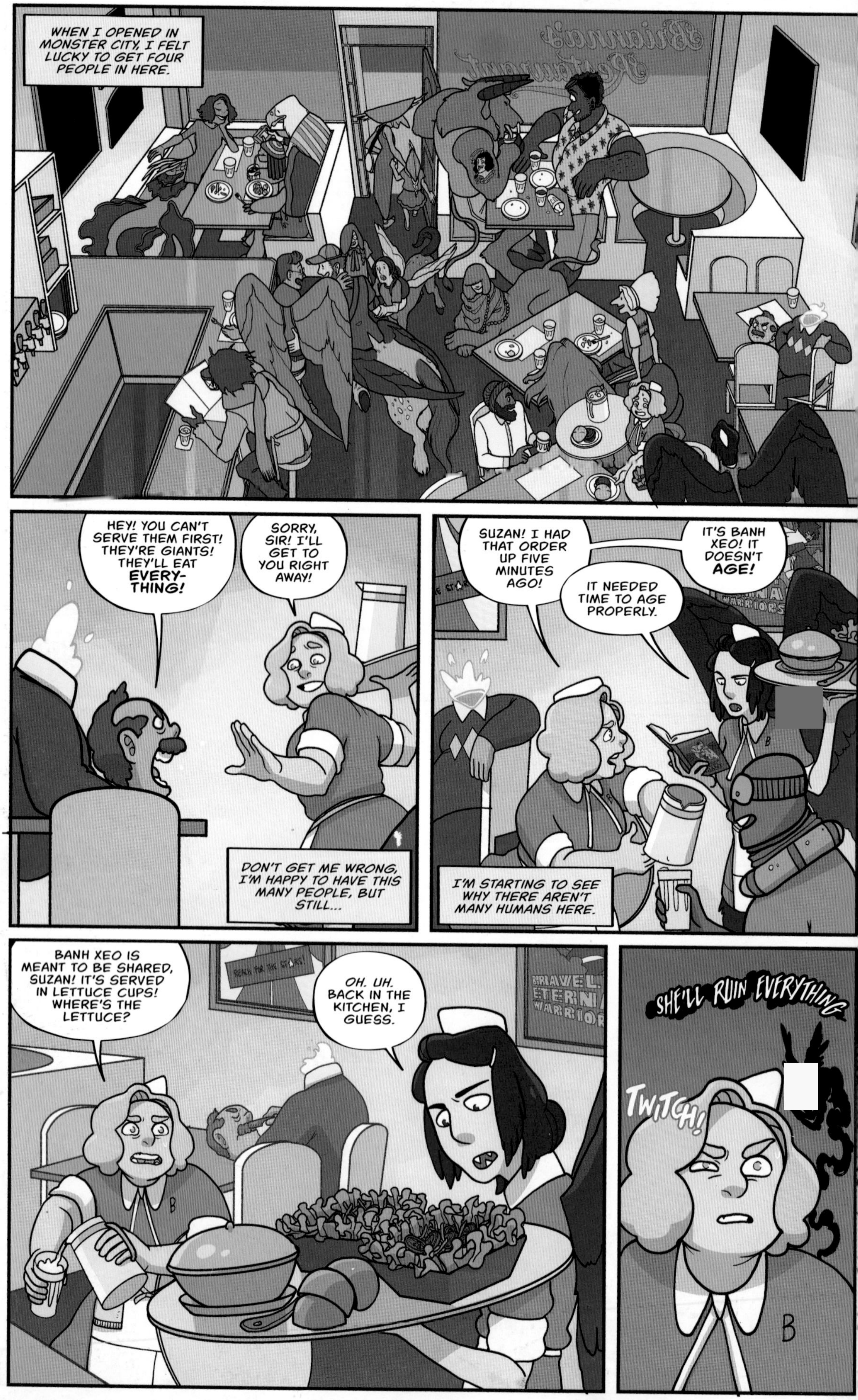

WHEN I OPENED IN MONSTER CITY, I FELT LUCKY TO GET FOUR PEOPLE IN HERE.
HEY! YOU CAN'T SERVE THEM FIRST! THEY'RE GIANTS! THEY'LL EAT **EVERYTHING!**
SORRY, SIR! I'LL GET TO YOU RIGHT AWAY!
DON'T GET ME WRONG, I'M HAPPY TO HAVE THIS MANY PEOPLE, BUT STILL...
SUZAN! I HAD THAT ORDER UP FIVE MINUTES AGO!
IT NEEDED TIME TO AGE PROPERLY.
IT'S BANH XEO! IT DOESN'T **AGE!**
I'M STARTING TO SEE WHY THERE AREN'T MANY HUMANS HERE.
BANH XEO IS MEANT TO BE SHARED, SUZAN! IT'S SERVED IN LETTUCE CUPS! WHERE'S THE LETTUCE?
REACH FOR THE STARS!
OH. UH. BACK IN THE KITCHEN, I GUESS.
SHE'LL RUIN EVERYTHING
TWITCH!

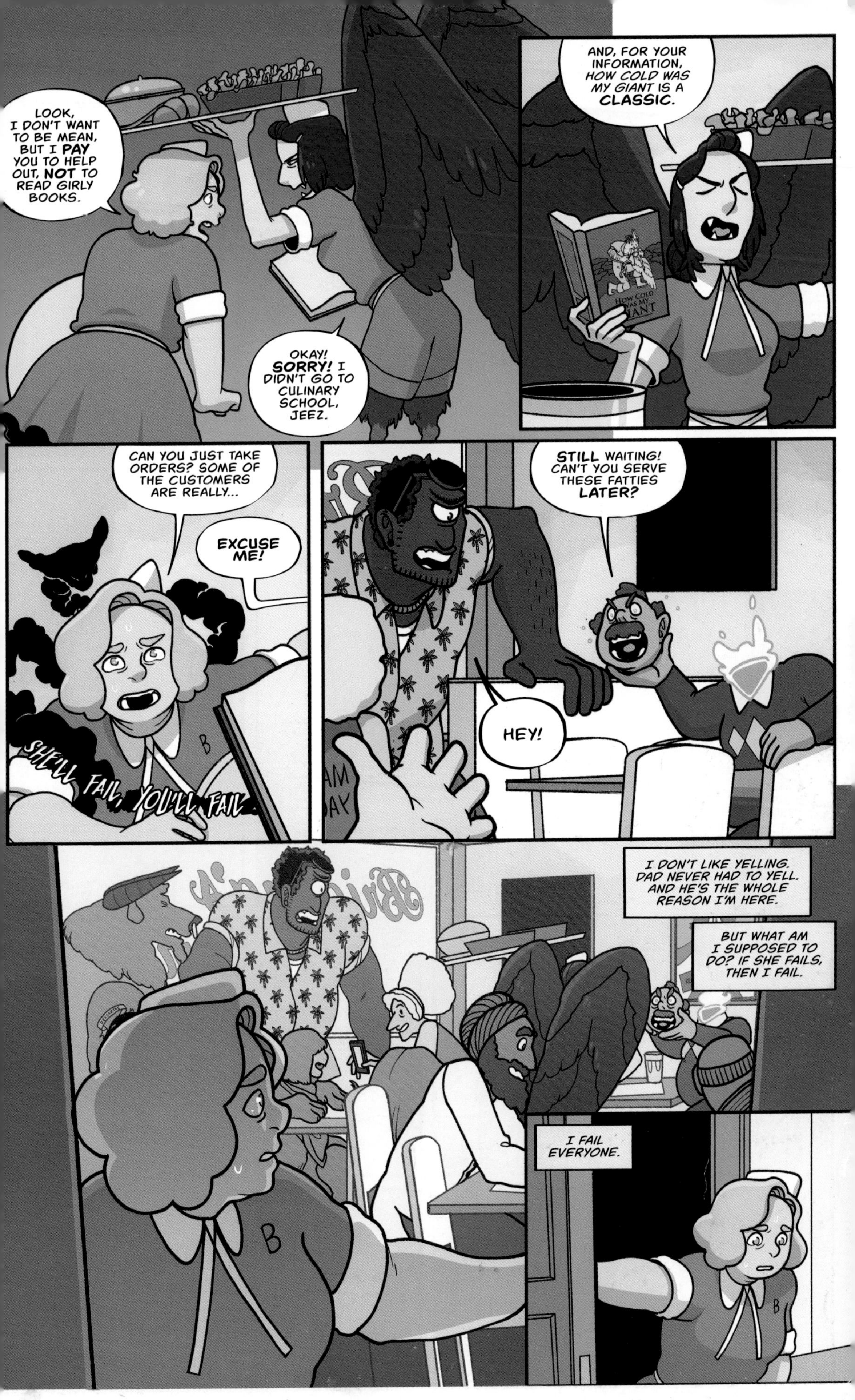
LOOK, I DON'T WANT TO BE MEAN, BUT I PAY YOU TO HELP OUT, NOT TO READ GIRLY BOOKS.
OKAY! SORRY! I DIDN'T GO TO CULINARY SCHOOL, JEEZ.
AND, FOR YOUR INFORMATION, HOW COLD WAS MY GIANT IS A CLASSIC.
HOW COLD WAS MY GIANT
CAN YOU JUST TAKE ORDERS? SOME OF THE CUSTOMERS ARE REALLY...
EXCUSE ME!
SHE'LL FAIL, YOU'LL FAIL
STILL WAITING! CAN'T YOU SERVE THESE FATTIES LATER?
HEY!
I DON'T LIKE YELLING. DAD NEVER HAD TO YELL. AND HE'S THE WHOLE REASON I'M HERE.
BUT WHAT AM I SUPPOSED TO DO? IF SHE FAILS, THEN I FAIL.
I FAIL EVERYONE.

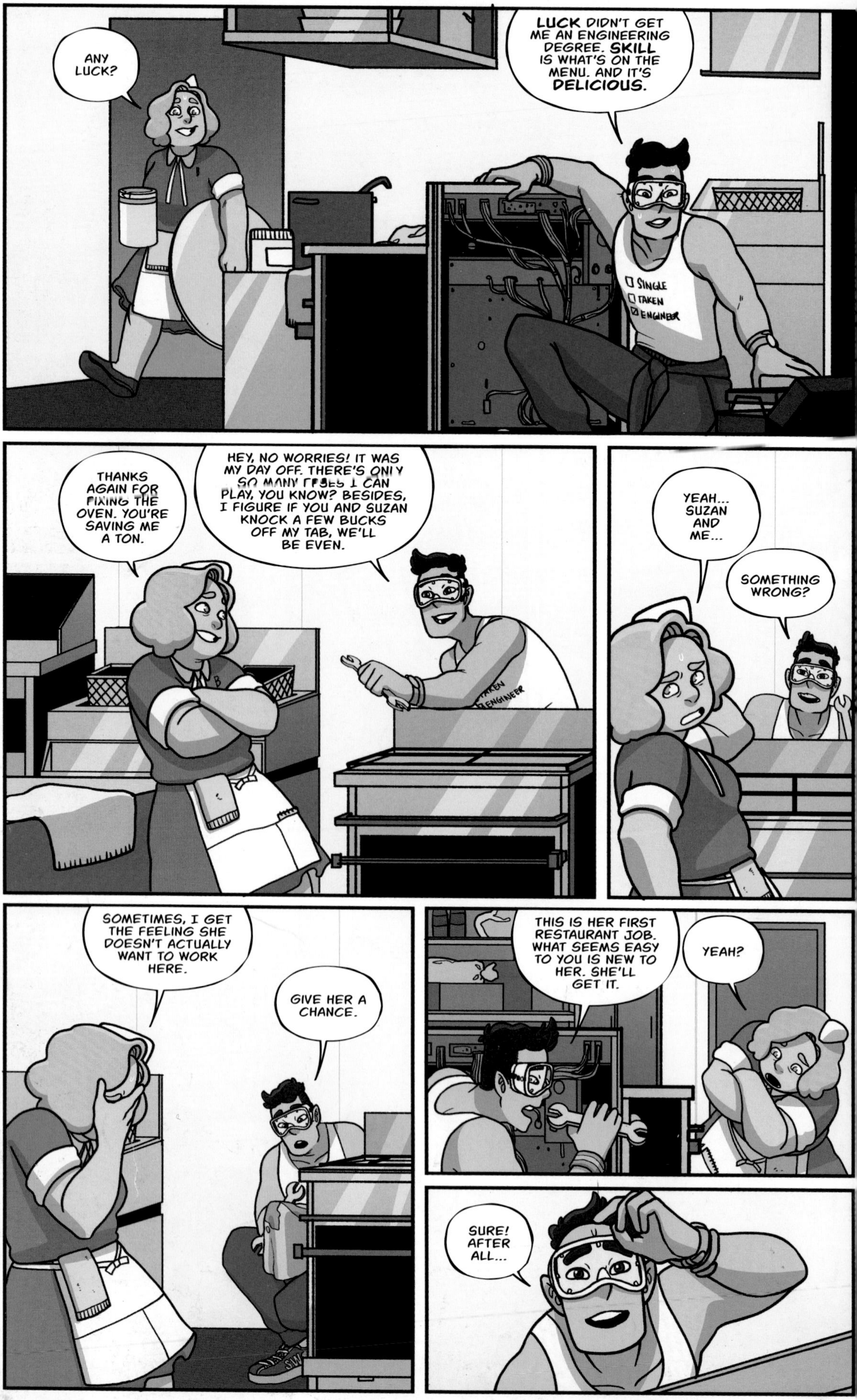
ANY LUCK?
LUCK DIDN'T GET ME AN ENGINEERING DEGREE. SKILL IS WHAT'S ON THE MENU. AND IT'S DELICIOUS.
SINGLE
TAKEN
ENGINEER
THANKS AGAIN FOR FIXING THE OVEN. YOU'RE SAVING ME A TON.
HEY, NO WORRIES! IT WAS MY DAY OFF. THERE'S ONLY SO MANY FPSES I CAN PLAY, YOU KNOW? BESIDES, I FIGURE IF YOU AND SUZAN KNOCK A FEW BUCKS OFF MY TAB, WE'LL BE EVEN.
YEAH... SUZAN AND ME...
SOMETHING WRONG?
SOMETIMES, I GET THE FEELING SHE DOESN'T ACTUALLY WANT TO WORK HERE.
GIVE HER A CHANCE.
THIS IS HER FIRST RESTAURANT JOB. WHAT SEEMS EASY TO YOU IS NEW TO HER. SHE'LL GET IT.
YEAH?
SURE! AFTER ALL...

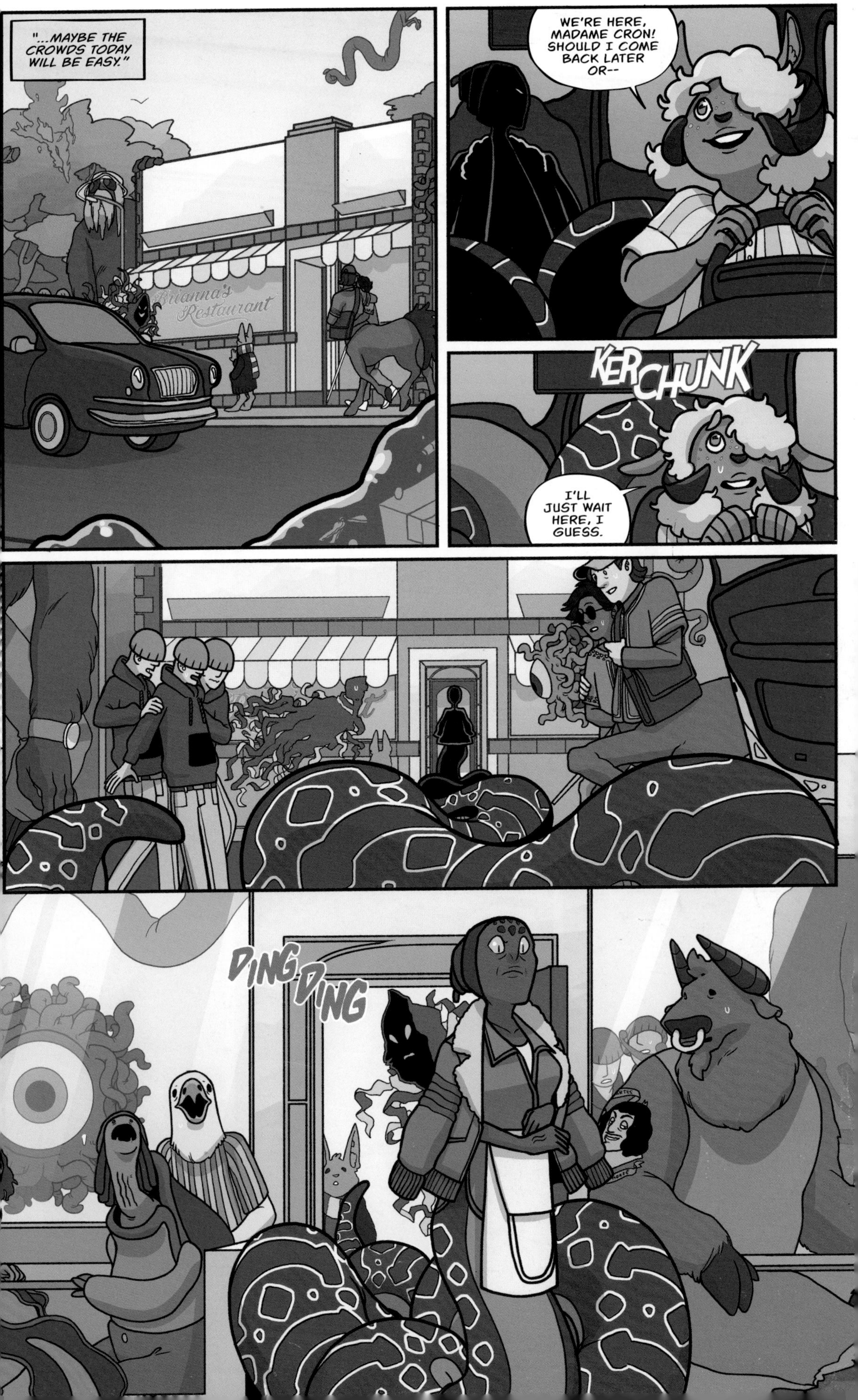
"...MAYBE THE CROWDS TODAY WILL BE EASY."
Brianna's Restaurant
WE'RE HERE, MADAME CRON! SHOULD I COME BACK LATER OR--
KERCHUNK
I'LL JUST WAIT HERE, I GUESS.
DING DING

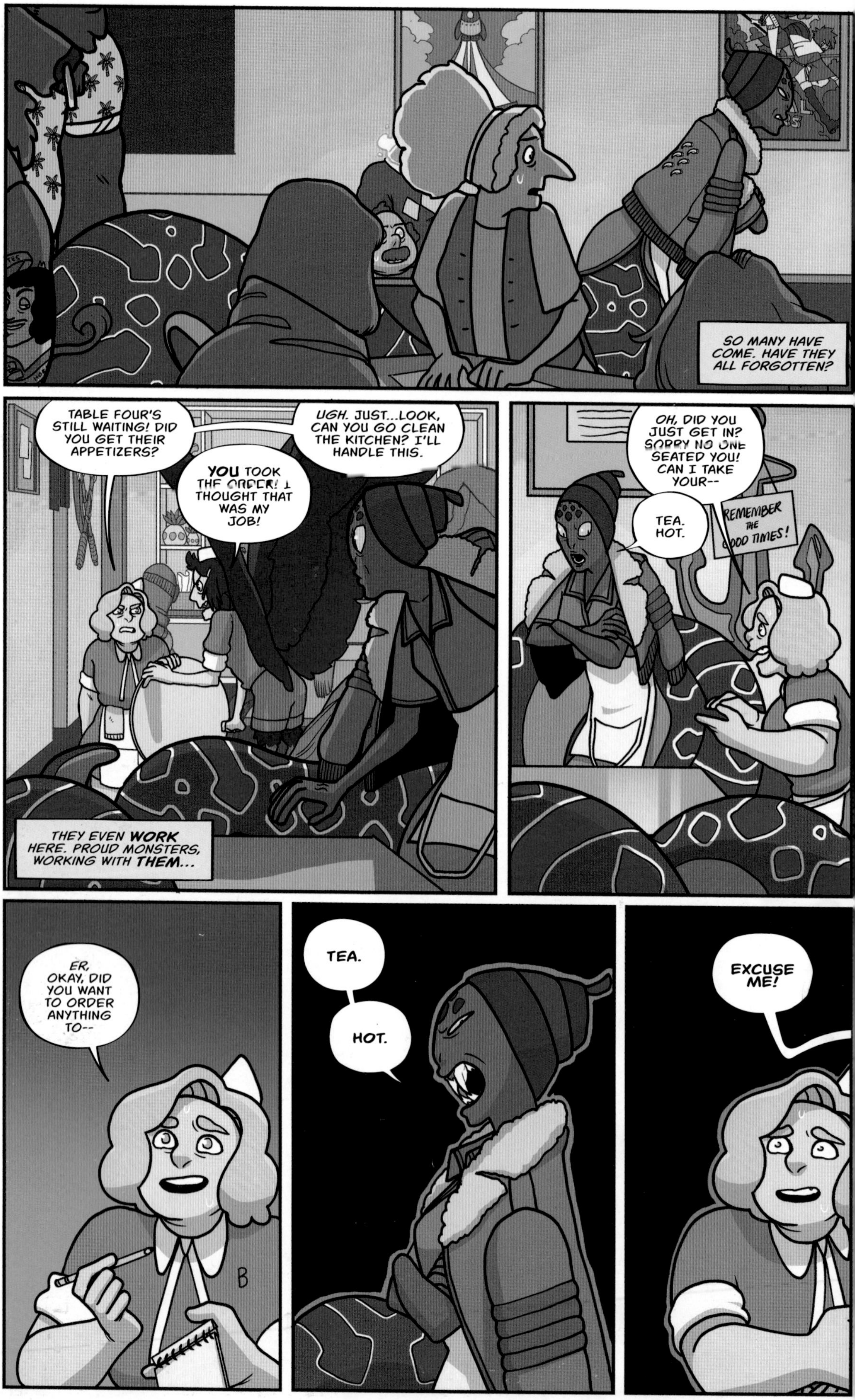
SO MANY HAVE COME. HAVE THEY ALL FORGOTTEN?
TABLE FOUR'S STILL WAITING! DID YOU GET THEIR APPETIZERS?
UGH. JUST...LOOK, CAN YOU GO CLEAN THE KITCHEN? I'LL HANDLE THIS.
YOU TOOK THE ORDER! I THOUGHT THAT WAS MY JOB!
THEY EVEN WORK HERE. PROUD MONSTERS, WORKING WITH THEM...
OH, DID YOU JUST GET IN? SORRY NO ONE SEATED YOU! CAN I TAKE YOUR--
TEA. HOT.
REMEMBER THE GOOD TIMES!
ER, OKAY, DID YOU WANT TO ORDER ANYTHING TO--
TEA.
HOT.
EXCUSE ME!

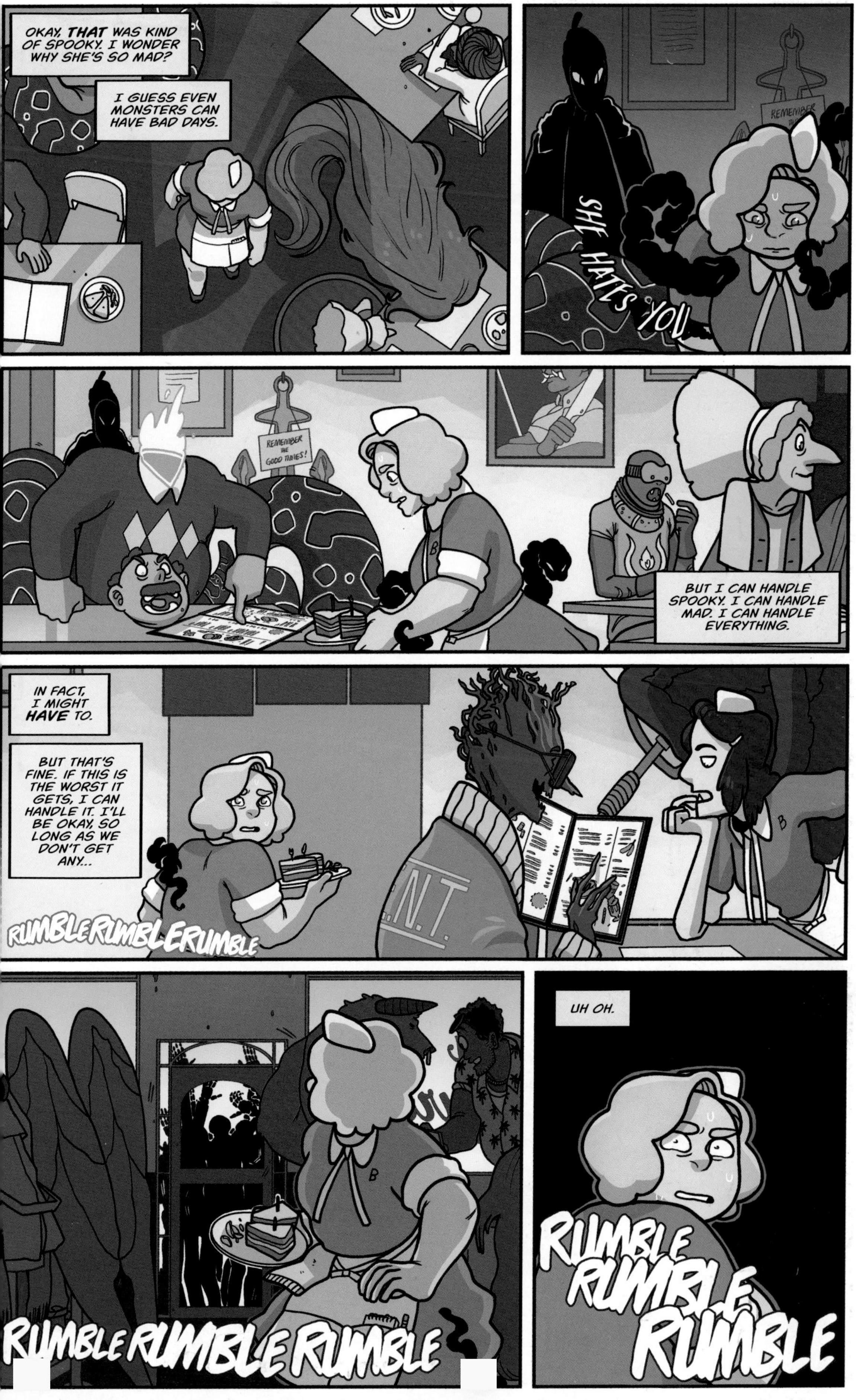
OKAY, THAT WAS KIND OF SPOOKY. I WONDER WHY SHE'S SO MAD?
I GUESS EVEN MONSTERS CAN HAVE BAD DAYS.
SHE HATES YOU
REMEMBER THE GOOD TIMES!
BUT I CAN HANDLE SPOOKY. I CAN HANDLE MAD. I CAN HANDLE EVERYTHING.
IN FACT, I MIGHT HAVE TO.
BUT THAT'S FINE. IF THIS IS THE WORST IT GETS, I CAN HANDLE IT. I'LL BE OKAY, SO LONG AS WE DON'T GET ANY...
RUMBLE RUMBLE RUMBLE
RUMBLE RUMBLE RUMBLE
UH OH.
RUMBLE RUMBLE RUMBLE

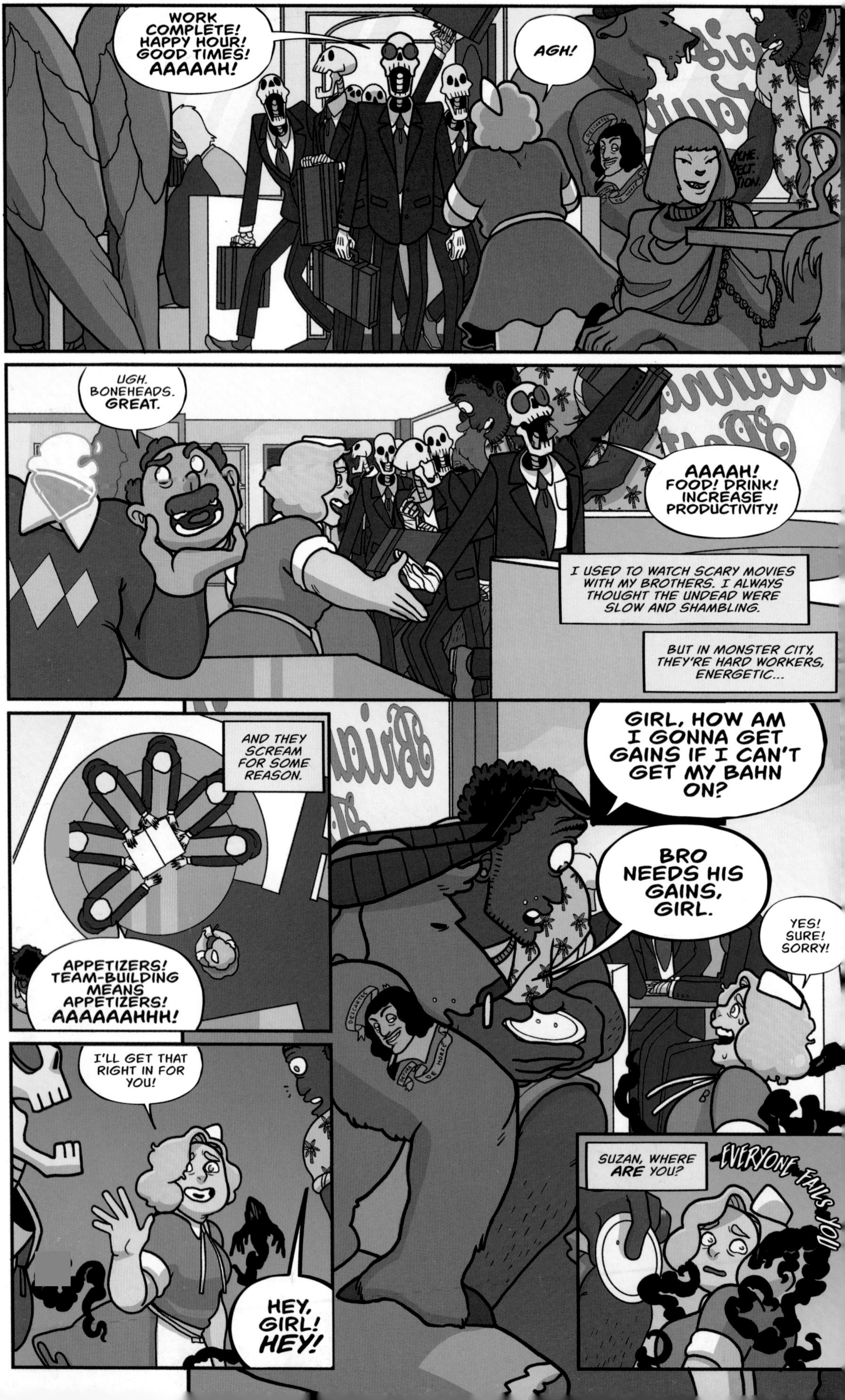
WORK COMPLETE! HAPPY HOUR! GOOD TIMES! AAAAAH!
AGH!
UGH. BONEHEADS. GREAT.
AAAAH! FOOD! DRINK! INCREASE PRODUCTIVITY!
I USED TO WATCH SCARY MOVIES WITH MY BROTHERS. I ALWAYS THOUGHT THE UNDEAD WERE SLOW AND SHAMBLING.
BUT IN MONSTER CITY, THEY'RE HARD WORKERS, ENERGETIC...
AND THEY SCREAM FOR SOME REASON.
APPETIZERS! TEAM-BUILDING MEANS APPETIZERS! AAAAAAHHH!
GIRL, HOW AM I GONNA GET GAINS IF I CAN'T GET MY BAHN ON?
BRO NEEDS HIS GAINS, GIRL.
YES! SURE! SORRY!
I'LL GET THAT RIGHT IN FOR YOU!
HEY, GIRL! HEY!
SUZAN, WHERE ARE YOU?
EVERYONE FAILS YOU

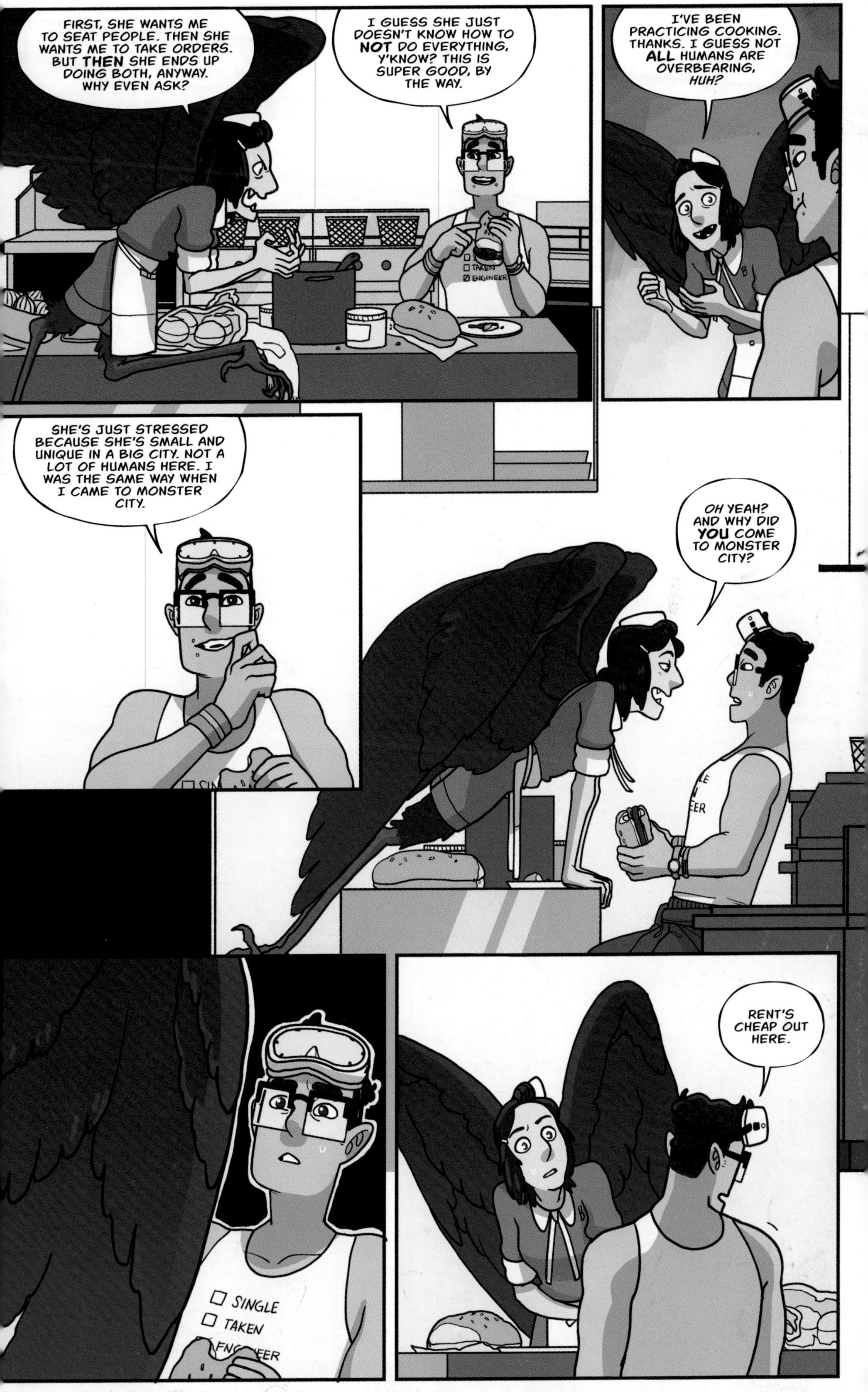
FIRST, SHE WANTS ME TO SEAT PEOPLE. THEN SHE WANTS ME TO TAKE ORDERS. BUT THEN SHE ENDS UP DOING BOTH, ANYWAY. WHY EVEN ASK?
I GUESS SHE JUST DOESN'T KNOW HOW TO NOT DO EVERYTHING, Y'KNOW? THIS IS SUPER GOOD, BY THE WAY.
SINGLE
TAKEN
ENGINEER
I'VE BEEN PRACTICING COOKING. THANKS. I GUESS NOT ALL HUMANS ARE OVERBEARING, HUH?
SHE'S JUST STRESSED BECAUSE SHE'S SMALL AND UNIQUE IN A BIG CITY. NOT A LOT OF HUMANS HERE. I WAS THE SAME WAY WHEN I CAME TO MONSTER CITY.
OH YEAH? AND WHY DID YOU COME TO MONSTER CITY?
SINGLE
TAKEN
RENT'S CHEAP OUT HERE.

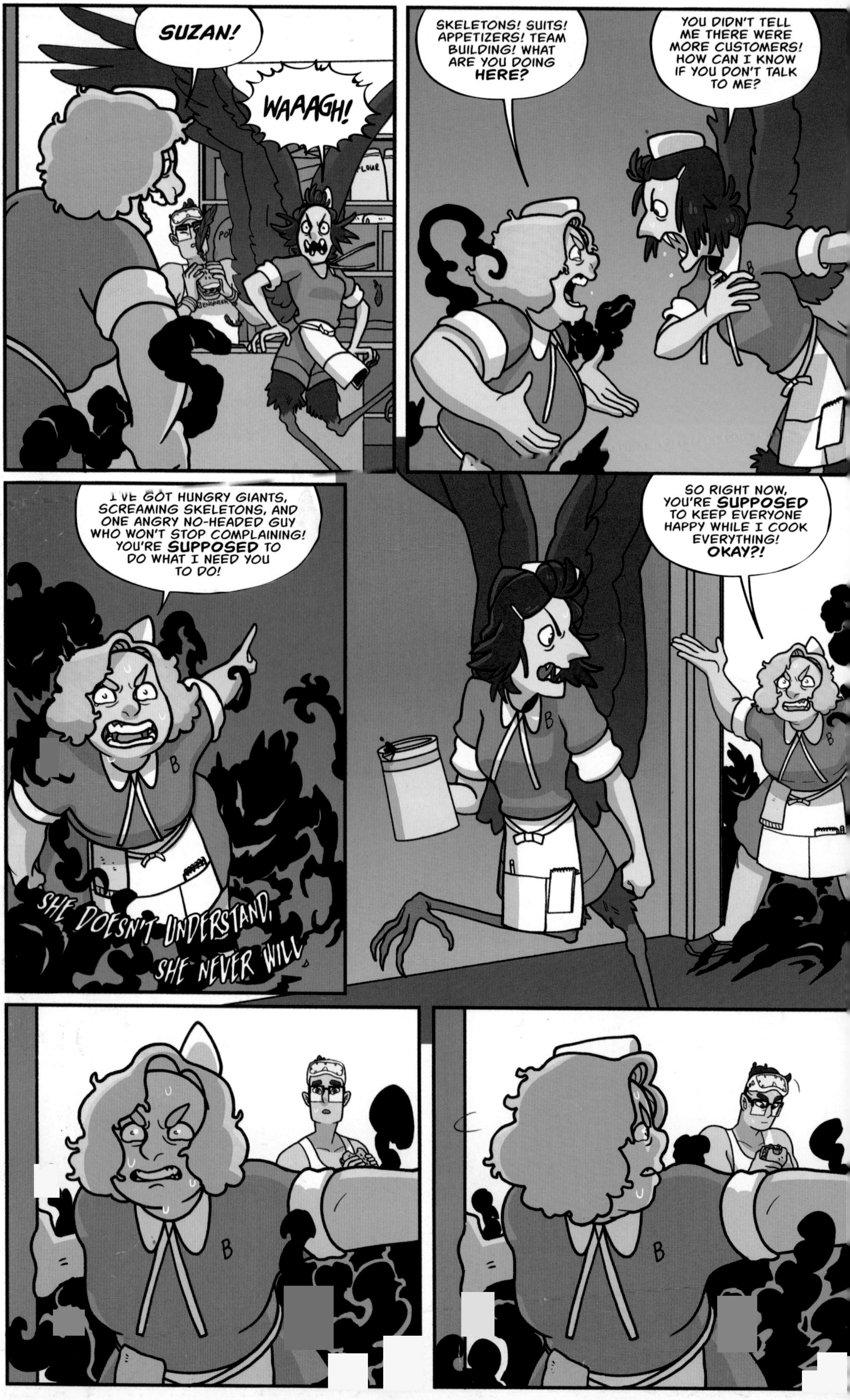
SUZAN!
WAAAGH!
SKELETONS! SUITS! APPETIZERS! TEAM BUILDING! WHAT ARE YOU DOING HERE?
YOU DIDN'T TELL ME THERE WERE MORE CUSTOMERS! HOW CAN I KNOW IF YOU DON'T TALK TO ME?
I'VE GOT HUNGRY GIANTS, SCREAMING SKELETONS, AND ONE ANGRY NO-HEADED GUY WHO WON'T STOP COMPLAINING! YOU'RE SUPPOSED TO DO WHAT I NEED YOU TO DO!
SHE DOESN'T UNDERSTAND, SHE NEVER WILL
SO RIGHT NOW, YOU'RE SUPPOSED TO KEEP EVERYONE HAPPY WHILE I COOK EVERYTHING! OKAY?!

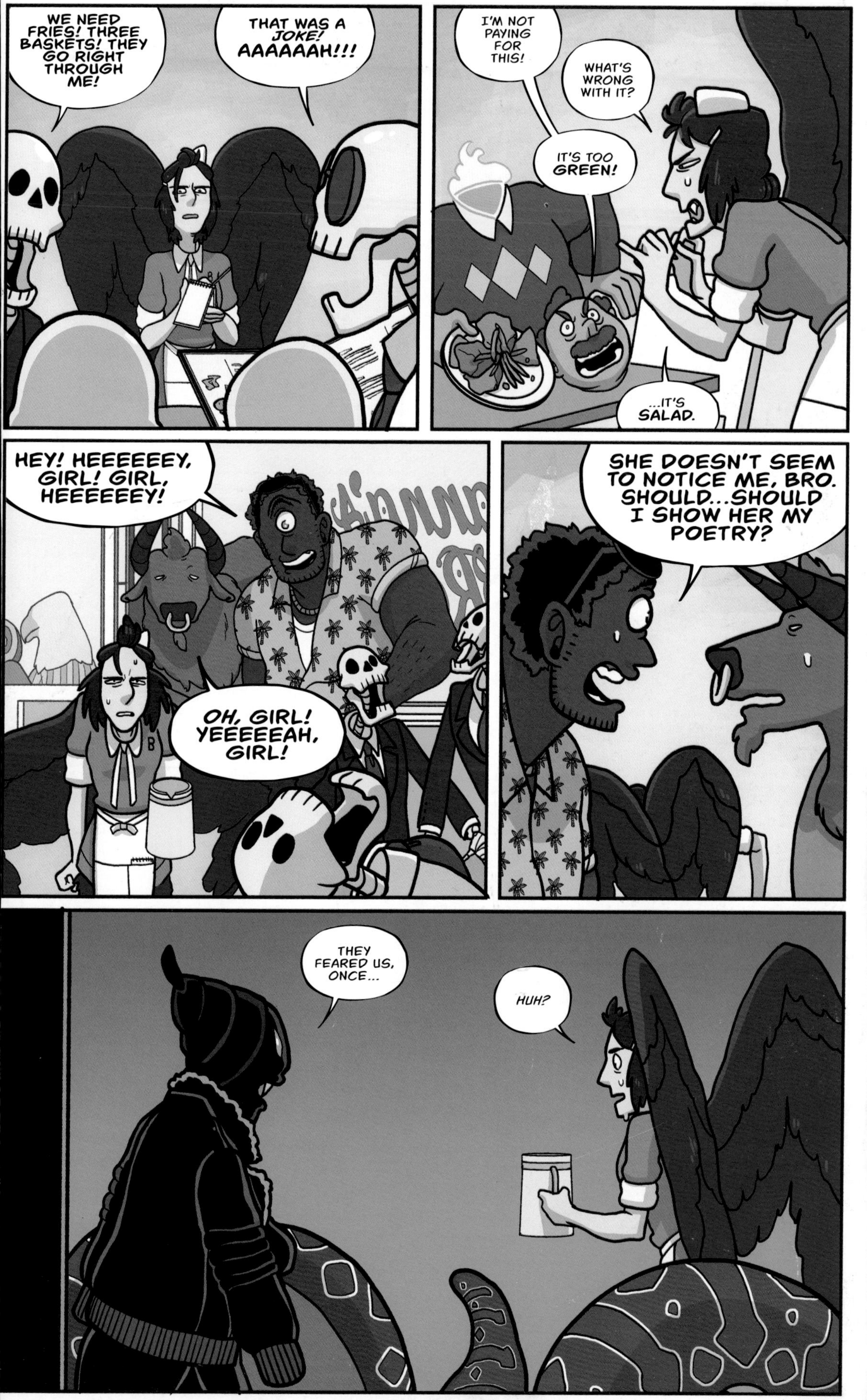
WE NEED FRIES! THREE BASKETS! THEY GO RIGHT THROUGH ME!
THAT WAS A *JOKE!* AAAAAAH!!!
I'M NOT PAYING FOR THIS!
WHAT'S WRONG WITH IT?
IT'S TOO GREEN!
...IT'S SALAD.
HEY! HEEEEEEY, GIRL! GIRL, HEEEEEEY!
OH, GIRL! YEEEEEAH, GIRL!
SHE DOESN'T SEEM TO NOTICE ME, BRO. SHOULD...SHOULD I SHOW HER MY POETRY?
THEY FEARED US, ONCE...
HUH?

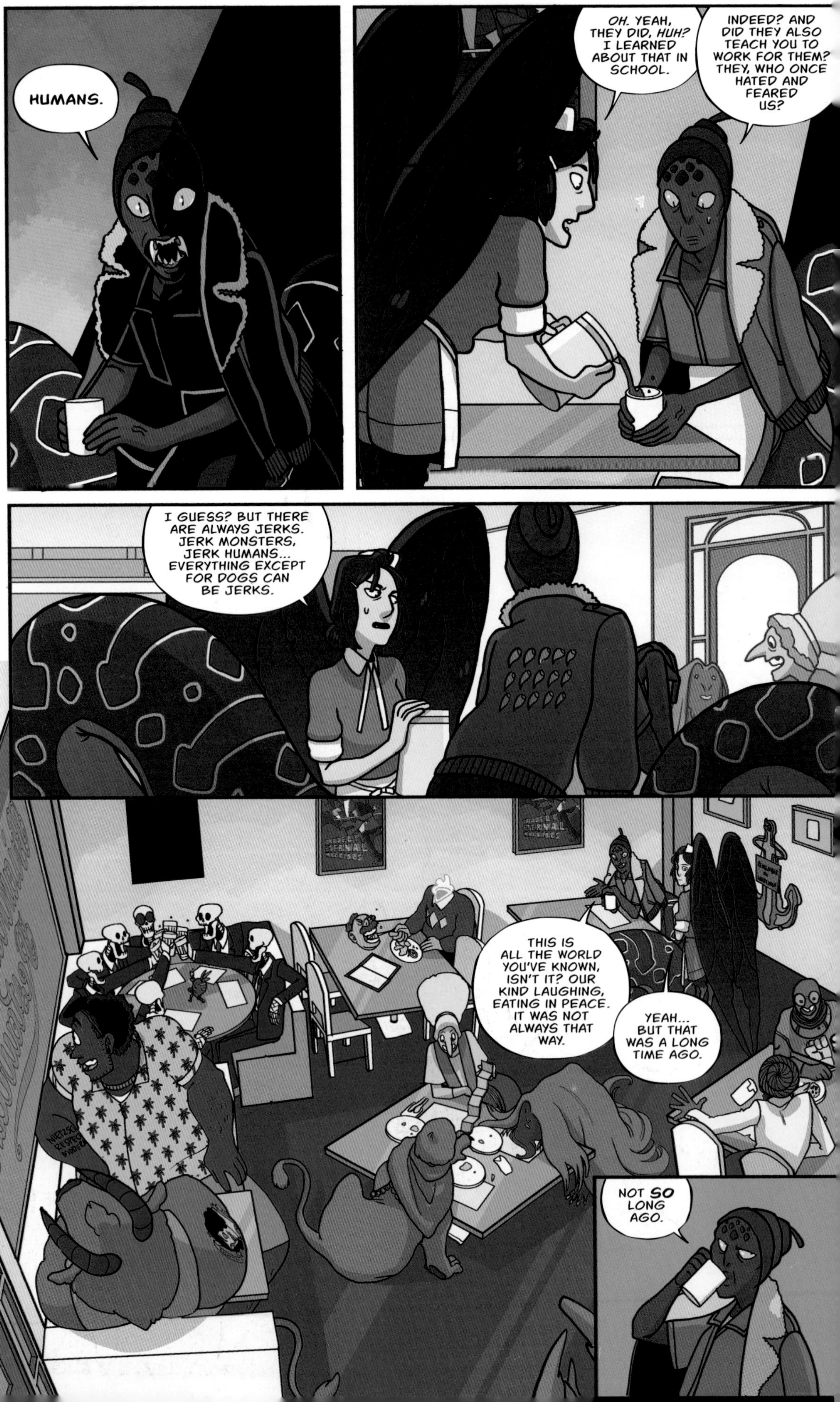
HUMANS.
OH. YEAH, THEY DID, *HUH?* I LEARNED ABOUT THAT IN SCHOOL.
INDEED? AND DID THEY ALSO TEACH YOU TO WORK FOR THEM? THEY, WHO ONCE HATED AND FEARED US?
I GUESS? BUT THERE ARE ALWAYS JERKS. JERK MONSTERS, JERK HUMANS... EVERYTHING EXCEPT FOR DOGS CAN BE JERKS.
THIS IS ALL THE WORLD YOU'VE KNOWN, ISN'T IT? OUR KIND LAUGHING, EATING IN PEACE. IT WAS NOT ALWAYS THAT WAY.
YEAH... BUT THAT WAS A LONG TIME AGO.
NOT **SO** LONG AGO.

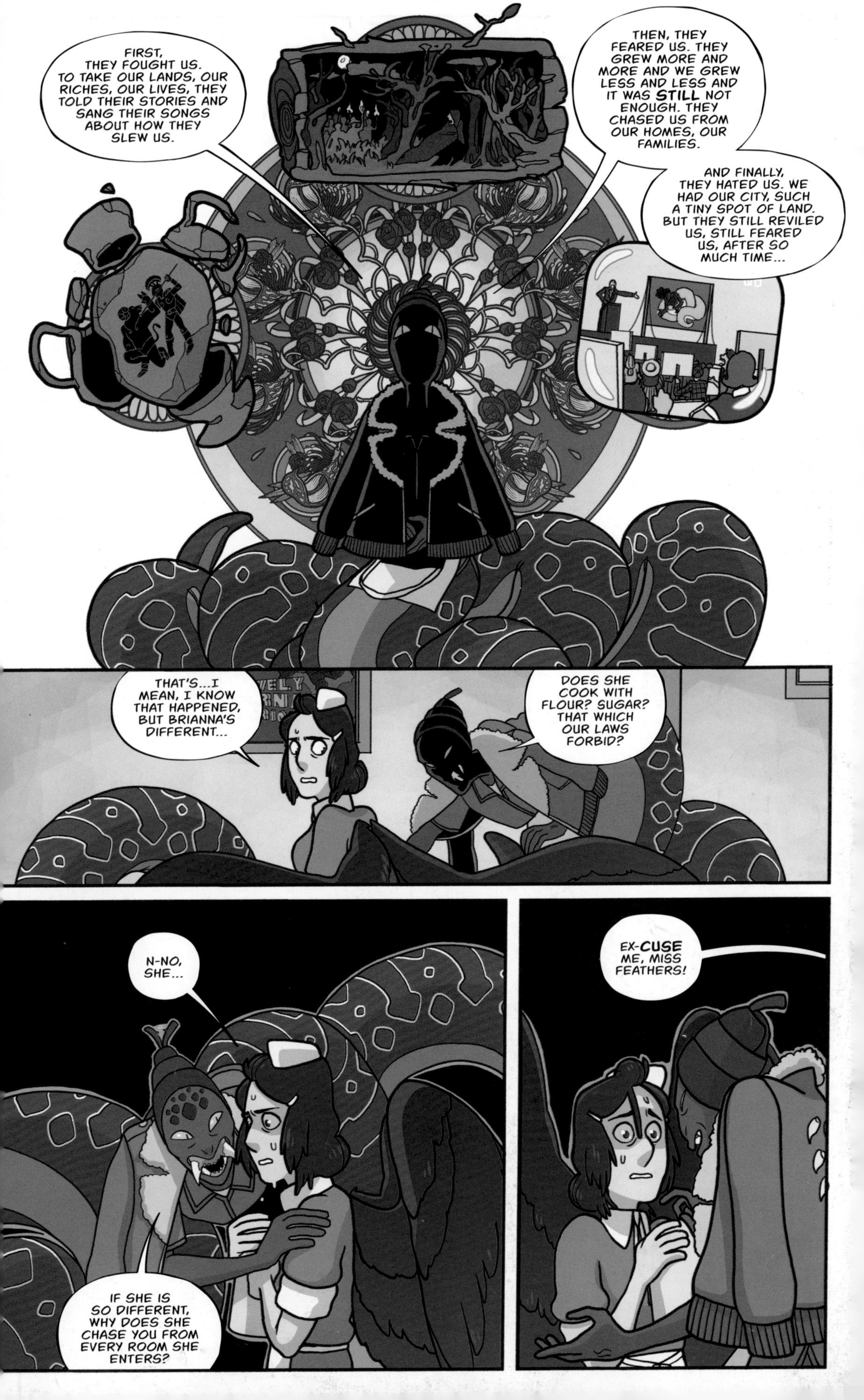
FIRST, THEY FOUGHT US. TO TAKE OUR LANDS, OUR RICHES, OUR LIVES, THEY TOLD THEIR STORIES AND SANG THEIR SONGS ABOUT HOW THEY SLEW US.
THEN, THEY FEARED US. THEY GREW MORE AND MORE AND WE GREW LESS AND LESS AND IT WAS STILL NOT ENOUGH. THEY CHASED US FROM OUR HOMES, OUR FAMILIES.
AND FINALLY, THEY HATED US. WE HAD OUR CITY, SUCH A TINY SPOT OF LAND. BUT THEY STILL REVILED US, STILL FEARED US, AFTER SO MUCH TIME...
THAT'S...I MEAN, I KNOW THAT HAPPENED, BUT BRIANNA'S DIFFERENT...
DOES SHE COOK WITH FLOUR? SUGAR? THAT WHICH OUR LAWS FORBID?
N-NO, SHE...
IF SHE IS SO DIFFERENT, WHY DOES SHE CHASE YOU FROM EVERY ROOM SHE ENTERS?
EX-CUSE ME, MISS FEATHERS!

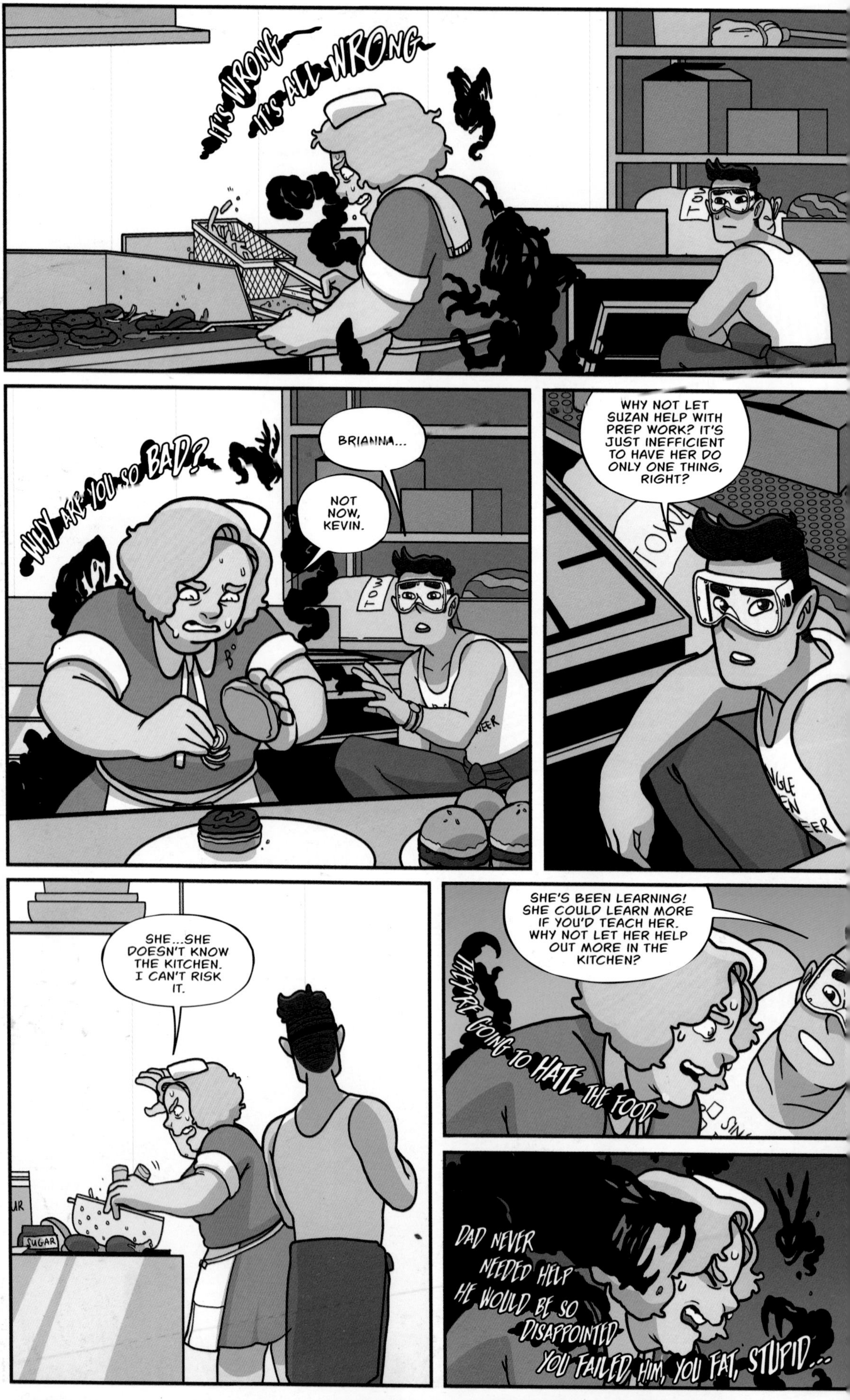

IT'S WRONG
IT'S ALL WRONG
WHY ARE YOU SO BAD?
BRIANNA...
NOT NOW, KEVIN.
WHY NOT LET SUZAN HELP WITH PREP WORK? IT'S JUST INEFFICIENT TO HAVE HER DO ONLY ONE THING, RIGHT?
SHE...SHE DOESN'T KNOW THE KITCHEN. I CAN'T RISK IT.
SHE'S BEEN LEARNING! SHE COULD LEARN MORE IF YOU'D TEACH HER. WHY NOT LET HER HELP OUT MORE IN THE KITCHEN?
THEY'RE GOING TO HATE THE FOOD
DAD NEVER
NEEDED HELP
HE WOULD BE SO
DISAPPOINTED
YOU FAILED HIM, YOU FAT, STUPID...
SUGAR

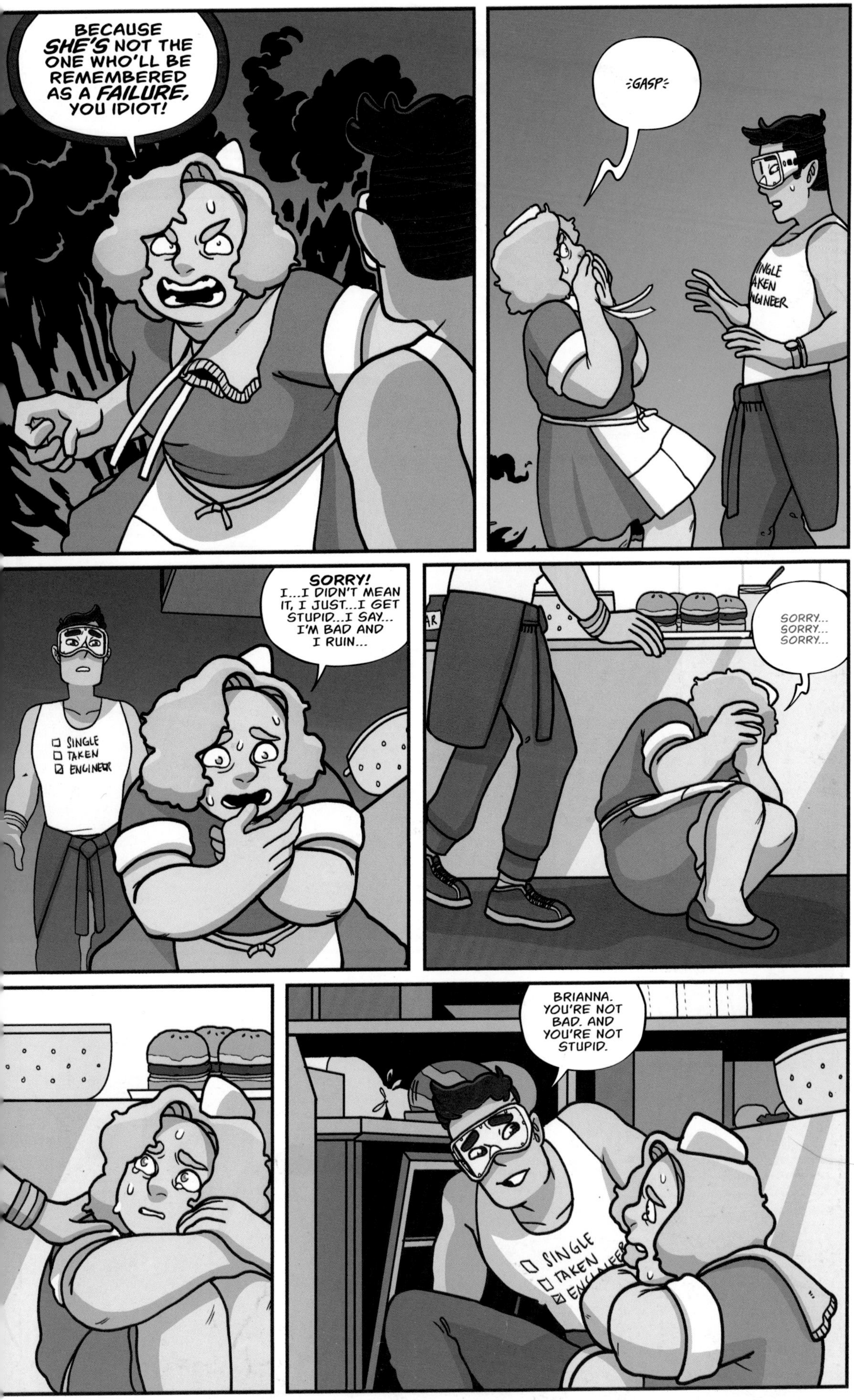
BECAUSE SHE'S NOT THE ONE WHO'LL BE REMEMBERED AS A FAILURE, YOU IDIOT!
GASP
SINGLE TAKEN ENGINEER
SORRY! I...I DIDN'T MEAN IT, I JUST...I GET STUPID...I SAY... I'M BAD AND I RUIN...
SINGLE TAKEN ENGINEER
SORRY... SORRY... SORRY...
BRIANNA. YOU'RE NOT BAD. AND YOU'RE NOT STUPID.

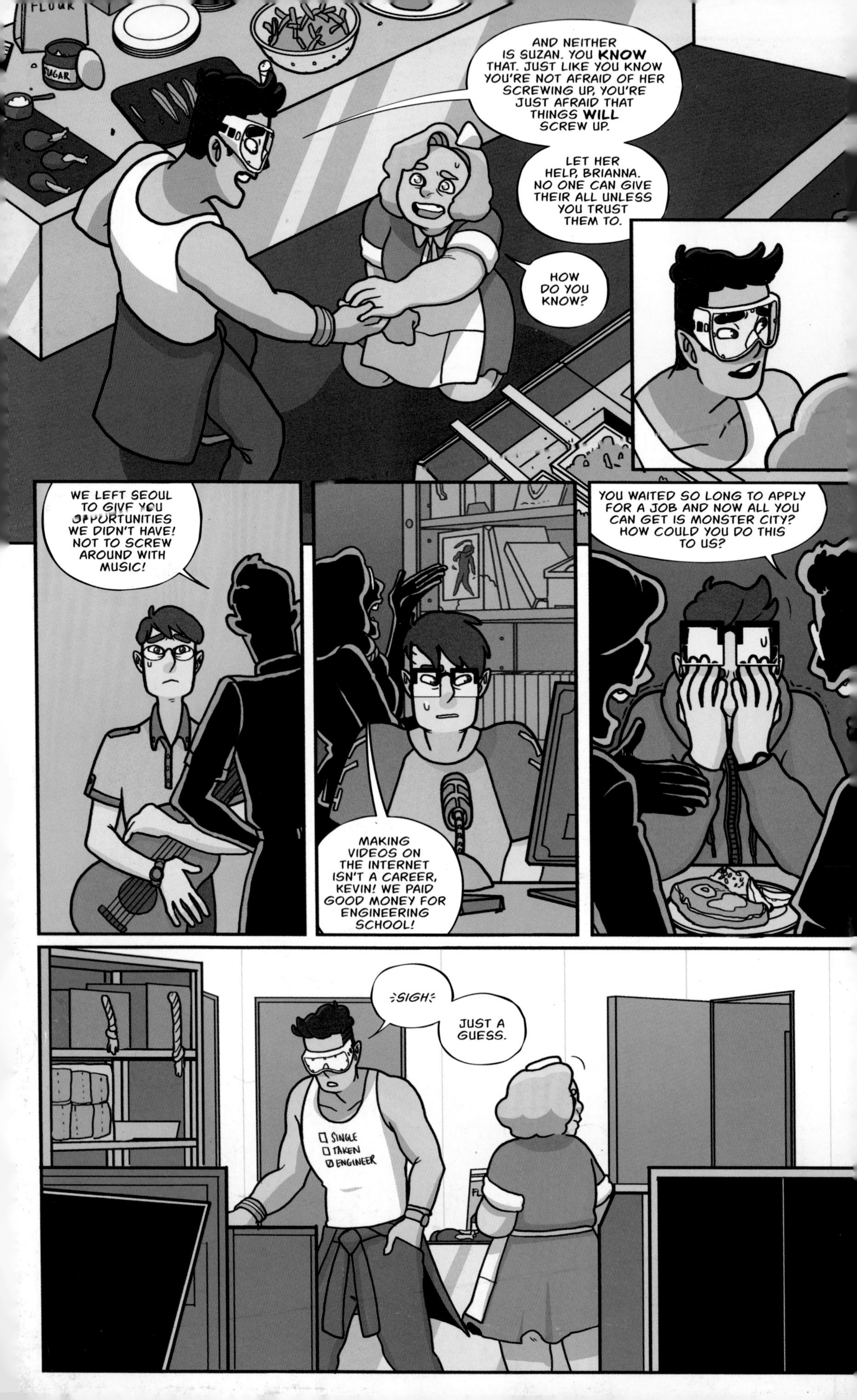
FLOUR
SUGAR
AND NEITHER IS SUZAN. YOU KNOW THAT. JUST LIKE YOU KNOW YOU'RE NOT AFRAID OF HER SCREWING UP, YOU'RE JUST AFRAID THAT THINGS WILL SCREW UP.
LET HER HELP, BRIANNA. NO ONE CAN GIVE THEIR ALL UNLESS YOU TRUST THEM TO.
HOW DO YOU KNOW?
WE LEFT SEOUL TO GIVE YOU OPPORTUNITIES WE DIDN'T HAVE! NOT TO SCREW AROUND WITH MUSIC!
MAKING VIDEOS ON THE INTERNET ISN'T A CAREER, KEVIN! WE PAID GOOD MONEY FOR ENGINEERING SCHOOL!
YOU WAITED SO LONG TO APPLY FOR A JOB AND NOW ALL YOU CAN GET IS MONSTER CITY? HOW COULD YOU DO THIS TO US?
SIGH
JUST A GUESS.
☐ SINGLE
☐ TAKEN
☑ ENGINEER

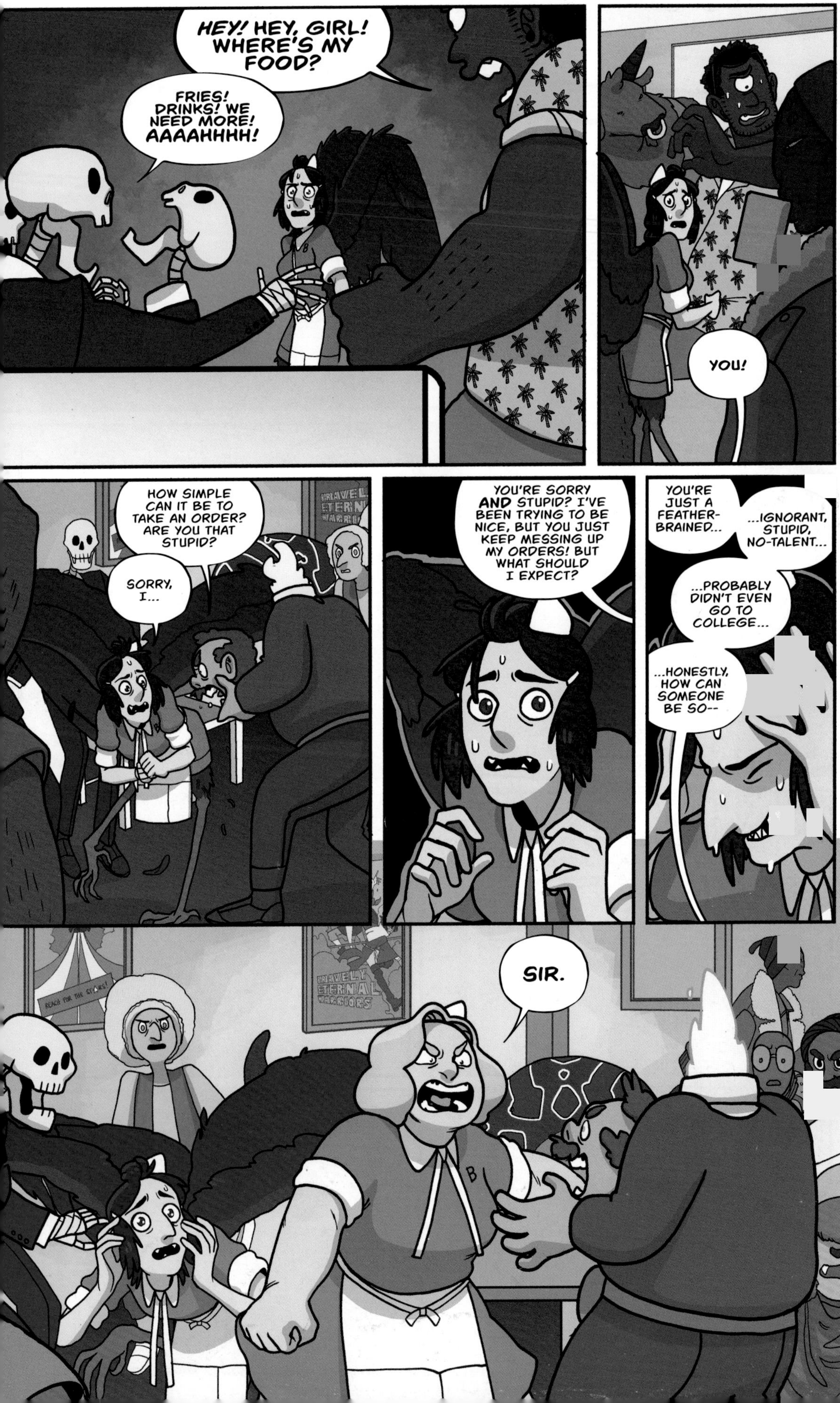
HEY! HEY, GIRL! WHERE'S MY FOOD?
FRIES! DRINKS! WE NEED MORE! AAAAHHHH!
YOU!
HOW SIMPLE CAN IT BE TO TAKE AN ORDER? ARE YOU THAT STUPID?
SORRY, I...
YOU'RE SORRY AND STUPID? I'VE BEEN TRYING TO BE NICE, BUT YOU JUST KEEP MESSING UP MY ORDERS! BUT WHAT SHOULD I EXPECT?
YOU'RE JUST A FEATHER-BRAINED...
...IGNORANT, STUPID, NO-TALENT...
...PROBABLY DIDN'T EVEN GO TO COLLEGE...
...HONESTLY, HOW CAN SOMEONE BE SO--
BRAVELY ETERNAL WARRIORS
REACH FOR THE STARS!
SIR.

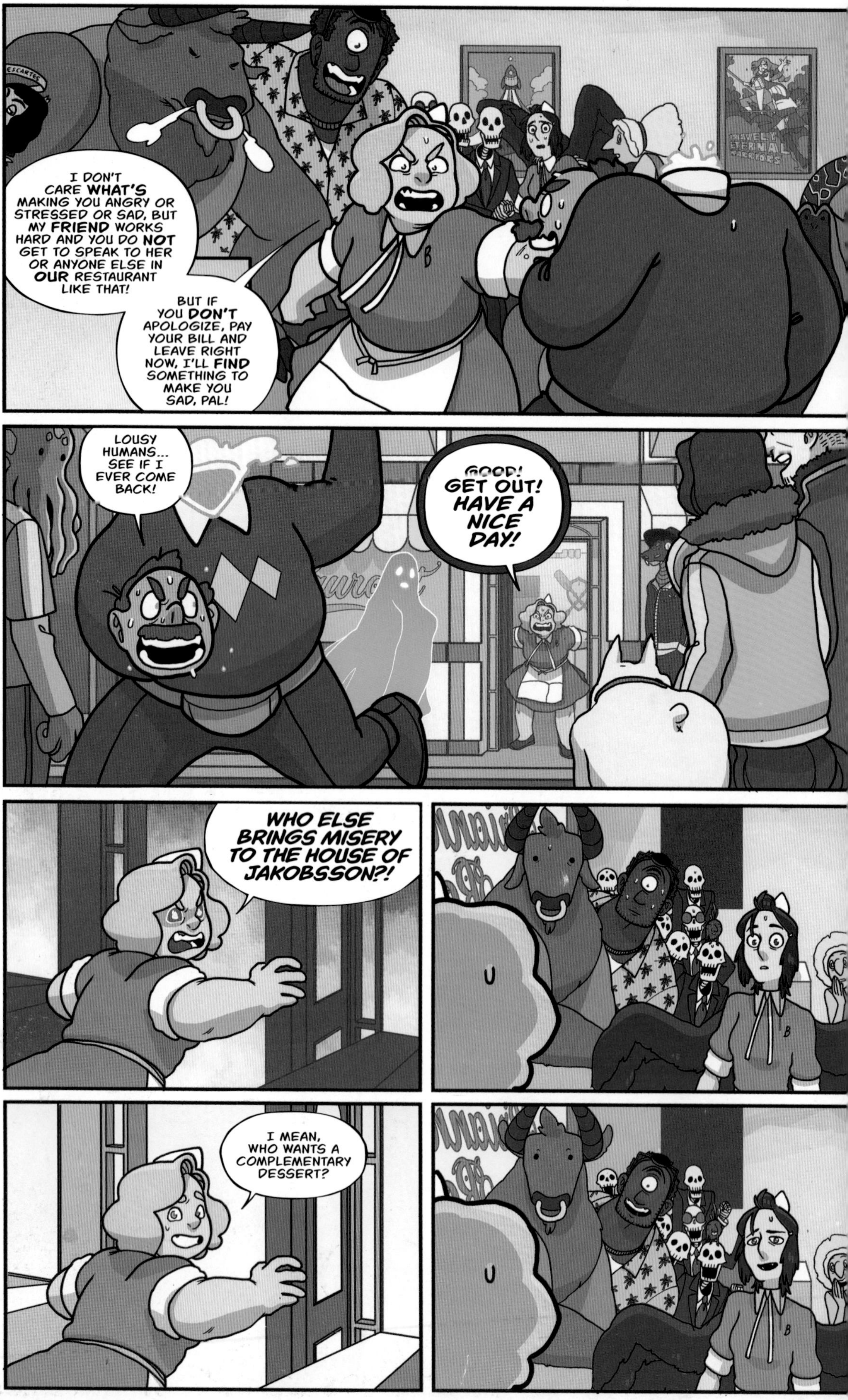
I DON'T CARE WHAT'S MAKING YOU ANGRY OR STRESSED OR SAD, BUT MY FRIEND WORKS HARD AND YOU DO NOT GET TO SPEAK TO HER OR ANYONE ELSE IN OUR RESTAURANT LIKE THAT!
BUT IF YOU DON'T APOLOGIZE, PAY YOUR BILL AND LEAVE RIGHT NOW, I'LL FIND SOMETHING TO MAKE YOU SAD, PAL!
LOUSY HUMANS... SEE IF I EVER COME BACK!
GOOD! GET OUT! HAVE A NICE DAY!
WHO ELSE BRINGS MISERY TO THE HOUSE OF JAKOBSSON?!
I MEAN, WHO WANTS A COMPLEMENTARY DESSERT?

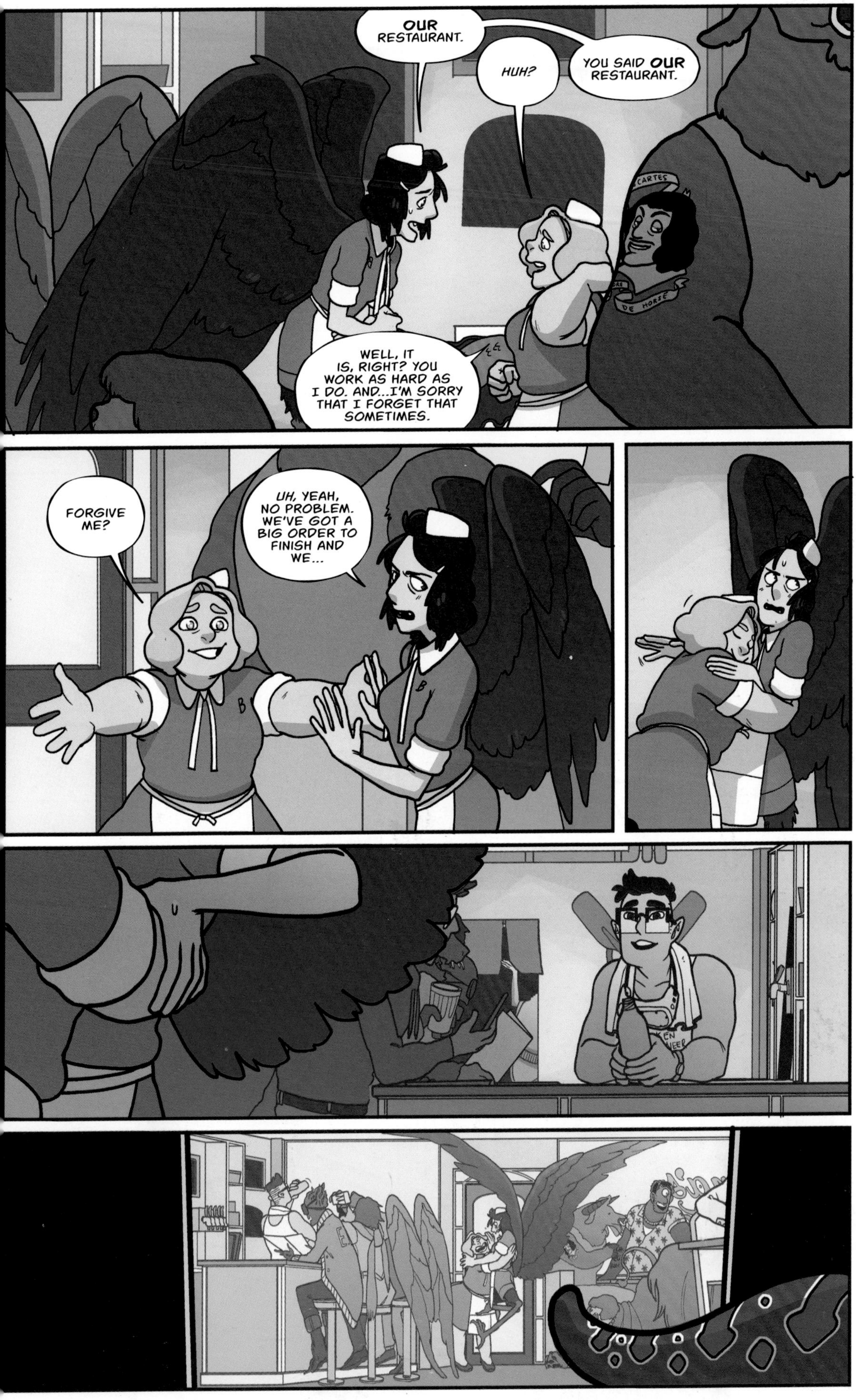
OUR RESTAURANT.
HUH?
YOU SAID OUR RESTAURANT.
CARTES
DE HORSE
WELL, IT IS, RIGHT? YOU WORK AS HARD AS I DO. AND...I'M SORRY THAT I FORGET THAT SOMETIMES.
FORGIVE ME?
UH, YEAH, NO PROBLEM. WE'VE GOT A BIG ORDER TO FINISH AND WE...

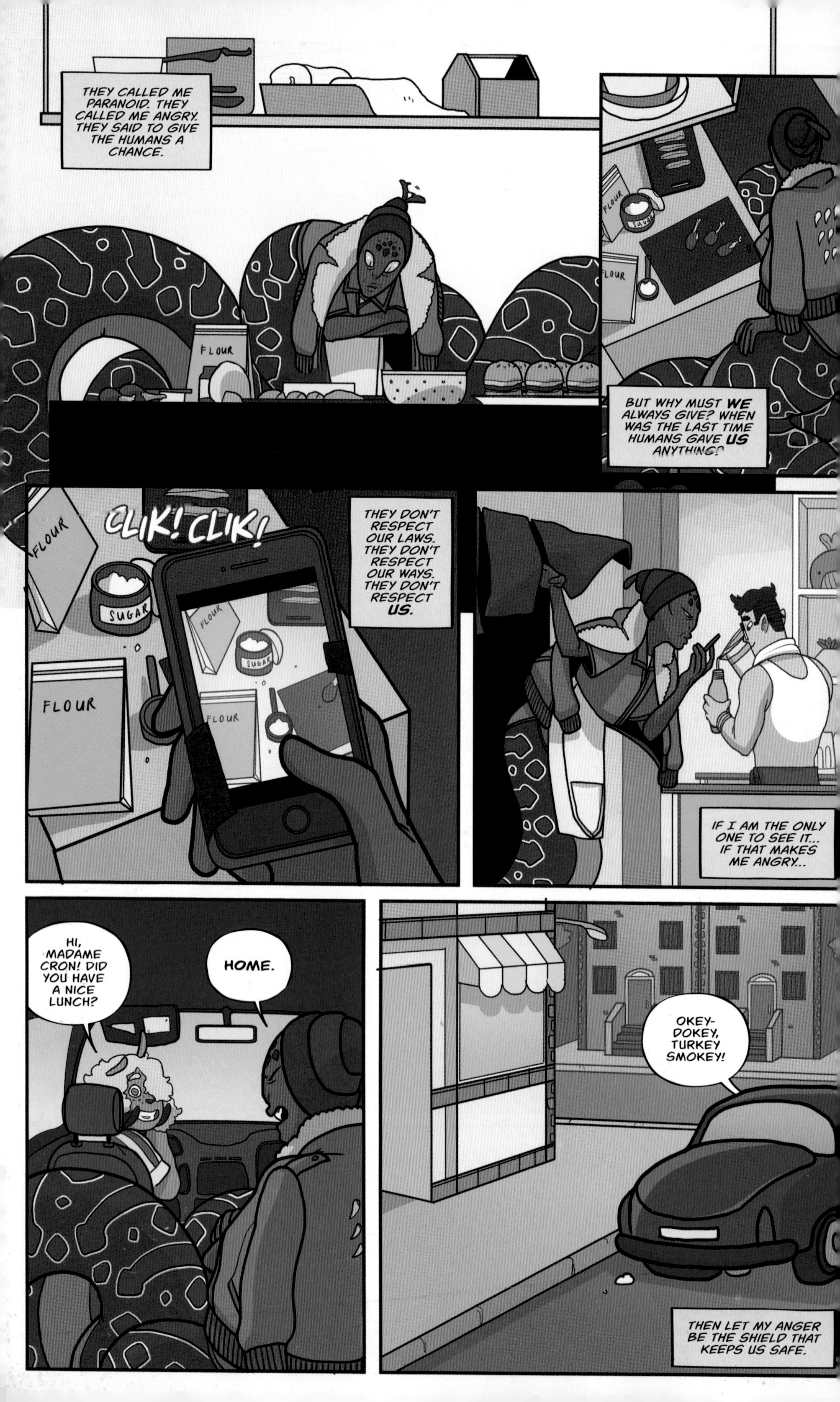

THEY CALLED ME PARANOID. THEY CALLED ME ANGRY. THEY SAID TO GIVE THE HUMANS A CHANCE.
FLOUR
[redacted]
FLOUR
SUGAR
FLOUR
BUT WHY MUST WE ALWAYS GIVE? WHEN WAS THE LAST TIME HUMANS GAVE US ANYTHING?
CLIK! CLIK!
FLOUR
SUGAR
FLOUR
THEY DON'T RESPECT OUR LAWS. THEY DON'T RESPECT OUR WAYS. THEY DON'T RESPECT US.
IF I AM THE ONLY ONE TO SEE IT... IF THAT MAKES ME ANGRY...
HI, MADAME CRON! DID YOU HAVE A NICE LUNCH?
HOME.
OKEY-DOKEY, TURKEY SMOKEY!
THEN LET MY ANGER BE THE SHIELD THAT KEEPS US SAFE.

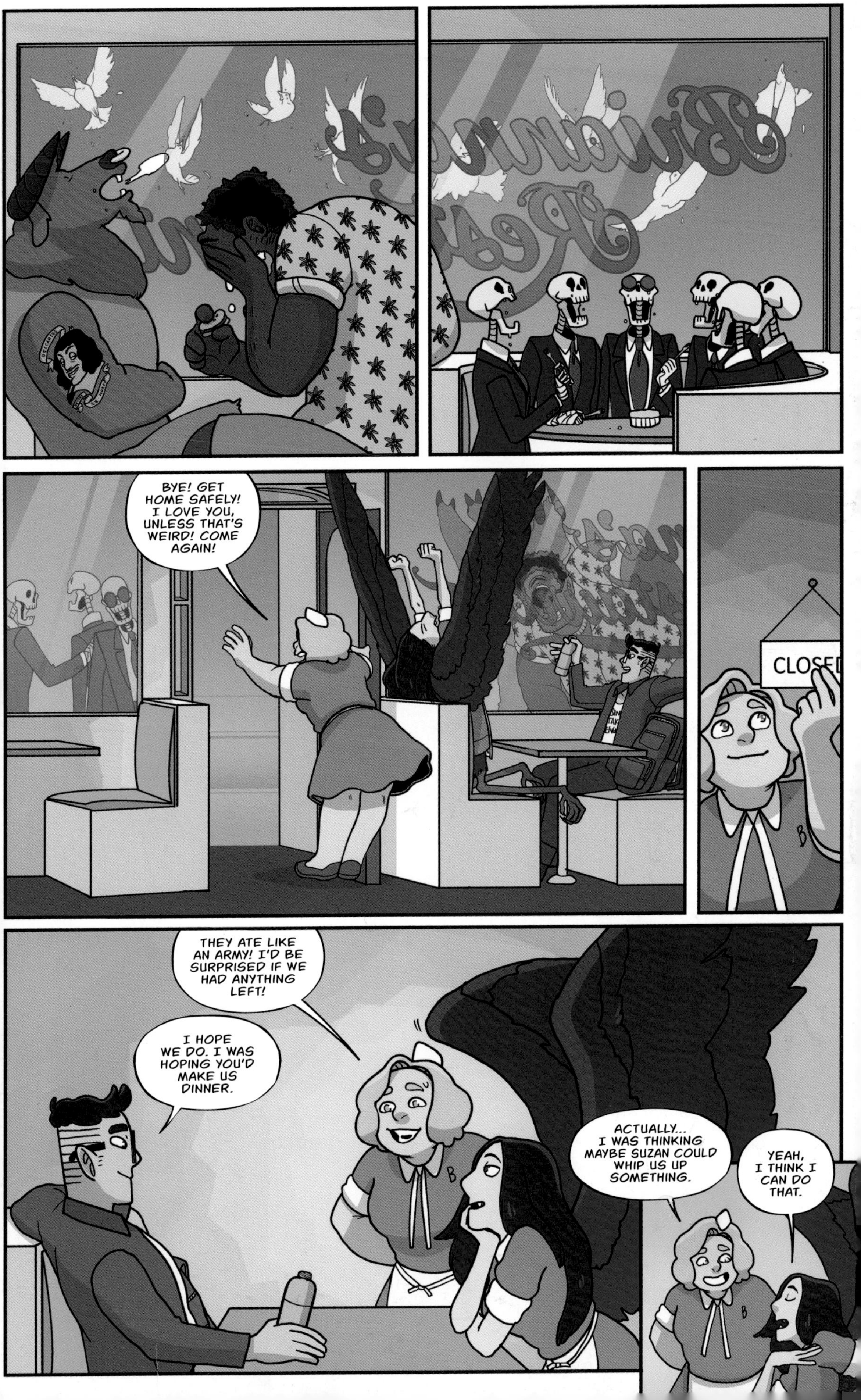

BYE! GET HOME SAFELY! I LOVE YOU, UNLESS THAT'S WEIRD! COME AGAIN!
CLOSED
THEY ATE LIKE AN ARMY! I'D BE SURPRISED IF WE HAD ANYTHING LEFT!
I HOPE WE DO. I WAS HOPING YOU'D MAKE US DINNER.
ACTUALLY... I WAS THINKING MAYBE SUZAN COULD WHIP US UP SOMETHING.
YEAH, I THINK I CAN DO THAT.

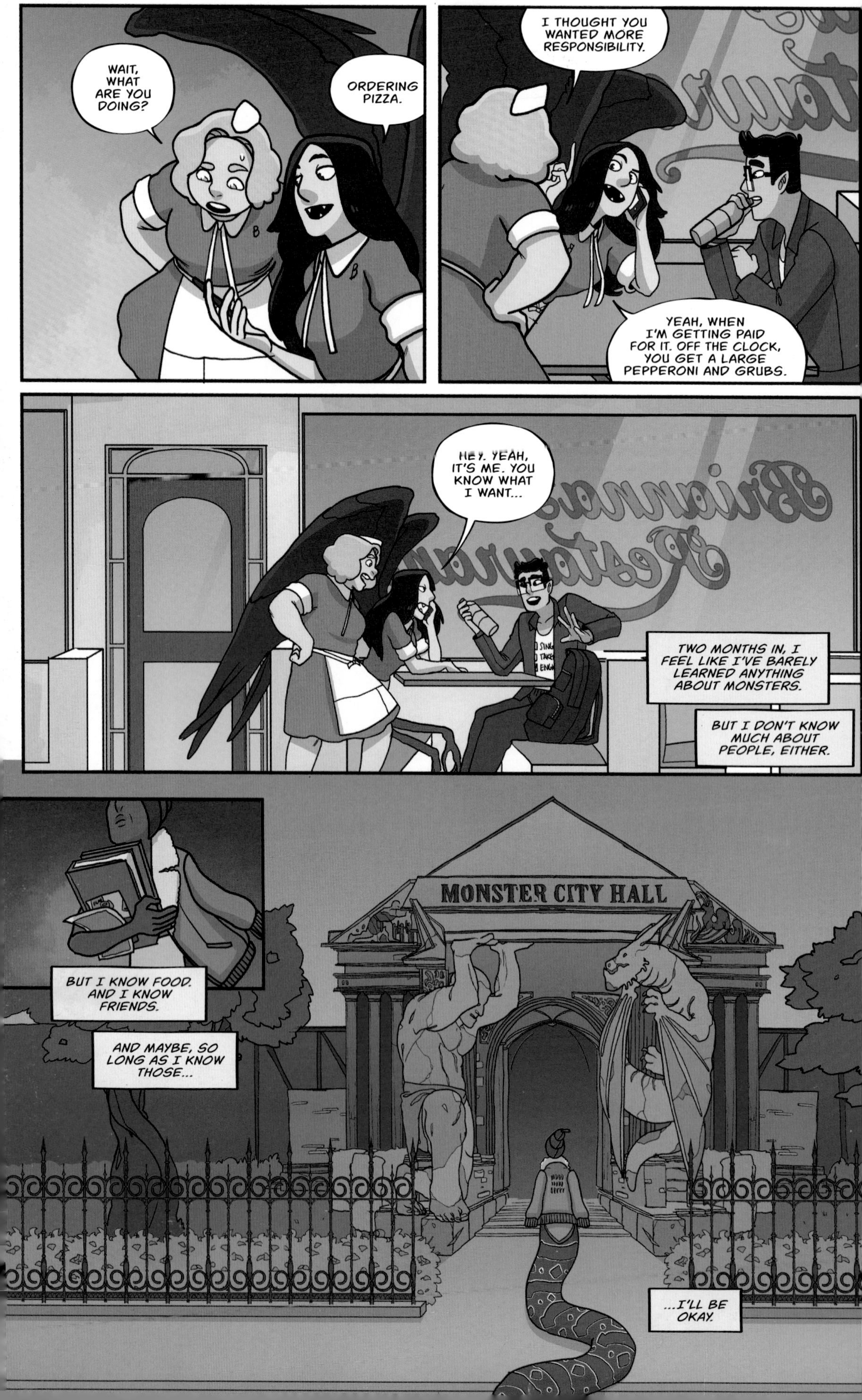
WAIT, WHAT ARE YOU DOING?
ORDERING PIZZA.
I THOUGHT YOU WANTED MORE RESPONSIBILITY.
YEAH, WHEN I'M GETTING PAID FOR IT. OFF THE CLOCK, YOU GET A LARGE PEPPERONI AND GRUBS.
HEY. YEAH, IT'S ME. YOU KNOW WHAT I WANT...
TWO MONTHS IN, I FEEL LIKE I'VE BARELY LEARNED ANYTHING ABOUT MONSTERS.
BUT I DON'T KNOW MUCH ABOUT PEOPLE, EITHER.
MONSTER CITY HALL
BUT I KNOW FOOD. AND I KNOW FRIENDS.
AND MAYBE, SO LONG AS I KNOW THOSE...
...I'LL BE OKAY.

chapter THREE

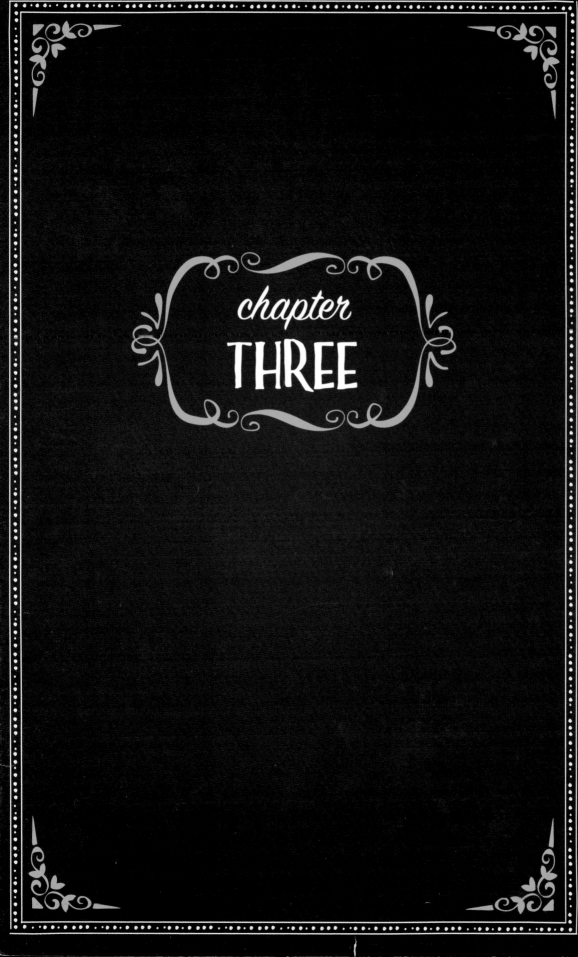

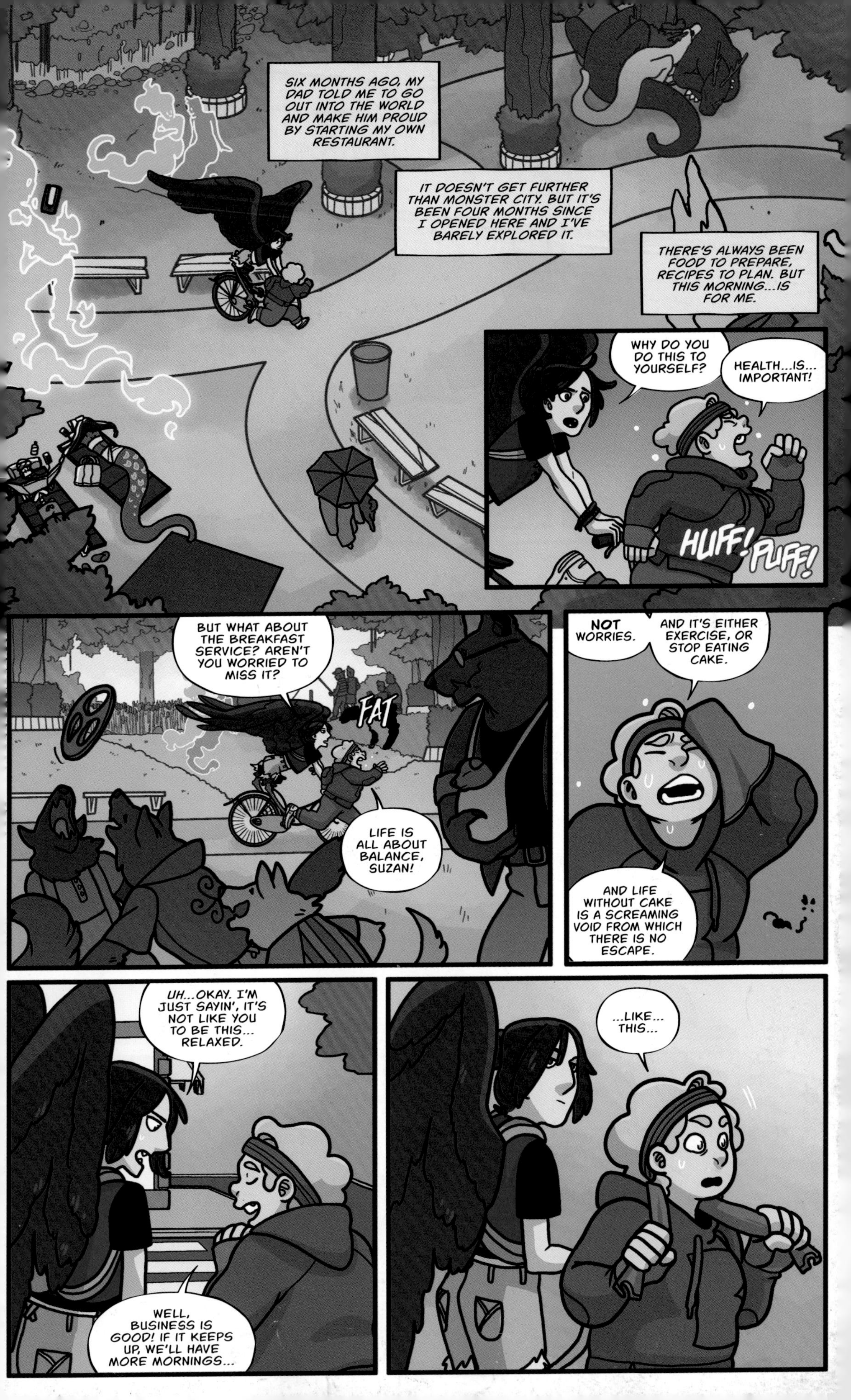
SIX MONTHS AGO, MY DAD TOLD ME TO GO OUT INTO THE WORLD AND MAKE HIM PROUD BY STARTING MY OWN RESTAURANT.
IT DOESN'T GET FURTHER THAN MONSTER CITY. BUT IT'S BEEN FOUR MONTHS SINCE I OPENED HERE AND I'VE BARELY EXPLORED IT.
THERE'S ALWAYS BEEN FOOD TO PREPARE, RECIPES TO PLAN. BUT THIS MORNING...IS FOR ME.
WHY DO YOU DO THIS TO YOURSELF?
HEALTH...IS... IMPORTANT!
HUFF! PUFF!
BUT WHAT ABOUT THE BREAKFAST SERVICE? AREN'T YOU WORRIED TO MISS IT?
FAT
LIFE IS ALL ABOUT BALANCE, SUZAN!
NOT WORRIES.
AND IT'S EITHER EXERCISE, OR STOP EATING CAKE.
AND LIFE WITHOUT CAKE IS A SCREAMING VOID FROM WHICH THERE IS NO ESCAPE.
UH...OKAY. I'M JUST SAYIN', IT'S NOT LIKE YOU TO BE THIS... RELAXED.
WELL, BUSINESS IS GOOD! IF IT KEEPS UP, WE'LL HAVE MORE MORNINGS...
...LIKE... THIS...

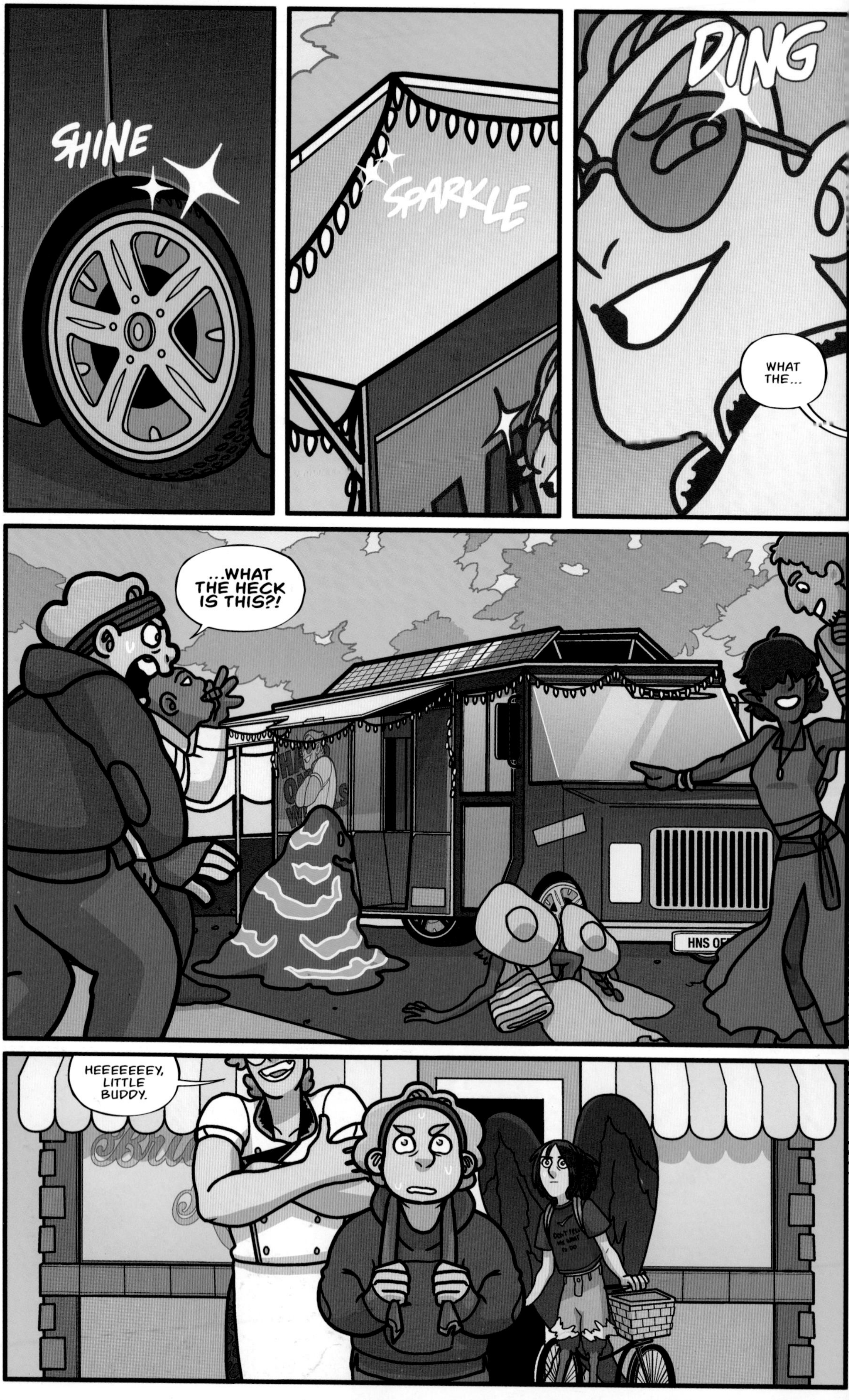
SHINE
SPARKLE
DING
WHAT THE...
...WHAT THE HECK IS THIS?!
HNS OF
HEEEEEEEY, LITTLE BUDDY.
DON'T TELL ME WHAT TO DO

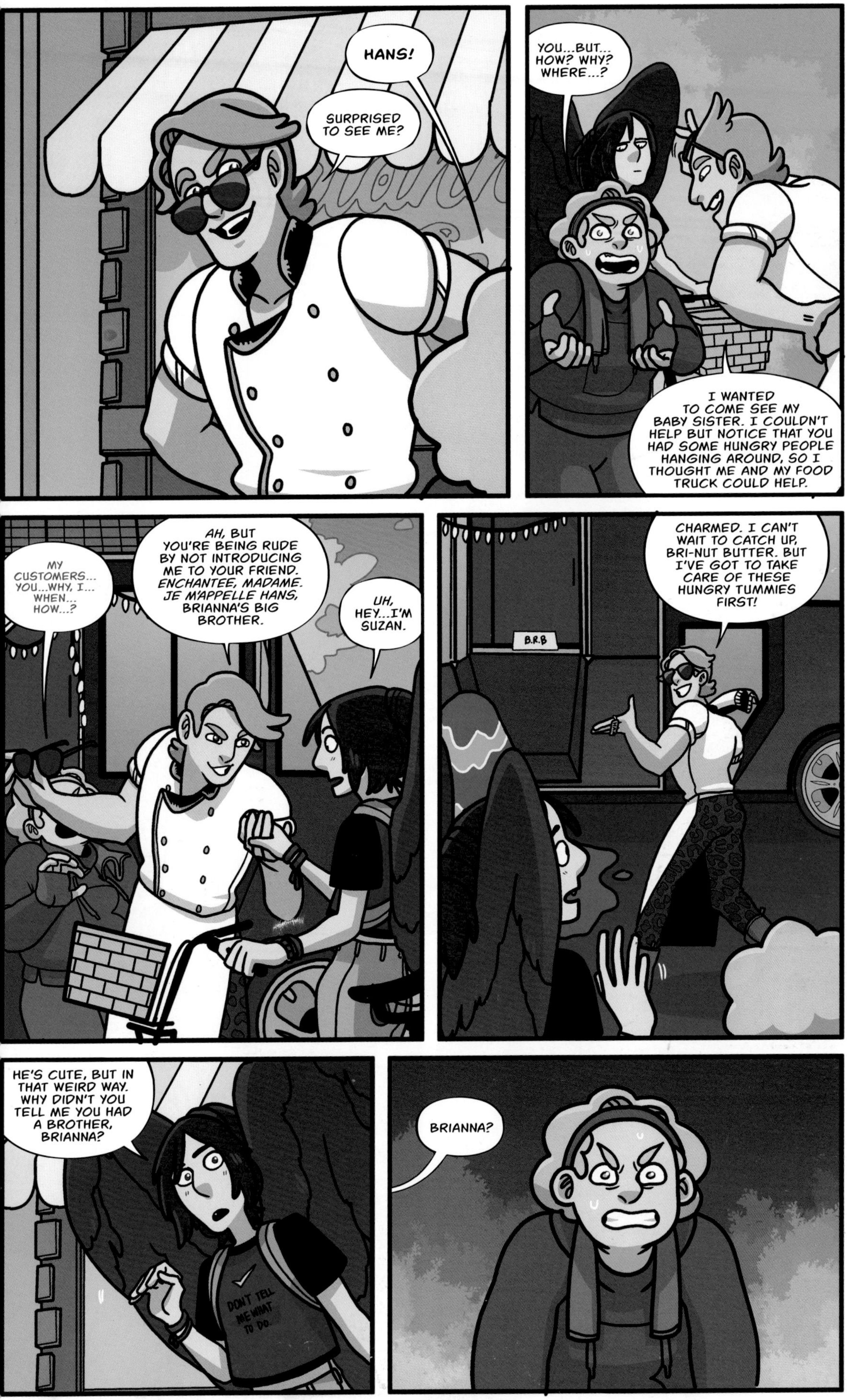
HANS!
SURPRISED TO SEE ME?
YOU...BUT... HOW? WHY? WHERE...?
I WANTED TO COME SEE MY BABY SISTER. I COULDN'T HELP BUT NOTICE THAT YOU HAD SOME HUNGRY PEOPLE HANGING AROUND, SO I THOUGHT ME AND MY FOOD TRUCK COULD HELP.
MY CUSTOMERS... YOU...WHY, I... WHEN... HOW...?
AH, BUT YOU'RE BEING RUDE BY NOT INTRODUCING ME TO YOUR FRIEND. *ENCHANTEE, MADAME. JE M'APPELLE HANS,* BRIANNA'S BIG BROTHER.
UH, HEY...I'M SUZAN.
B.R.B
CHARMED. I CAN'T WAIT TO CATCH UP, BRI-NUT BUTTER. BUT I'VE GOT TO TAKE CARE OF THESE HUNGRY TUMMIES FIRST!
HE'S CUTE, BUT IN THAT WEIRD WAY. WHY DIDN'T YOU TELL ME YOU HAD A BROTHER, BRIANNA?
DON'T TELL ME WHAT TO DO.
BRIANNA?

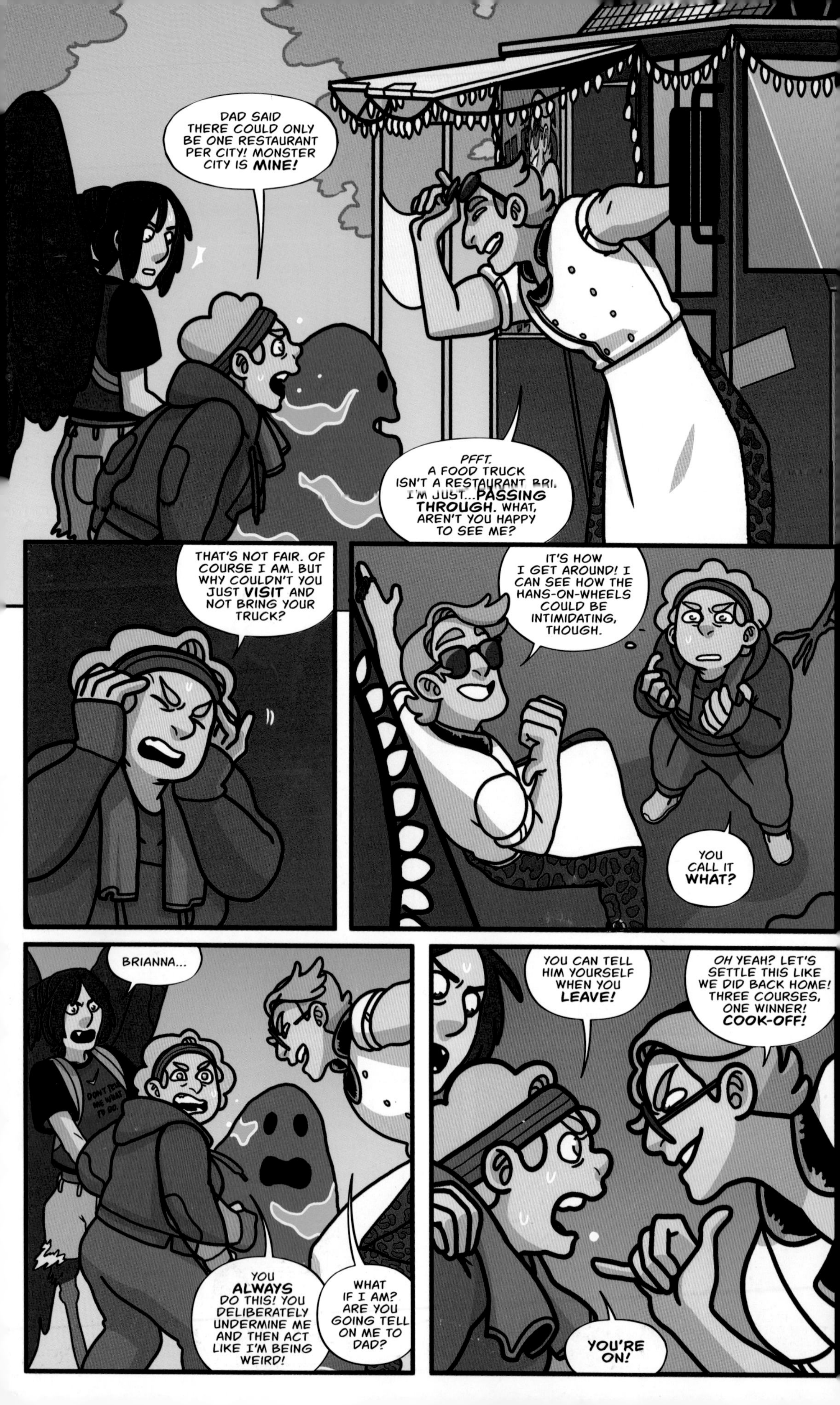
DAD SAID THERE COULD ONLY BE ONE RESTAURANT PER CITY! MONSTER CITY IS **MINE!**
PFFT. A FOOD TRUCK ISN'T A RESTAURANT, BRI. I'M JUST... **PASSING THROUGH.** WHAT, AREN'T YOU HAPPY TO SEE ME?
THAT'S NOT FAIR. OF COURSE I AM. BUT WHY COULDN'T YOU JUST **VISIT** AND NOT BRING YOUR TRUCK?
IT'S HOW I GET AROUND! I CAN SEE HOW THE HANS-ON-WHEELS COULD BE INTIMIDATING, THOUGH.
YOU CALL IT **WHAT?**
BRIANNA...
DON'T TELL ME WHAT I'D DO.
YOU **ALWAYS** DO THIS! YOU DELIBERATELY UNDERMINE ME AND THEN ACT LIKE I'M BEING WEIRD!
WHAT IF I AM? ARE YOU GOING TELL ON ME TO DAD?
YOU CAN TELL HIM YOURSELF WHEN YOU **LEAVE!**
OH YEAH? LET'S SETTLE THIS LIKE WE DID BACK HOME! THREE COURSES, ONE WINNER! **COOK-OFF!**
YOU'RE ON!

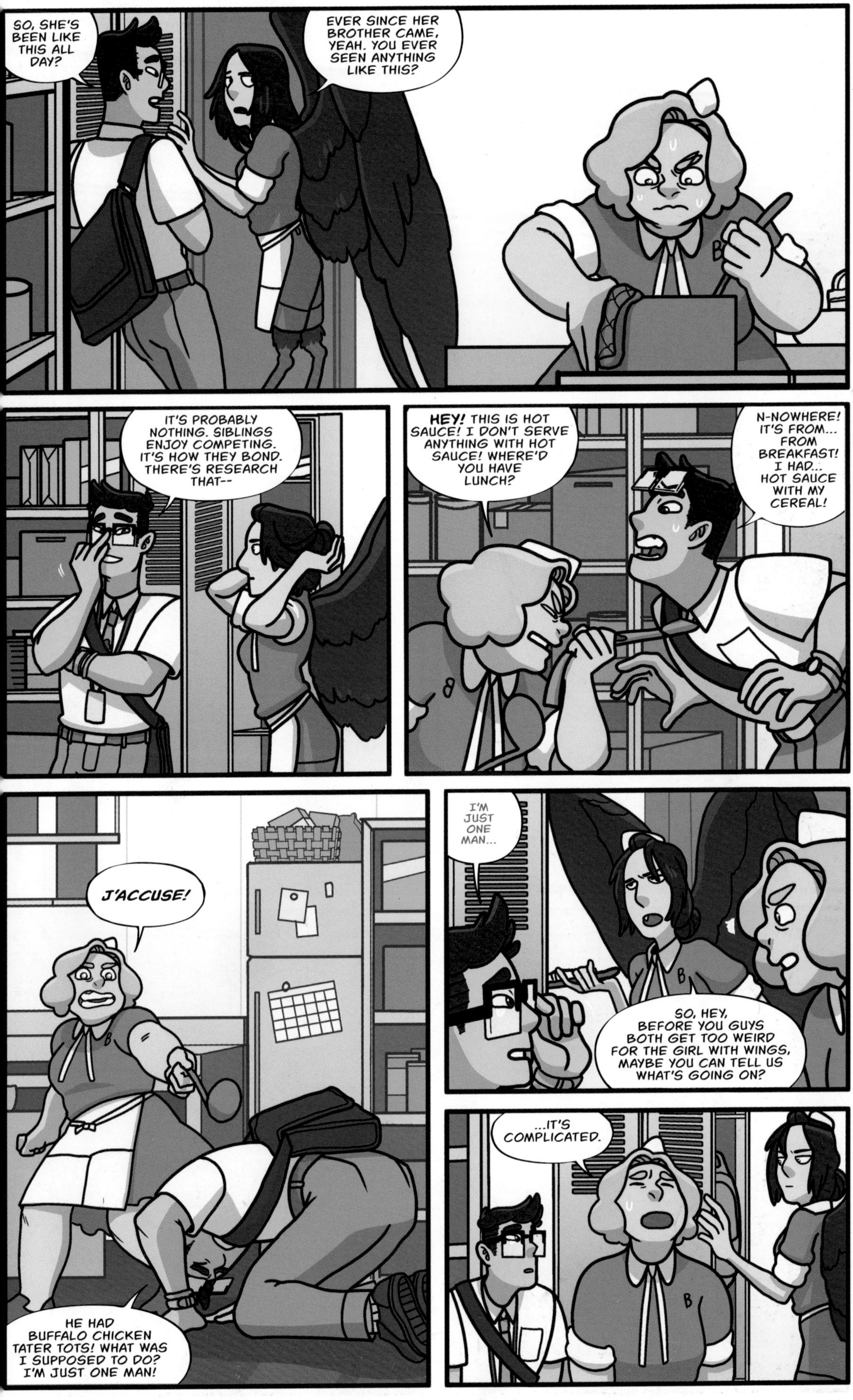
SO, SHE'S BEEN LIKE THIS ALL DAY?
EVER SINCE HER BROTHER CAME, YEAH. YOU EVER SEEN ANYTHING LIKE THIS?
IT'S PROBABLY NOTHING. SIBLINGS ENJOY COMPETING. IT'S HOW THEY BOND. THERE'S RESEARCH THAT--
HEY! THIS IS HOT SAUCE! I DON'T SERVE ANYTHING WITH HOT SAUCE! WHERE'D YOU HAVE LUNCH?
N-NOWHERE! IT'S FROM... FROM BREAKFAST! I HAD... HOT SAUCE WITH MY CEREAL!
J'ACCUSE!
HE HAD BUFFALO CHICKEN TATER TOTS! WHAT WAS I SUPPOSED TO DO? I'M JUST ONE MAN!
I'M JUST ONE MAN...
SO, HEY, BEFORE YOU GUYS BOTH GET TOO WEIRD FOR THE GIRL WITH WINGS, MAYBE YOU CAN TELL US WHAT'S GOING ON?
...IT'S COMPLICATED.

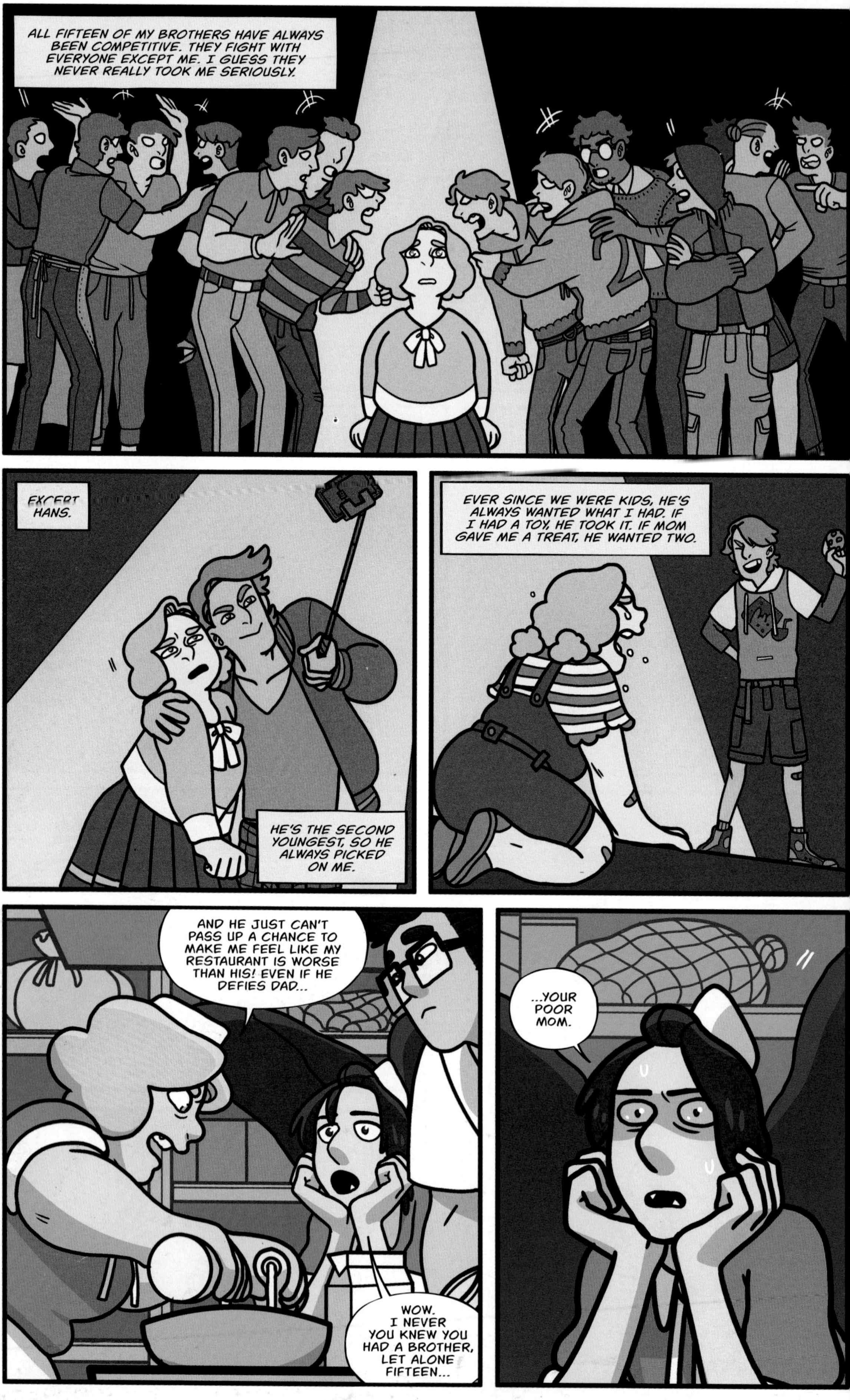
ALL FIFTEEN OF MY BROTHERS HAVE ALWAYS BEEN COMPETITIVE. THEY FIGHT WITH EVERYONE EXCEPT ME. I GUESS THEY NEVER REALLY TOOK ME SERIOUSLY.
EXCEPT HANS.
HE'S THE SECOND YOUNGEST, SO HE ALWAYS PICKED ON ME.
EVER SINCE WE WERE KIDS, HE'S ALWAYS WANTED WHAT I HAD. IF I HAD A TOY, HE TOOK IT. IF MOM GAVE ME A TREAT, HE WANTED TWO.
AND HE JUST CAN'T PASS UP A CHANCE TO MAKE ME FEEL LIKE MY RESTAURANT IS WORSE THAN HIS! EVEN IF HE DEFIES DAD...
WOW. I NEVER YOU KNEW YOU HAD A BROTHER, LET ALONE FIFTEEN...
...YOUR POOR MOM.

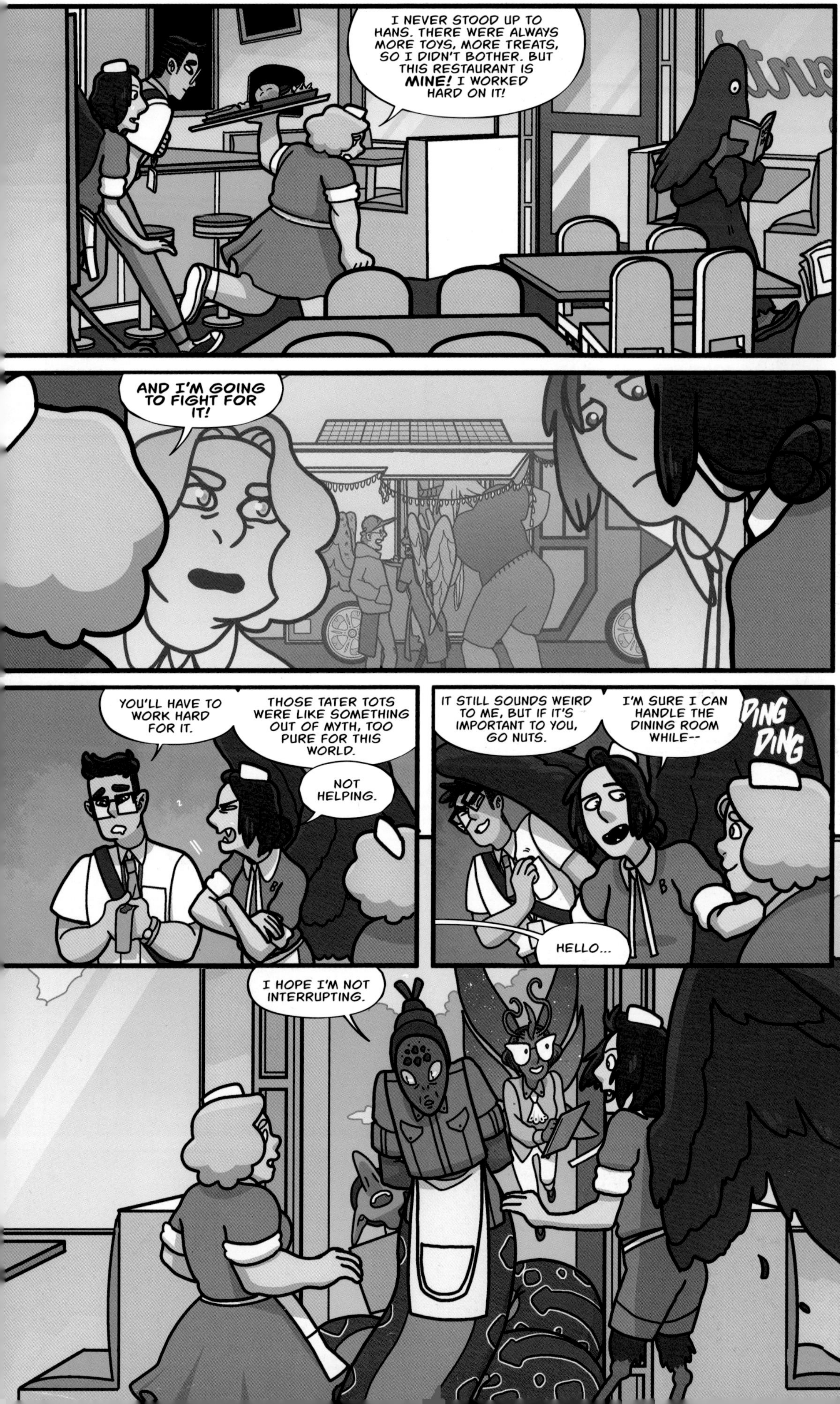
I NEVER STOOD UP TO HANS. THERE WERE ALWAYS MORE TOYS, MORE TREATS, SO I DIDN'T BOTHER. BUT THIS RESTAURANT IS **MINE!** I WORKED HARD ON IT!
AND I'M GOING TO FIGHT FOR IT!
YOU'LL HAVE TO WORK HARD FOR IT.
THOSE TATER TOTS WERE LIKE SOMETHING OUT OF MYTH, TOO PURE FOR THIS WORLD.
NOT HELPING.
IT STILL SOUNDS WEIRD TO ME, BUT IF IT'S IMPORTANT TO YOU, GO NUTS.
I'M SURE I CAN HANDLE THE DINING ROOM WHILE--
DING DING
HELLO...
I HOPE I'M NOT INTERRUPTING.

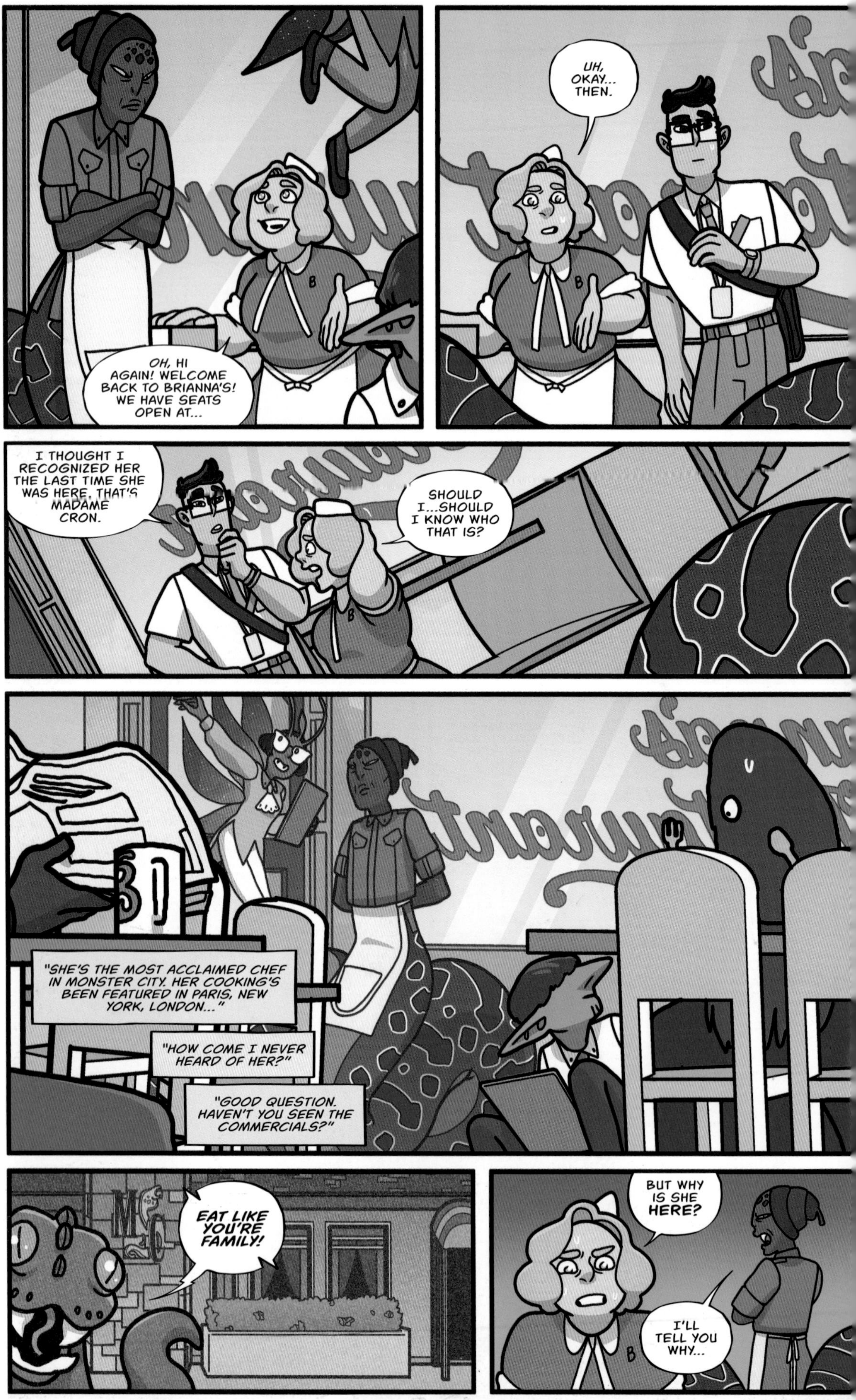
OH, HI AGAIN! WELCOME BACK TO BRIANNA'S! WE HAVE SEATS OPEN AT...
UH, OKAY... THEN.
I THOUGHT I RECOGNIZED HER THE LAST TIME SHE WAS HERE. THAT'S MADAME CRON.
SHOULD I...SHOULD I KNOW WHO THAT IS?
"SHE'S THE MOST ACCLAIMED CHEF IN MONSTER CITY. HER COOKING'S BEEN FEATURED IN PARIS, NEW YORK, LONDON..."
"HOW COME I NEVER HEARD OF HER?"
"GOOD QUESTION. HAVEN'T YOU SEEN THE COMMERCIALS?"
EAT LIKE YOU'RE FAMILY!
BUT WHY IS SHE HERE?
I'LL TELL YOU WHY...

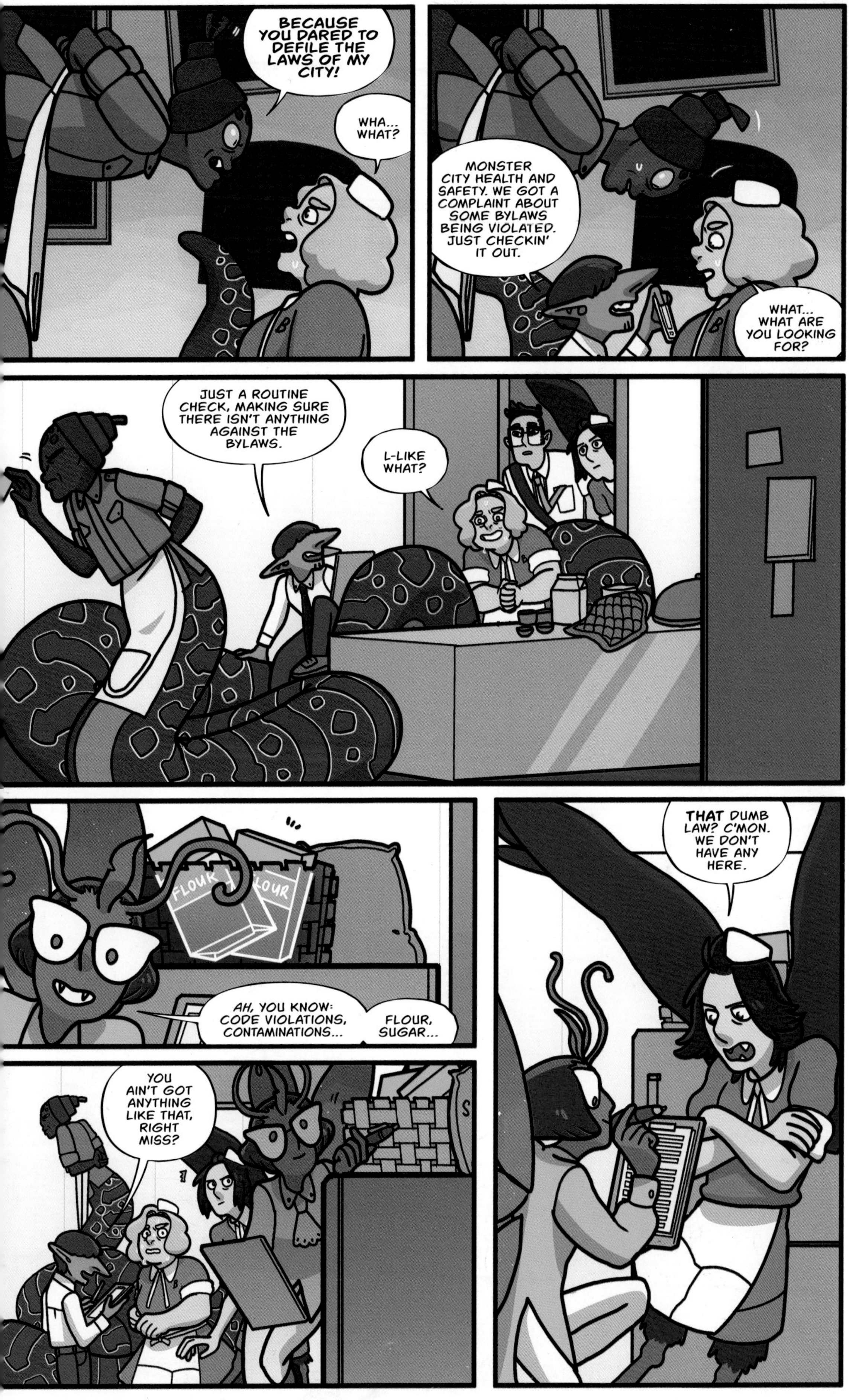
BECAUSE YOU DARED TO DEFILE THE LAWS OF MY CITY!
WHA... WHAT?
MONSTER CITY HEALTH AND SAFETY. WE GOT A COMPLAINT ABOUT SOME BYLAWS BEING VIOLATED. JUST CHECKIN' IT OUT.
WHAT... WHAT ARE YOU LOOKING FOR?
JUST A ROUTINE CHECK, MAKING SURE THERE ISN'T ANYTHING AGAINST THE BYLAWS.
L-LIKE WHAT?
FLOUR
FLOUR
AH, YOU KNOW: CODE VIOLATIONS, CONTAMINATIONS...
FLOUR, SUGAR...
THAT DUMB LAW? C'MON. WE DON'T HAVE ANY HERE.
YOU AIN'T GOT ANYTHING LIKE THAT, RIGHT MISS?

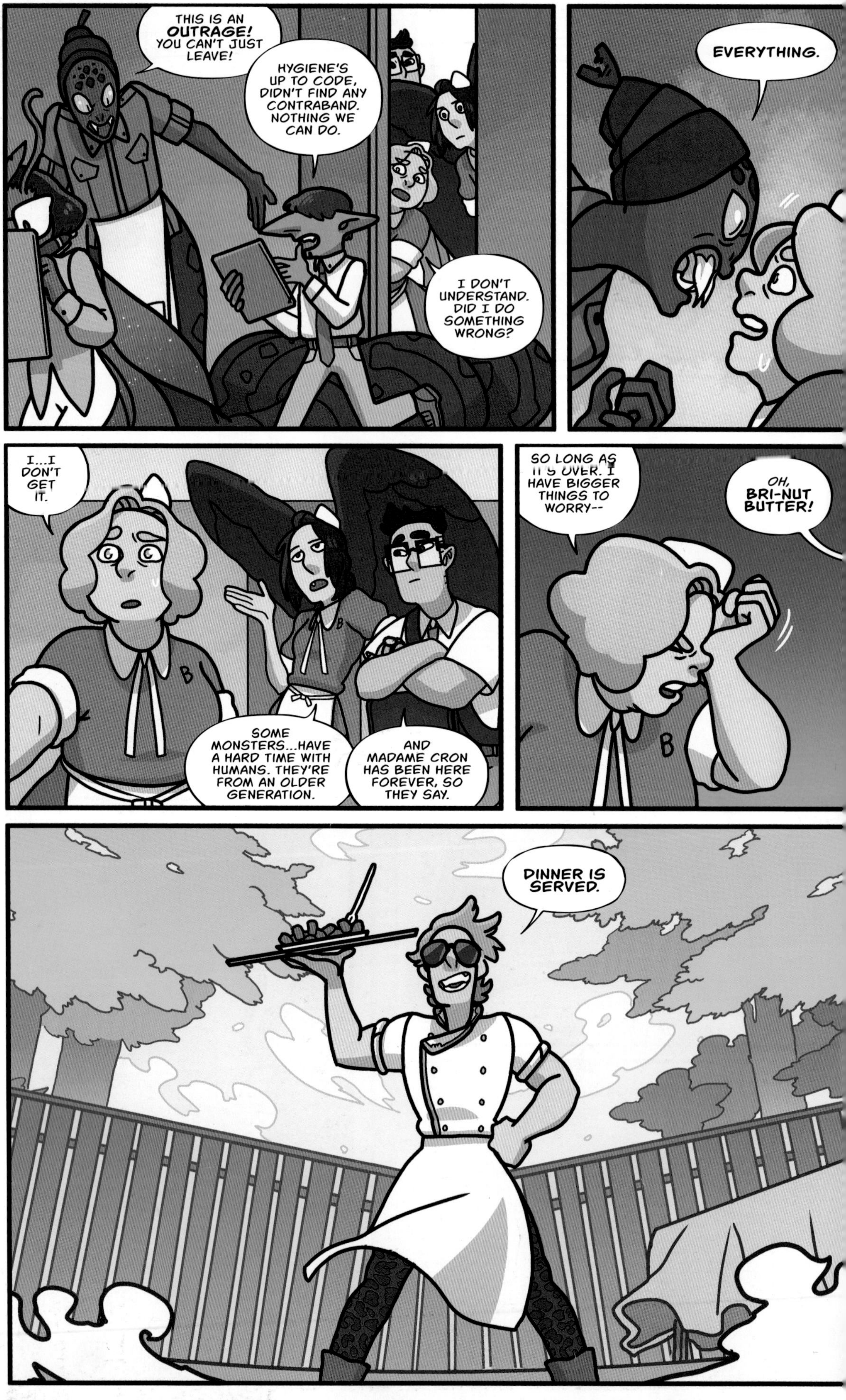
THIS IS AN OUTRAGE! YOU CAN'T JUST LEAVE!
HYGIENE'S UP TO CODE, DIDN'T FIND ANY CONTRABAND. NOTHING WE CAN DO.
I DON'T UNDERSTAND. DID I DO SOMETHING WRONG?
EVERYTHING.
I...I DON'T GET IT.
SOME MONSTERS...HAVE A HARD TIME WITH HUMANS. THEY'RE FROM AN OLDER GENERATION.
AND MADAME CRON HAS BEEN HERE FOREVER, SO THEY SAY.
SO LONG AS IT'S OVER. I HAVE BIGGER THINGS TO WORRY--
OH, BRI-NUT BUTTER!
DINNER IS SERVED.

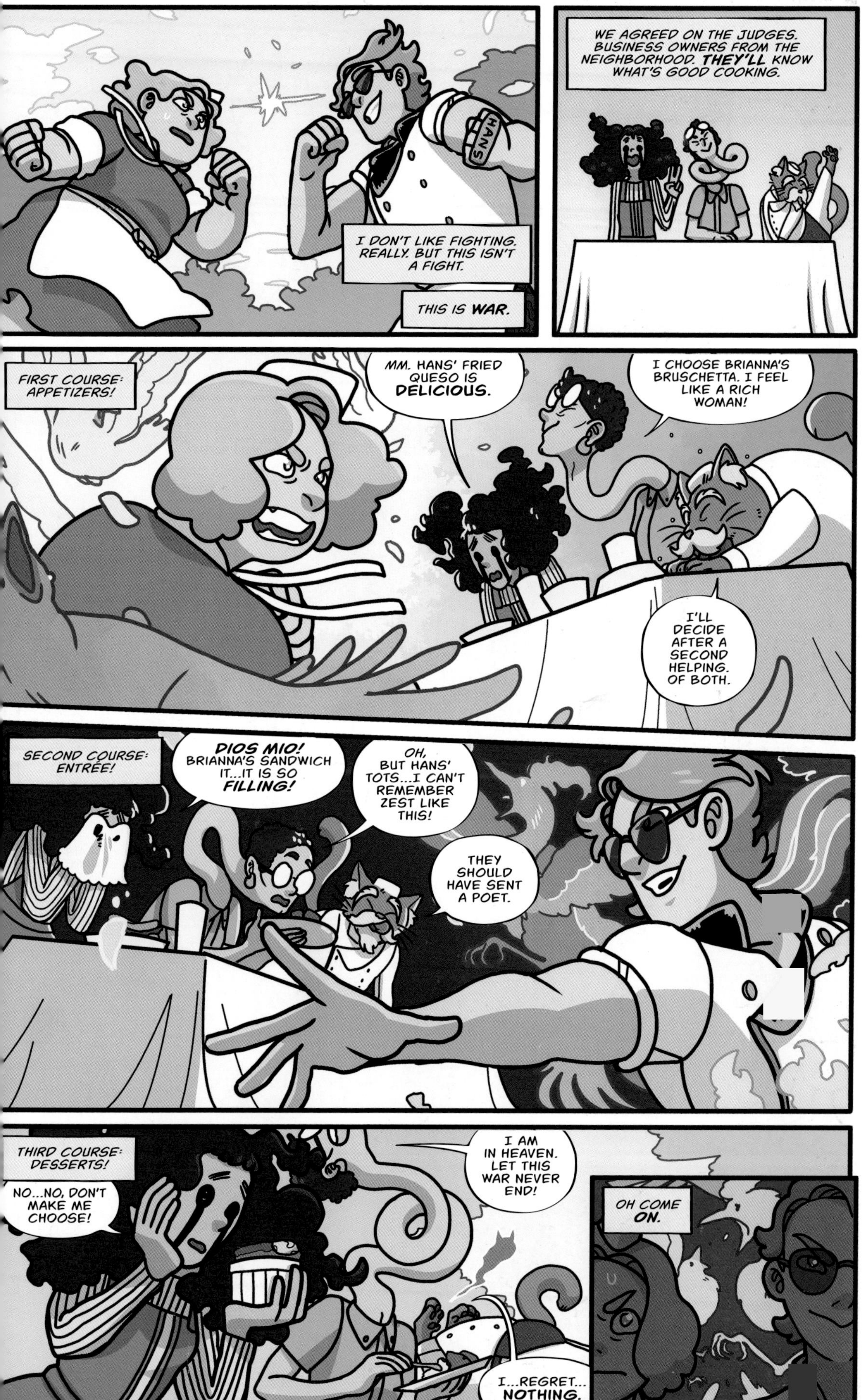

I DON'T LIKE FIGHTING. REALLY. BUT THIS ISN'T A FIGHT.
THIS IS **WAR.**
WE AGREED ON THE JUDGES. BUSINESS OWNERS FROM THE NEIGHBORHOOD. **THEY'LL** KNOW WHAT'S GOOD COOKING.
FIRST COURSE: APPETIZERS!
MM. HANS' FRIED QUESO IS **DELICIOUS.**
I CHOOSE BRIANNA'S BRUSCHETTA. I FEEL LIKE A RICH WOMAN!
I'LL DECIDE AFTER A SECOND HELPING. OF BOTH.
SECOND COURSE: ENTRÉE!
DIOS MIO! BRIANNA'S SANDWICH IT...IT IS SO **FILLING!**
OH, BUT HANS' TOTS...I CAN'T REMEMBER ZEST LIKE THIS!
THEY SHOULD HAVE SENT A POET.
THIRD COURSE: DESSERTS!
NO...NO, DON'T MAKE ME CHOOSE!
I AM IN HEAVEN. LET THIS WAR NEVER END!
I...REGRET... **NOTHING.**
OH COME **ON.**

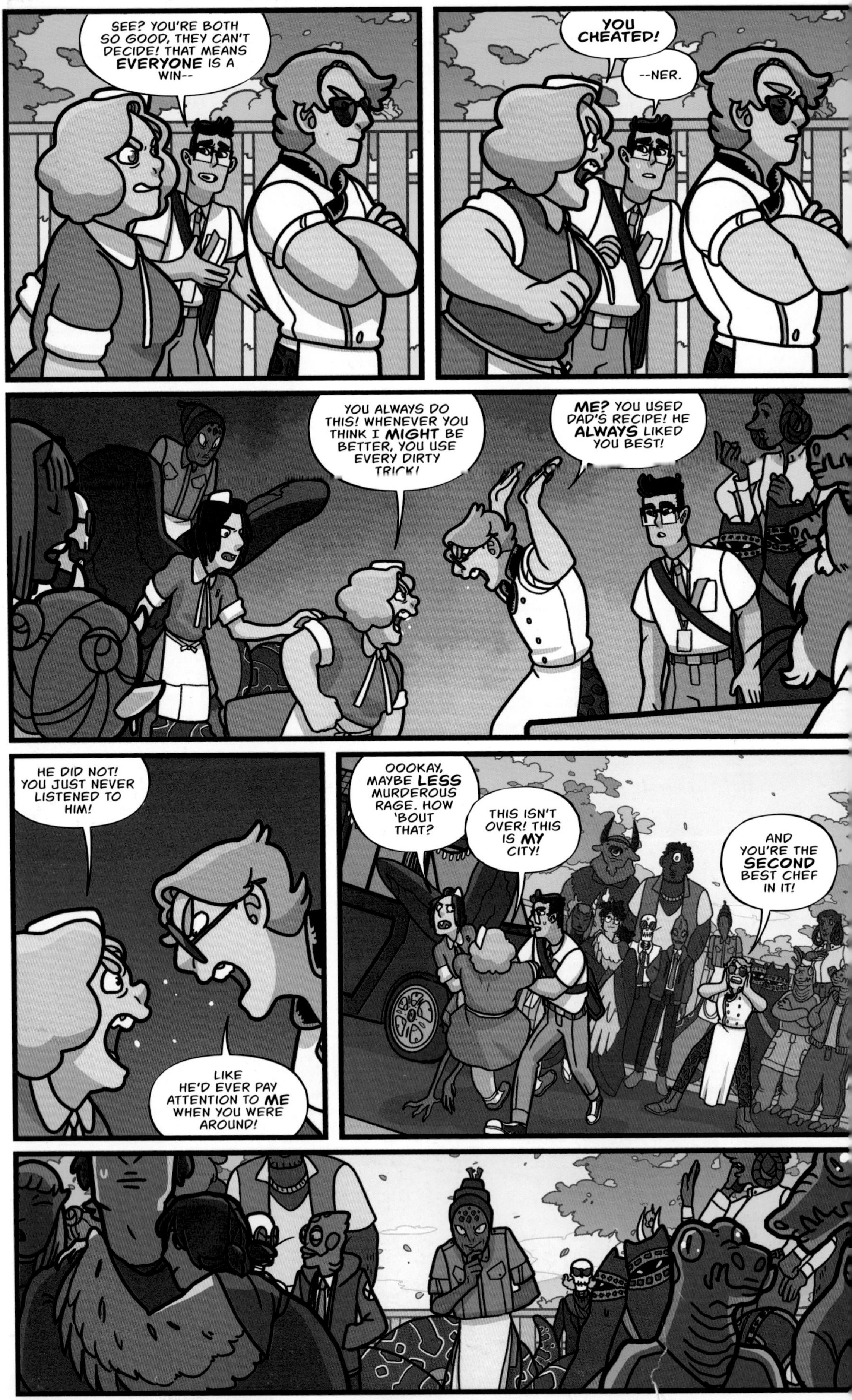
SEE? YOU'RE BOTH SO GOOD, THEY CAN'T DECIDE! THAT MEANS EVERYONE IS A WIN--
YOU CHEATED!
--NER.
YOU ALWAYS DO THIS! WHENEVER YOU THINK I MIGHT BE BETTER, YOU USE EVERY DIRTY TRICK!
ME? YOU USED DAD'S RECIPE! HE ALWAYS LIKED YOU BEST!
HE DID NOT! YOU JUST NEVER LISTENED TO HIM!
LIKE HE'D EVER PAY ATTENTION TO ME WHEN YOU WERE AROUND!
OOOKAY, MAYBE LESS MURDEROUS RAGE. HOW 'BOUT THAT?
THIS ISN'T OVER! THIS IS MY CITY!
AND YOU'RE THE SECOND BEST CHEF IN IT!

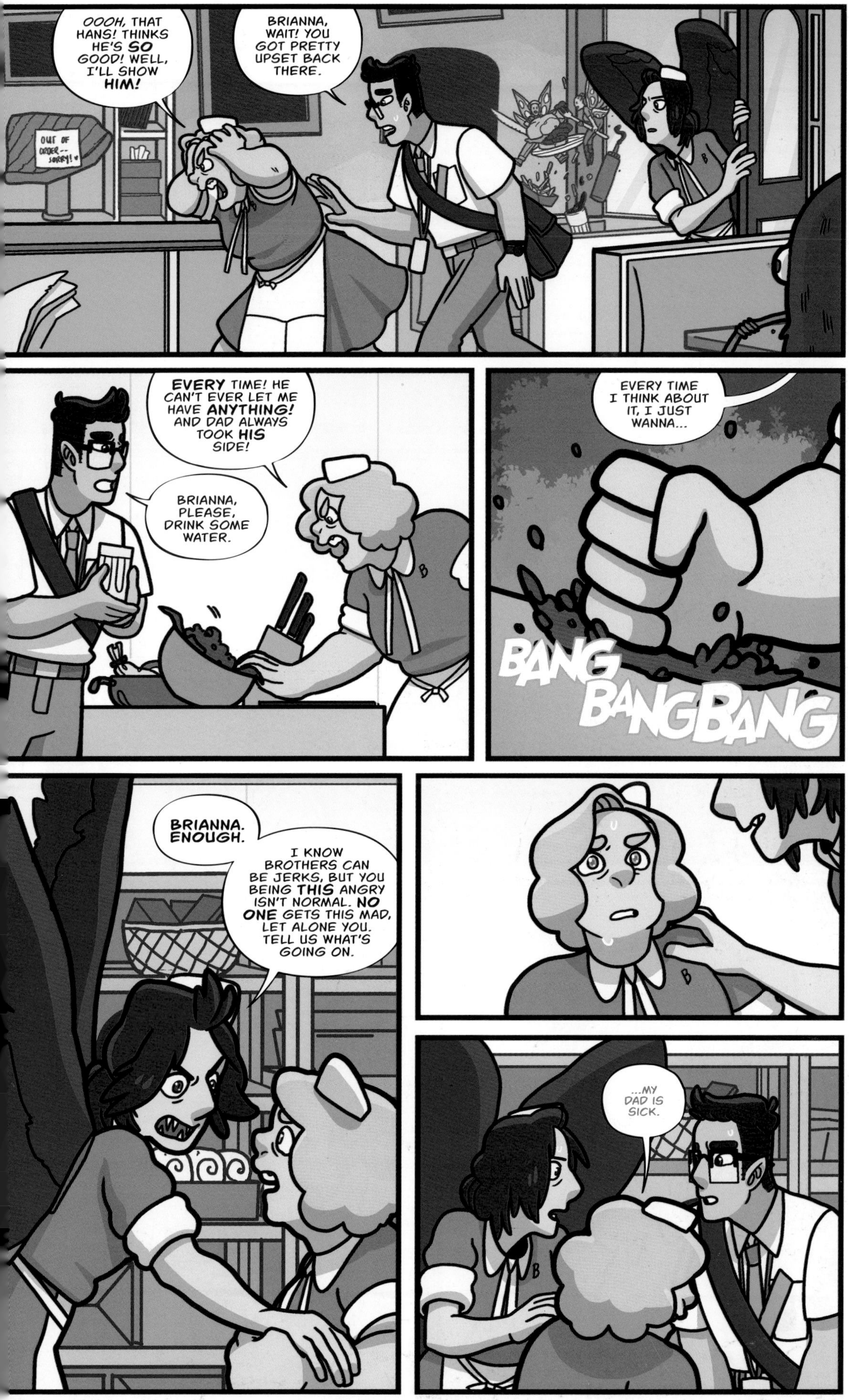
OOOH, THAT HANS! THINKS HE'S SO GOOD! WELL, I'LL SHOW HIM!
BRIANNA, WAIT! YOU GOT PRETTY UPSET BACK THERE.
OUT OF ORDER-- SORRY!
EVERY TIME! HE CAN'T EVER LET ME HAVE ANYTHING! AND DAD ALWAYS TOOK HIS SIDE!
BRIANNA, PLEASE, DRINK SOME WATER.
EVERY TIME I THINK ABOUT IT, I JUST WANNA...
BANG
BANGBANG
BRIANNA. ENOUGH.
I KNOW BROTHERS CAN BE JERKS, BUT YOU BEING THIS ANGRY ISN'T NORMAL. NO ONE GETS THIS MAD, LET ALONE YOU. TELL US WHAT'S GOING ON.
...MY DAD IS SICK.

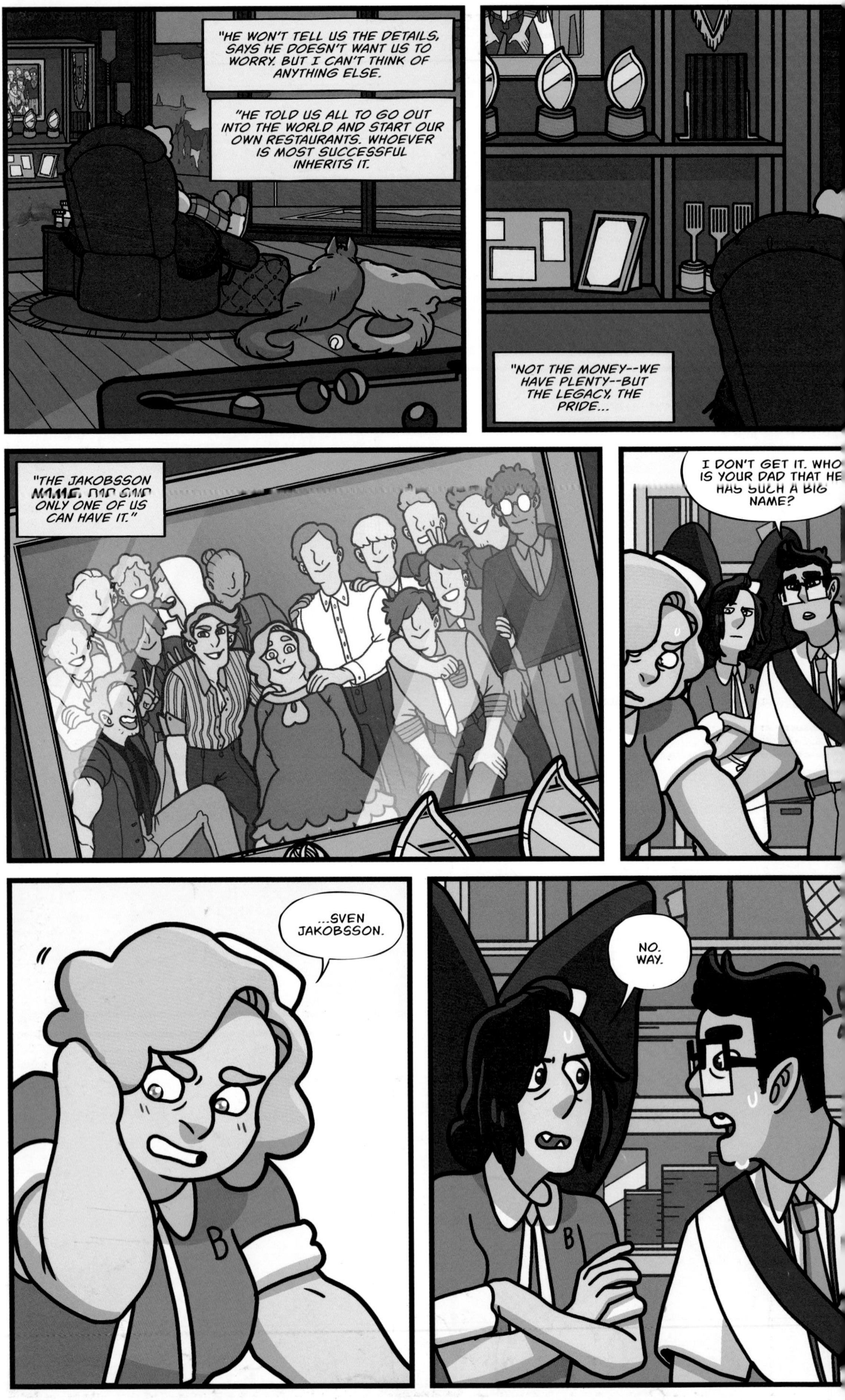
"HE WON'T TELL US THE DETAILS, SAYS HE DOESN'T WANT US TO WORRY. BUT I CAN'T THINK OF ANYTHING ELSE.
"HE TOLD US ALL TO GO OUT INTO THE WORLD AND START OUR OWN RESTAURANTS. WHOEVER IS MOST SUCCESSFUL INHERITS IT.
"NOT THE MONEY--WE HAVE PLENTY--BUT THE LEGACY, THE PRIDE...
"THE JAKOBSSON
ONLY ONE OF US CAN HAVE IT."
I DON'T GET IT. WHO IS YOUR DAD THAT HE HAS SUCH A BIG NAME?
...SVEN JAKOBSSON.
NO. WAY.

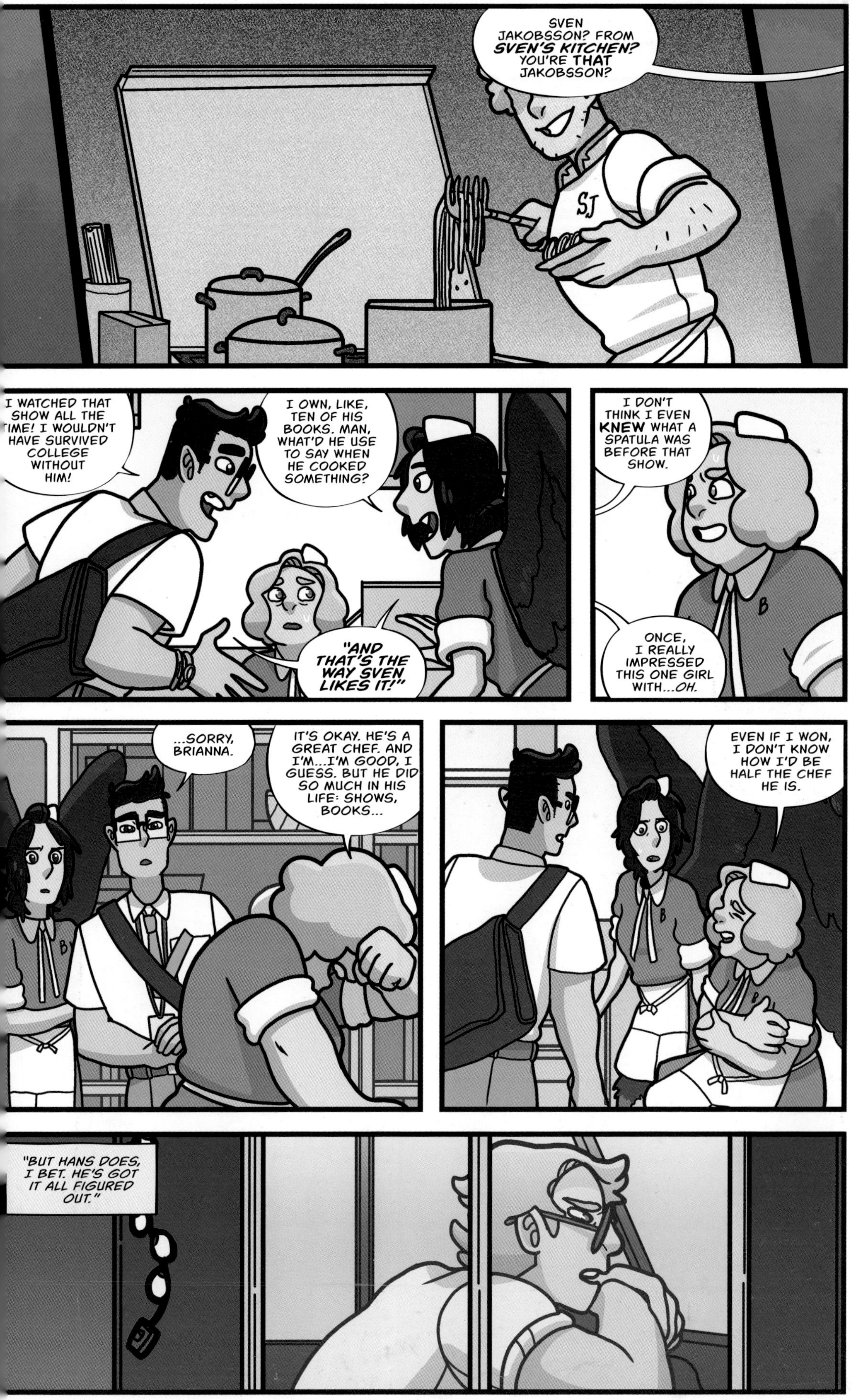
SVEN JAKOBSSON? FROM *SVEN'S KITCHEN?* YOU'RE **THAT** JAKOBSSON?
SJ
I WATCHED THAT SHOW ALL THE TIME! I WOULDN'T HAVE SURVIVED COLLEGE WITHOUT HIM!
I OWN, LIKE, TEN OF HIS BOOKS. MAN, WHAT'D HE USE TO SAY WHEN HE COOKED SOMETHING?
"AND THAT'S THE WAY SVEN LIKES IT!"
I DON'T THINK I EVEN **KNEW** WHAT A SPATULA WAS BEFORE THAT SHOW.
ONCE, I REALLY IMPRESSED THIS ONE GIRL WITH...*OH.*
...SORRY, BRIANNA.
IT'S OKAY. HE'S A GREAT CHEF. AND I'M...I'M GOOD, I GUESS. BUT HE DID SO MUCH IN HIS LIFE: SHOWS, BOOKS...
EVEN IF I WON, I DON'T KNOW HOW I'D BE HALF THE CHEF HE IS.
"BUT HANS DOES, I BET. HE'S GOT IT ALL FIGURED OUT."

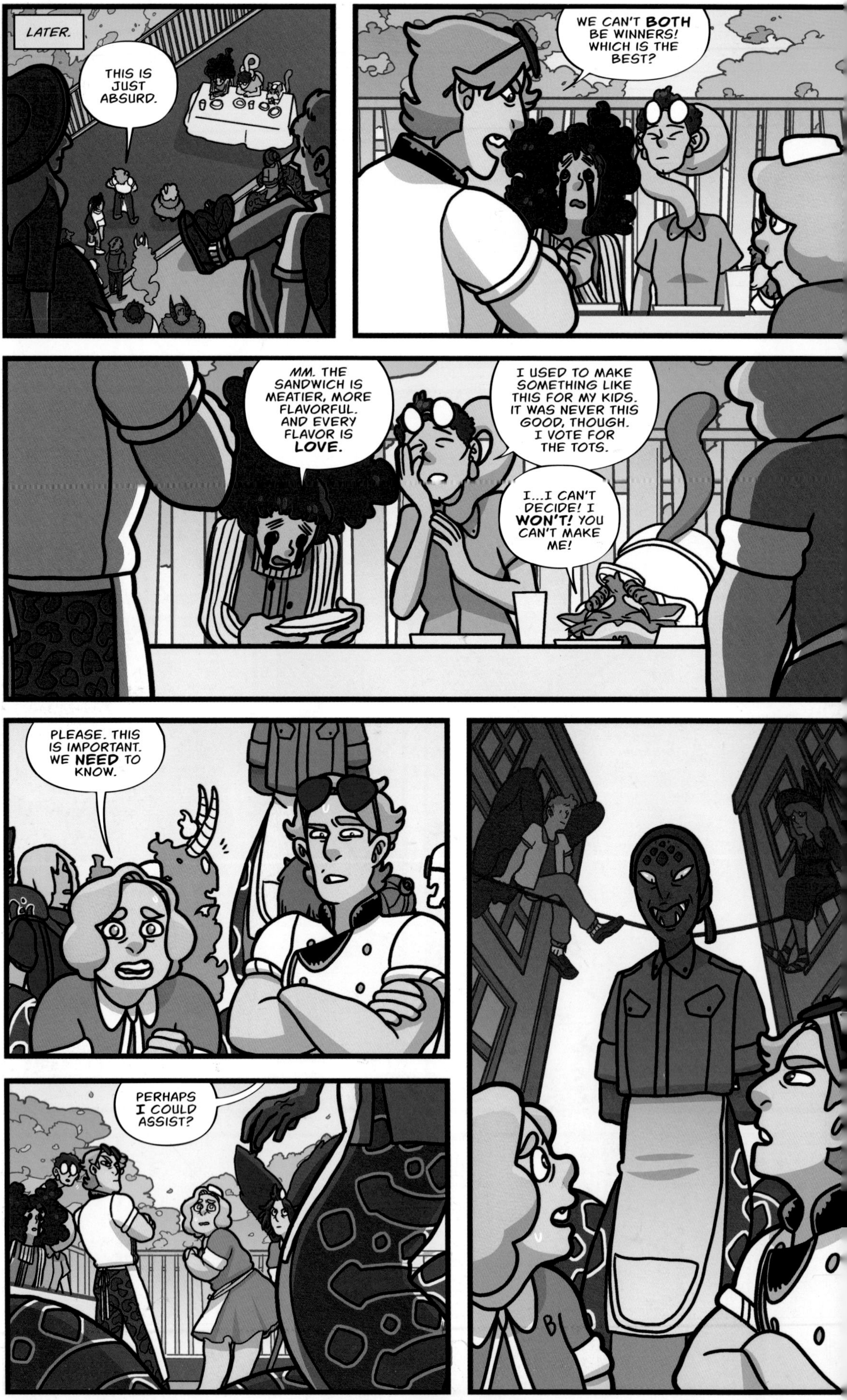
LATER.
THIS IS JUST ABSURD.
WE CAN'T **BOTH** BE WINNERS! WHICH IS THE BEST?
MM. THE SANDWICH IS MEATIER, MORE FLAVORFUL. AND EVERY FLAVOR IS **LOVE.**
I USED TO MAKE SOMETHING LIKE THIS FOR MY KIDS. IT WAS NEVER THIS GOOD, THOUGH. I VOTE FOR THE TOTS.
I...I CAN'T DECIDE! I **WON'T!** YOU CAN'T MAKE ME!
PLEASE. THIS IS IMPORTANT. WE **NEED** TO KNOW.
PERHAPS **I** COULD ASSIST?

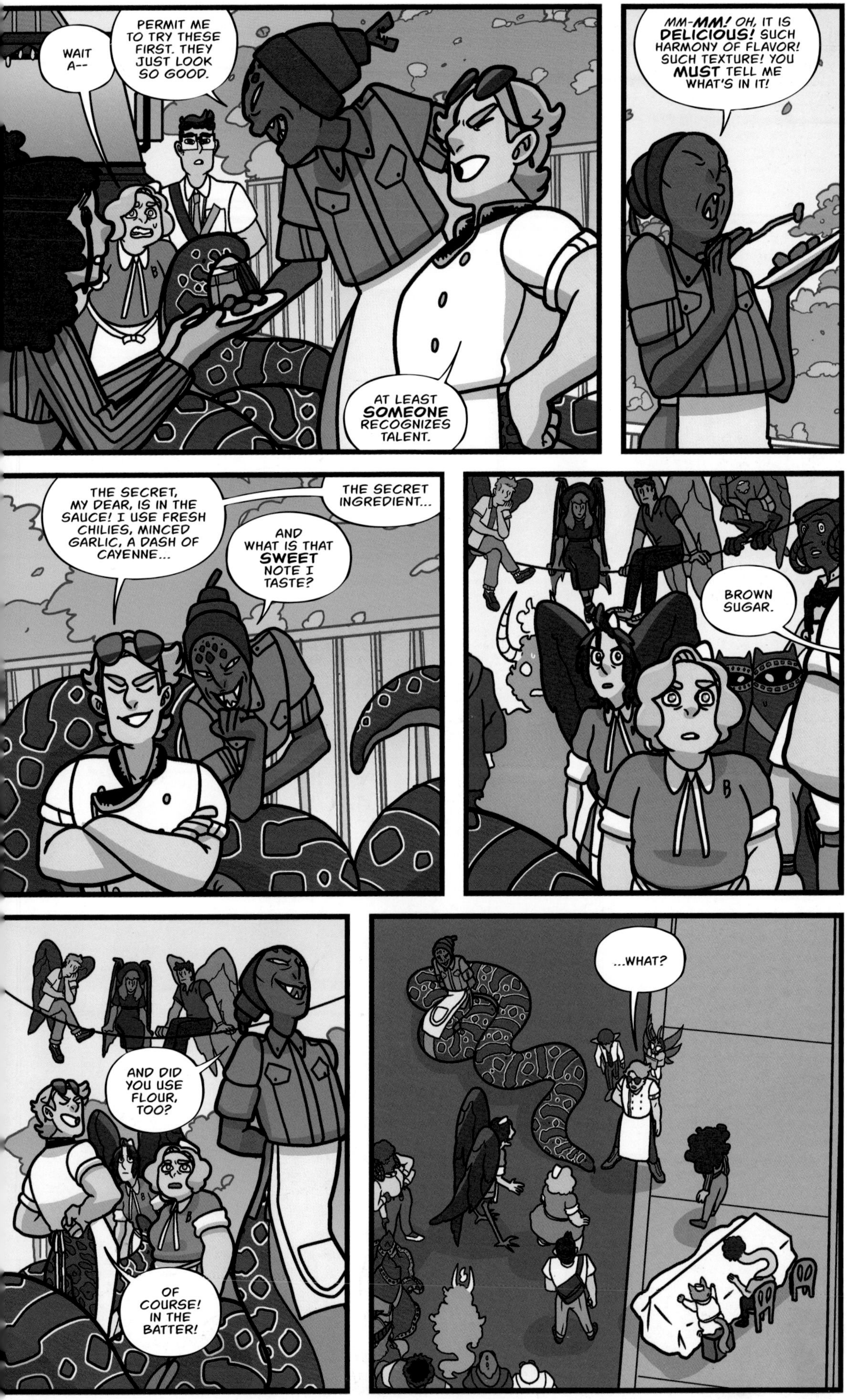
PERMIT ME TO TRY THESE FIRST. THEY JUST LOOK SO GOOD.
WAIT A--
AT LEAST SOMEONE RECOGNIZES TALENT.
MM-MM! OH, IT IS DELICIOUS! SUCH HARMONY OF FLAVOR! SUCH TEXTURE! YOU MUST TELL ME WHAT'S IN IT!
THE SECRET, MY DEAR, IS IN THE SAUCE! I USE FRESH CHILIES, MINCED GARLIC, A DASH OF CAYENNE...
AND WHAT IS THAT SWEET NOTE I TASTE?
THE SECRET INGREDIENT...
BROWN SUGAR.
AND DID YOU USE FLOUR, TOO?
OF COURSE! IN THE BATTER!
...WHAT?

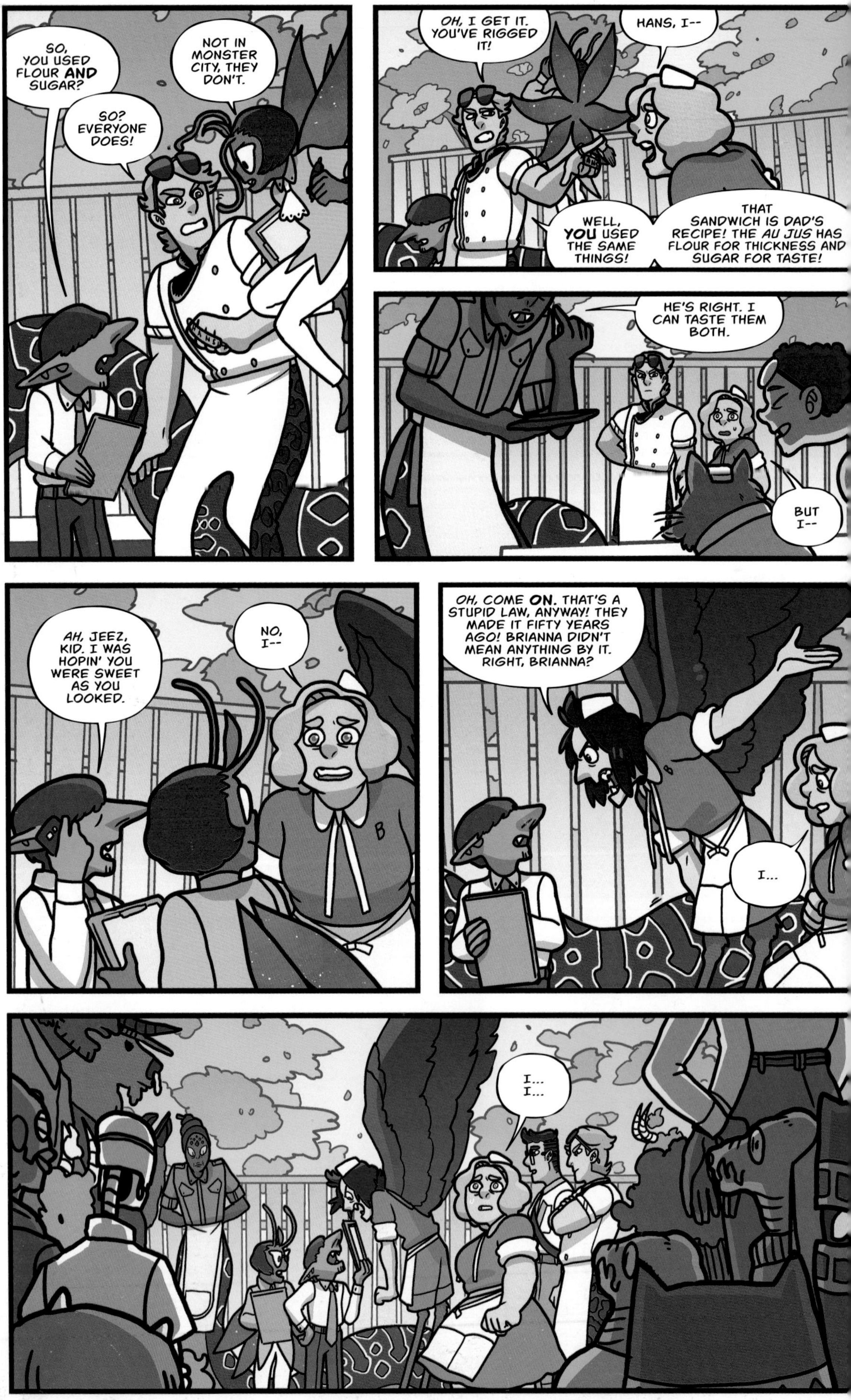
SO, YOU USED FLOUR AND SUGAR?
SO? EVERYONE DOES!
NOT IN MONSTER CITY, THEY DON'T.
OH, I GET IT. YOU'VE RIGGED IT!
HANS, I--
WELL, YOU USED THE SAME THINGS!
THAT SANDWICH IS DAD'S RECIPE! THE AU JUS HAS FLOUR FOR THICKNESS AND SUGAR FOR TASTE!
HE'S RIGHT. I CAN TASTE THEM BOTH.
BUT I--
AH, JEEZ, KID. I WAS HOPIN' YOU WERE SWEET AS YOU LOOKED.
NO, I--
OH, COME ON. THAT'S A STUPID LAW, ANYWAY! THEY MADE IT FIFTY YEARS AGO! BRIANNA DIDN'T MEAN ANYTHING BY IT. RIGHT, BRIANNA?
I...
I... I...

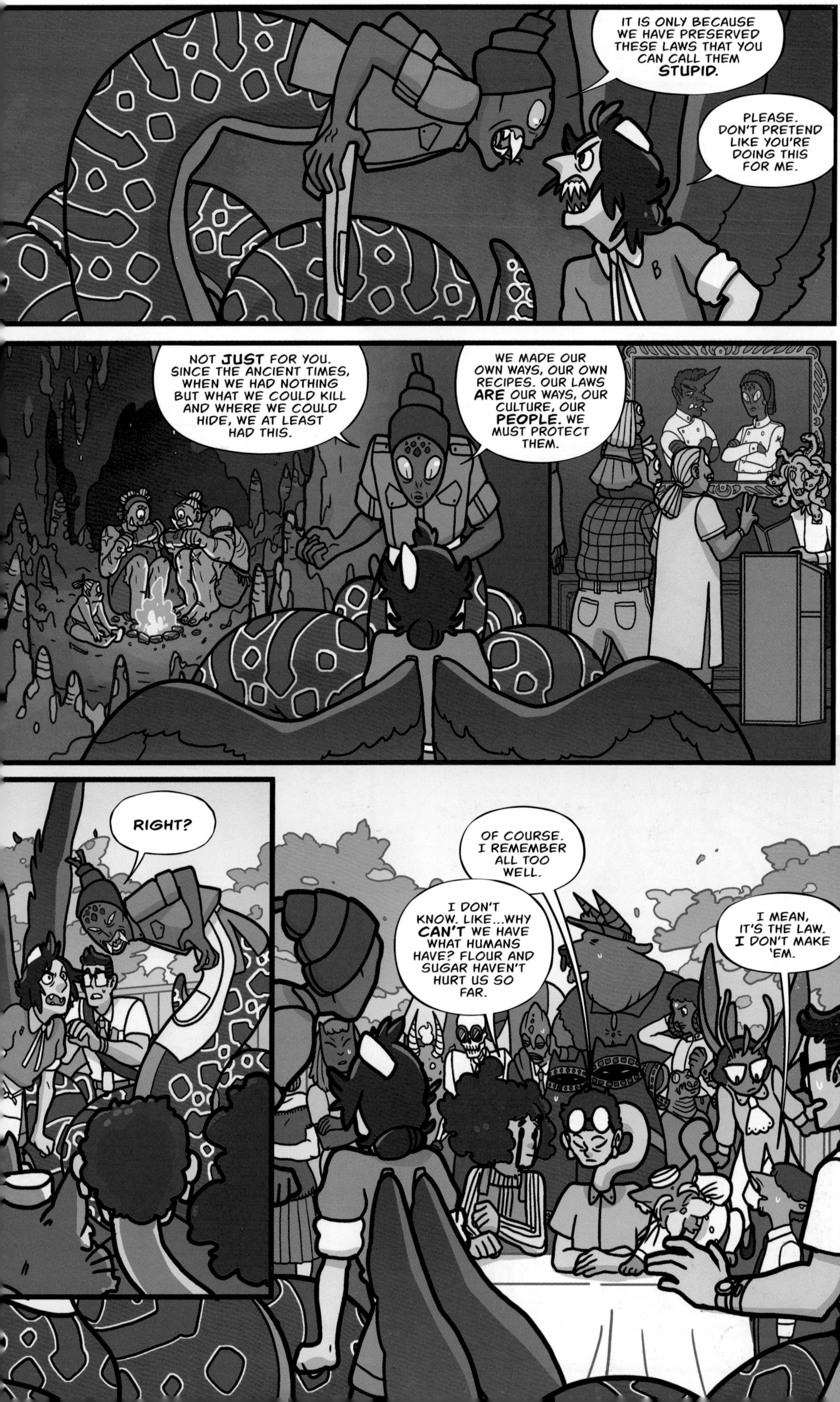
IT IS ONLY BECAUSE WE HAVE PRESERVED THESE LAWS THAT YOU CAN CALL THEM STUPID.
PLEASE. DON'T PRETEND LIKE YOU'RE DOING THIS FOR ME.
NOT JUST FOR YOU. SINCE THE ANCIENT TIMES, WHEN WE HAD NOTHING BUT WHAT WE COULD KILL AND WHERE WE COULD HIDE, WE AT LEAST HAD THIS.
WE MADE OUR OWN WAYS, OUR OWN RECIPES. OUR LAWS ARE OUR WAYS, OUR CULTURE, OUR PEOPLE. WE MUST PROTECT THEM.
RIGHT?
OF COURSE. I REMEMBER ALL TOO WELL.
I DON'T KNOW. LIKE...WHY CAN'T WE HAVE WHAT HUMANS HAVE? FLOUR AND SUGAR HAVEN'T HURT US SO FAR.
I MEAN, IT'S THE LAW. I DON'T MAKE 'EM.

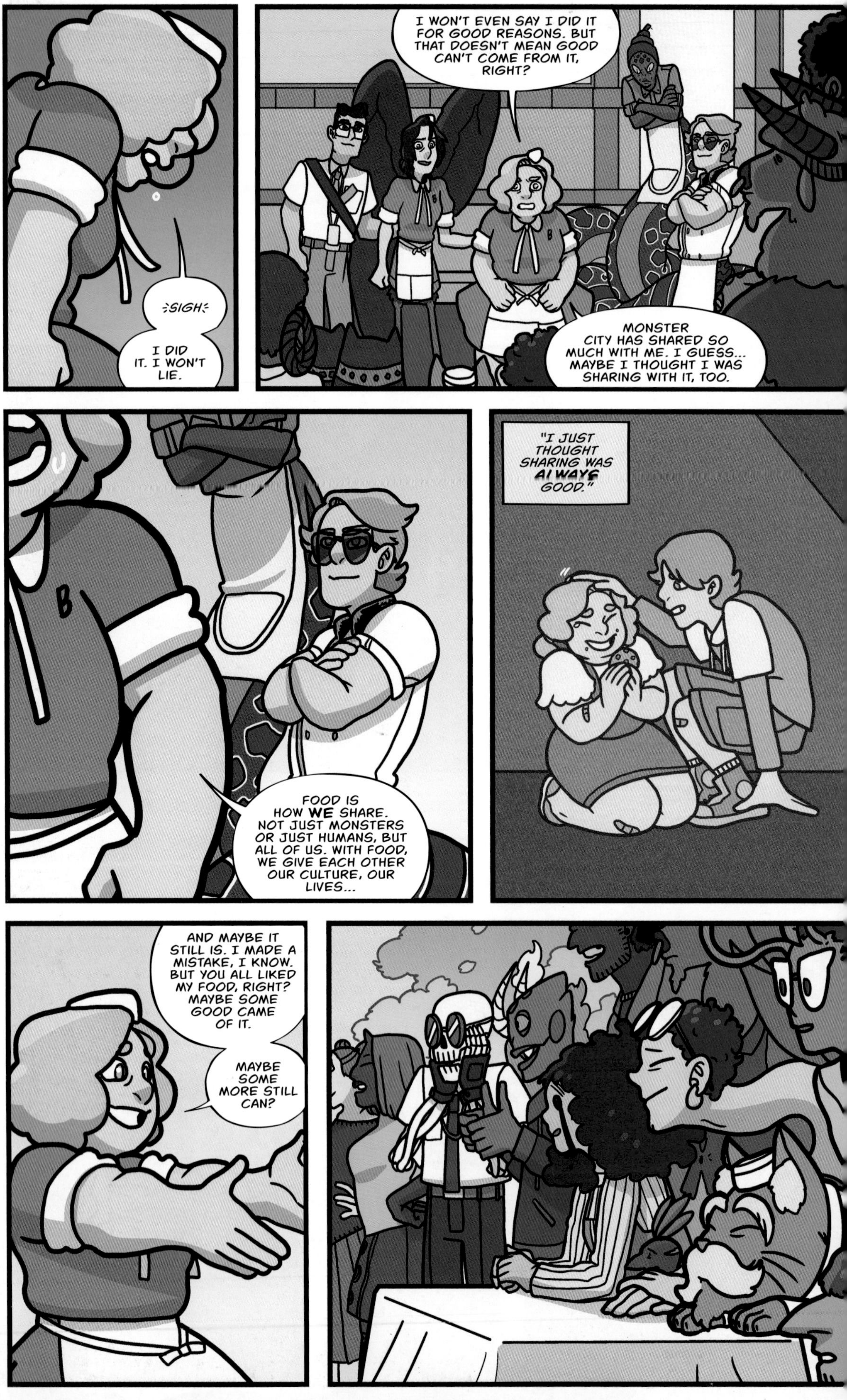
SIGH
I DID IT. I WON'T LIE.
I WON'T EVEN SAY I DID IT FOR GOOD REASONS. BUT THAT DOESN'T MEAN GOOD CAN'T COME FROM IT, RIGHT?
MONSTER CITY HAS SHARED SO MUCH WITH ME. I GUESS... MAYBE I THOUGHT I WAS SHARING WITH IT, TOO.
FOOD IS HOW WE SHARE. NOT JUST MONSTERS OR JUST HUMANS, BUT ALL OF US. WITH FOOD, WE GIVE EACH OTHER OUR CULTURE, OUR LIVES...
"I JUST THOUGHT SHARING WAS ALWAYS GOOD."
AND MAYBE IT STILL IS. I MADE A MISTAKE, I KNOW. BUT YOU ALL LIKED MY FOOD, RIGHT? MAYBE SOME GOOD CAME OF IT.
MAYBE SOME MORE STILL CAN?

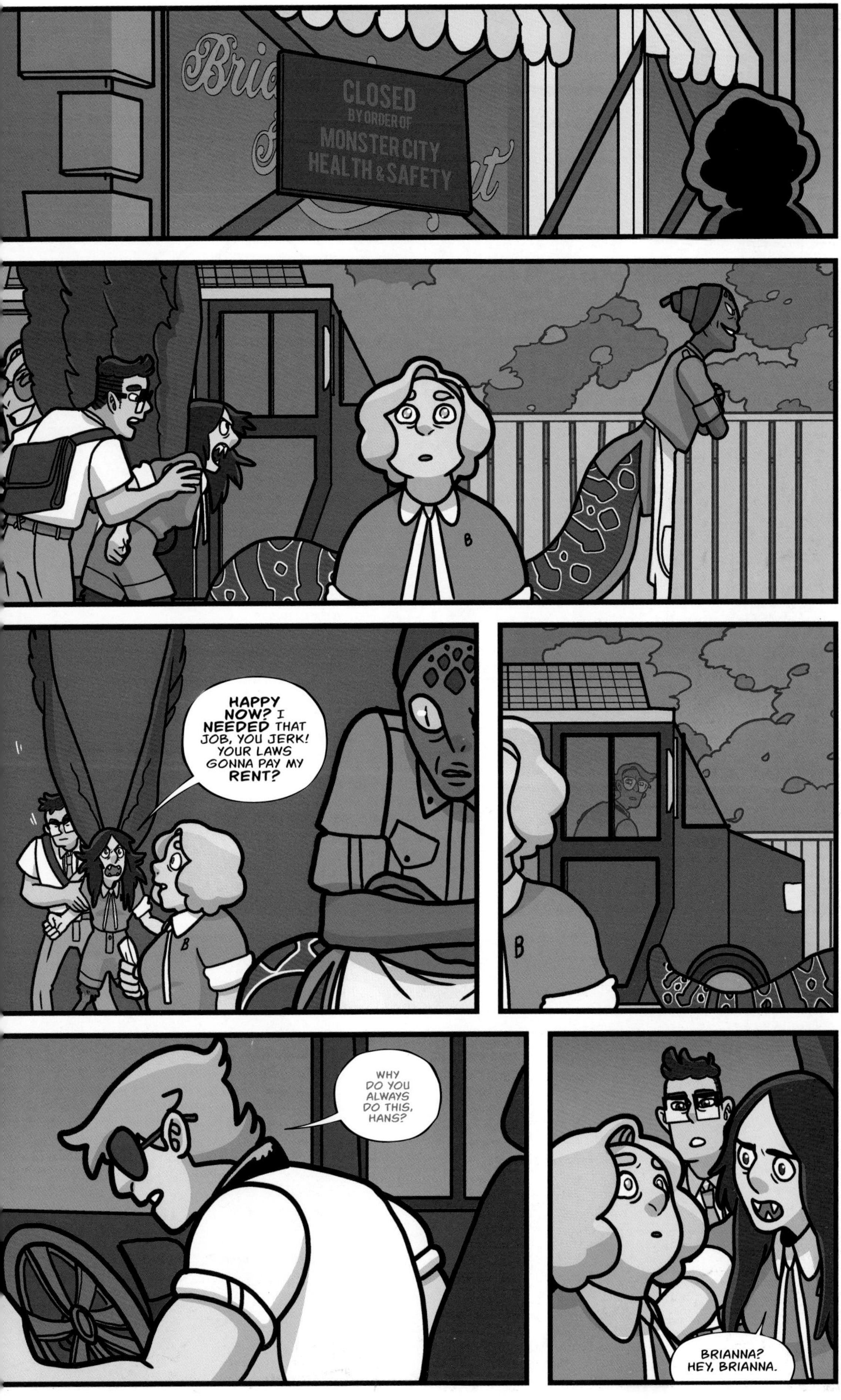

CLOSED BY ORDER OF MONSTER CITY HEALTH & SAFETY
HAPPY NOW? I NEEDED THAT JOB, YOU JERK! YOUR LAWS GONNA PAY MY RENT?
WHY DO YOU ALWAYS DO THIS, HANS?
BRIANNA? HEY, BRIANNA.

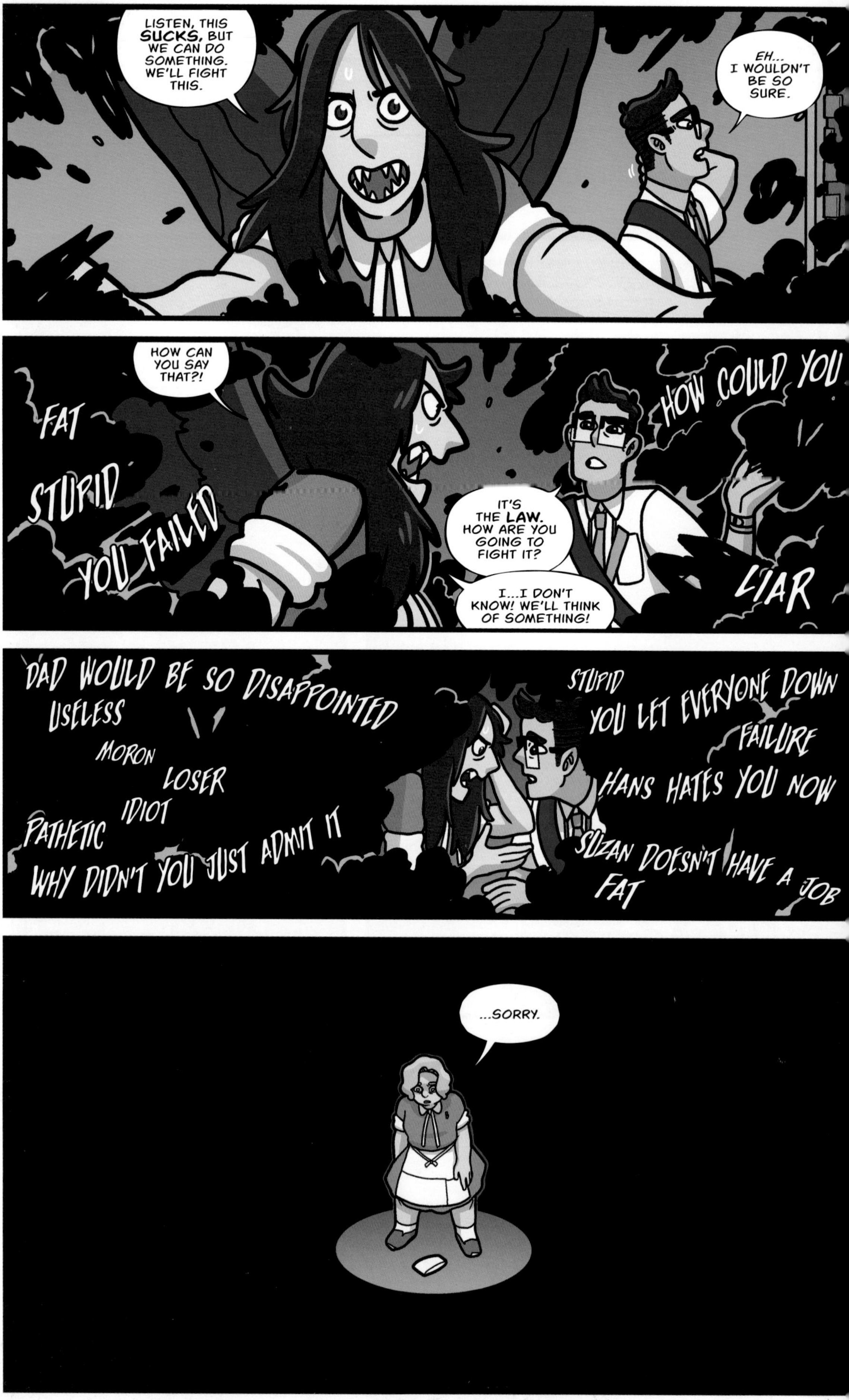

LISTEN, THIS SUCKS, BUT WE CAN DO SOMETHING. WE'LL FIGHT THIS.
EH... I WOULDN'T BE SO SURE.
HOW CAN YOU SAY THAT?!
FAT
STUPID
YOU FAILED
HOW COULD YOU
IT'S THE LAW. HOW ARE YOU GOING TO FIGHT IT?
I...I DON'T KNOW! WE'LL THINK OF SOMETHING!
LIAR
DAD WOULD BE SO DISAPPOINTED
USELESS
MORON
LOSER
IDIOT
PATHETIC
WHY DIDN'T YOU JUST ADMIT IT
STUPID
YOU LET EVERYONE DOWN
FAILURE
HANS HATES YOU NOW
SUZAN DOESN'T HAVE A JOB
FAT
...SORRY.

chapter
FOUR

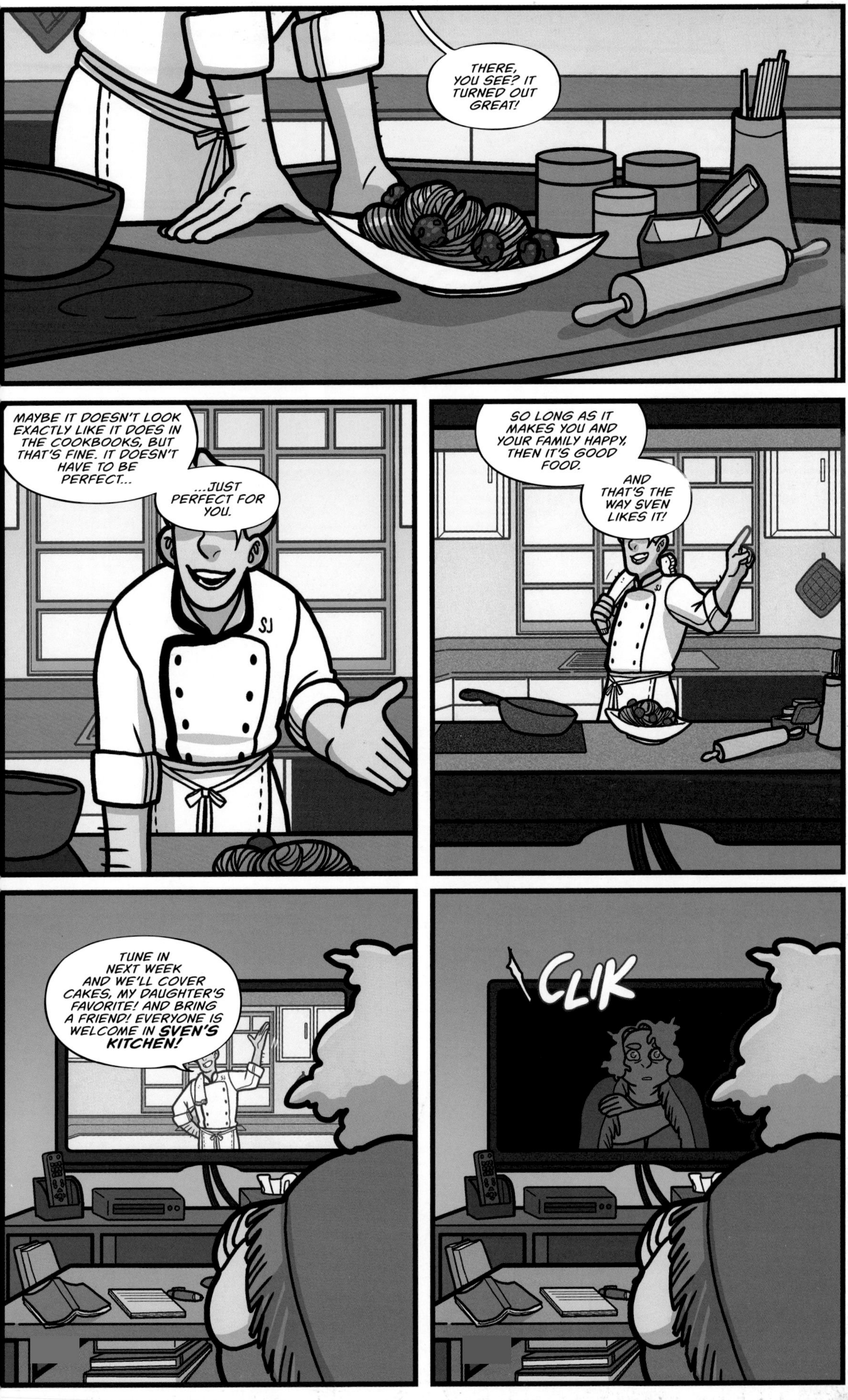
THERE, YOU SEE? IT TURNED OUT GREAT!
MAYBE IT DOESN'T LOOK EXACTLY LIKE IT DOES IN THE COOKBOOKS, BUT THAT'S FINE. IT DOESN'T HAVE TO BE PERFECT...
...JUST PERFECT FOR YOU.
SJ
SO LONG AS IT MAKES YOU AND YOUR FAMILY HAPPY, THEN IT'S GOOD FOOD.
AND THAT'S THE WAY SVEN LIKES IT!
TUNE IN NEXT WEEK AND WE'LL COVER CAKES, MY DAUGHTER'S FAVORITE! AND BRING A FRIEND! EVERYONE IS WELCOME IN **SVEN'S KITCHEN!**
CLIK

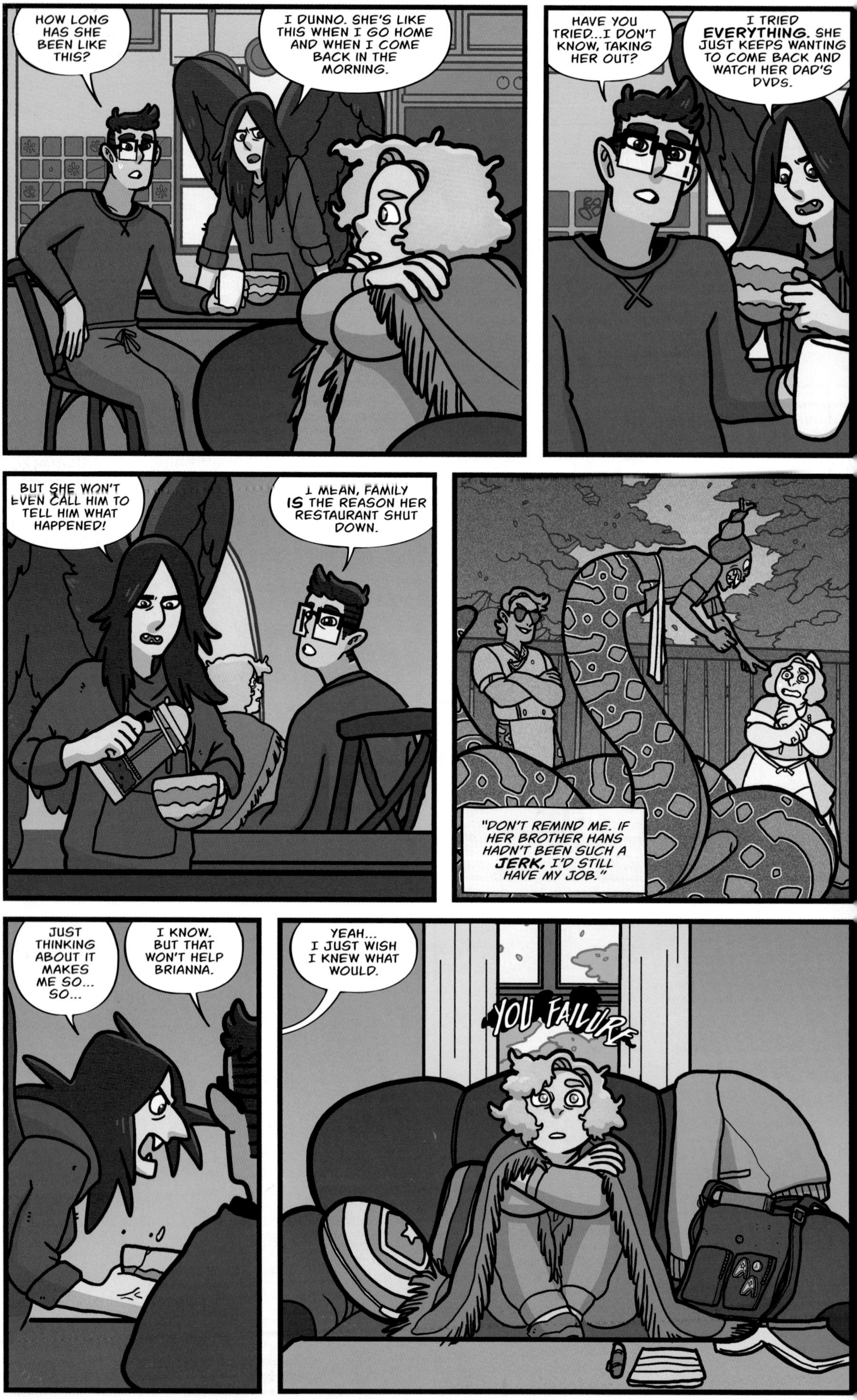
HOW LONG HAS SHE BEEN LIKE THIS?
I DUNNO. SHE'S LIKE THIS WHEN I GO HOME AND WHEN I COME BACK IN THE MORNING.
HAVE YOU TRIED...I DON'T KNOW, TAKING HER OUT?
I TRIED **EVERYTHING.** SHE JUST KEEPS WANTING TO COME BACK AND WATCH HER DAD'S DVDS.
BUT SHE WON'T EVEN CALL HIM TO TELL HIM WHAT HAPPENED!
I MEAN, FAMILY **IS** THE REASON HER RESTAURANT SHUT DOWN.
"DON'T REMIND ME. IF HER BROTHER HANS HADN'T BEEN SUCH A **JERK,** I'D STILL HAVE MY JOB."
JUST THINKING ABOUT IT MAKES ME SO... SO...
I KNOW. BUT THAT WON'T HELP BRIANNA.
YEAH... I JUST WISH I KNEW WHAT WOULD.
YOU FAILURE

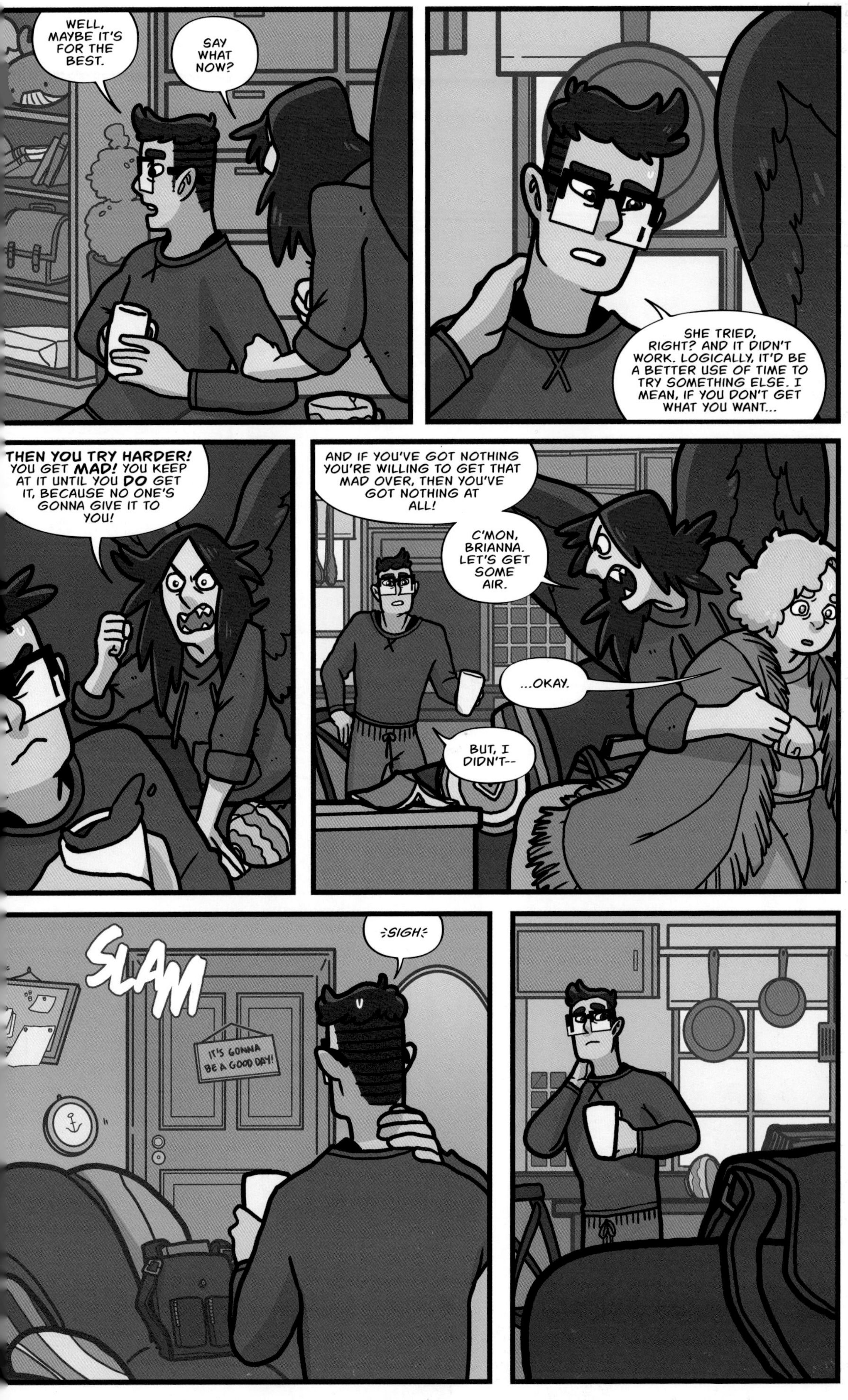
WELL, MAYBE IT'S FOR THE BEST.
SAY WHAT NOW?
SHE TRIED, RIGHT? AND IT DIDN'T WORK. LOGICALLY, IT'D BE A BETTER USE OF TIME TO TRY SOMETHING ELSE. I MEAN, IF YOU DON'T GET WHAT YOU WANT...
THEN YOU TRY HARDER! YOU GET MAD! YOU KEEP AT IT UNTIL YOU DO GET IT, BECAUSE NO ONE'S GONNA GIVE IT TO YOU!
AND IF YOU'VE GOT NOTHING YOU'RE WILLING TO GET THAT MAD OVER, THEN YOU'VE GOT NOTHING AT ALL!
C'MON, BRIANNA. LET'S GET SOME AIR.
...OKAY.
BUT, I DIDN'T--
SLAM
IT'S GONNA BE A GOOD DAY!
SIGH

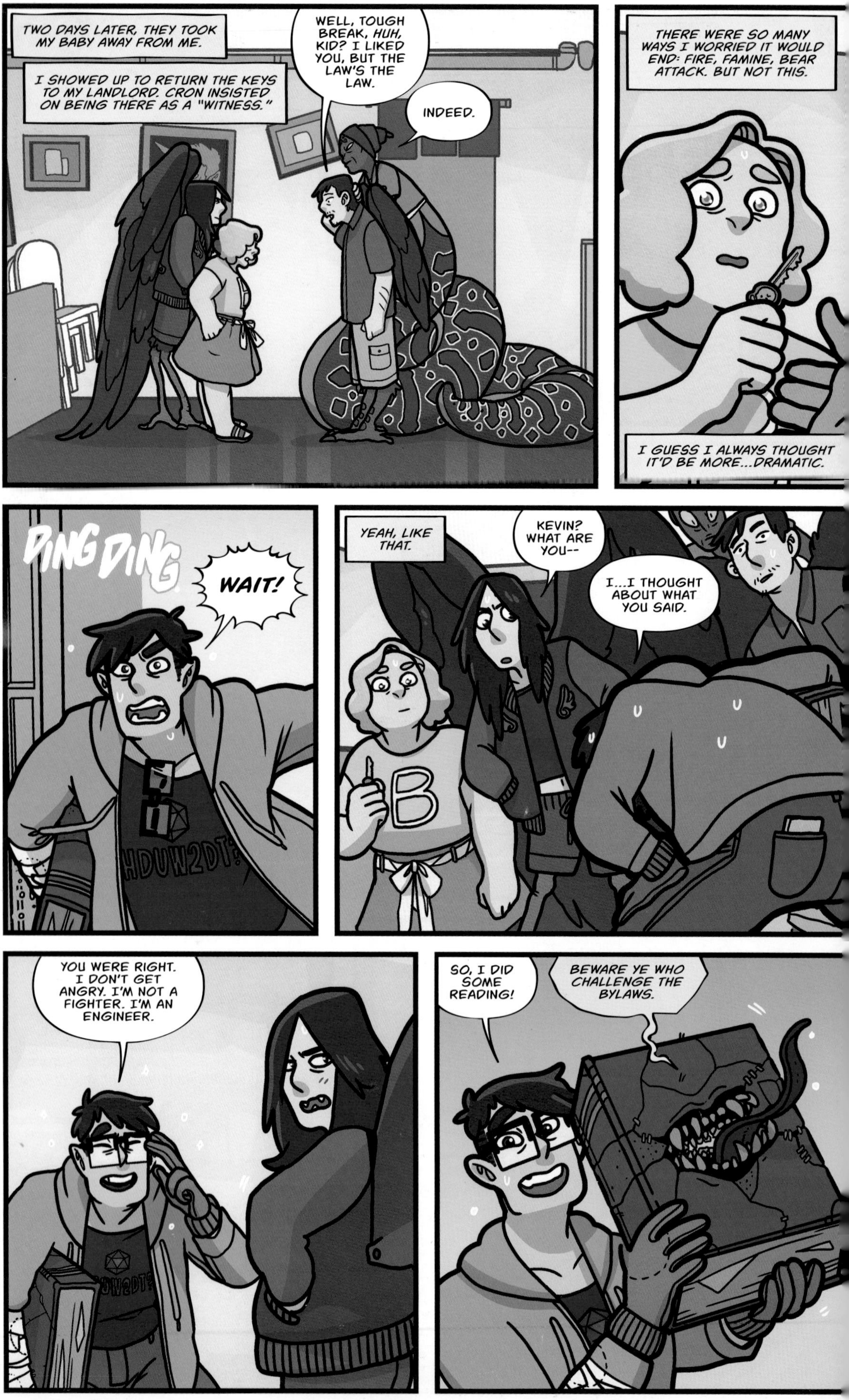
TWO DAYS LATER, THEY TOOK MY BABY AWAY FROM ME.
I SHOWED UP TO RETURN THE KEYS TO MY LANDLORD. CRON INSISTED ON BEING THERE AS A "WITNESS."
WELL, TOUGH BREAK, HUH, KID? I LIKED YOU, BUT THE LAW'S THE LAW.
INDEED.
THERE WERE SO MANY WAYS I WORRIED IT WOULD END: FIRE, FAMINE, BEAR ATTACK. BUT NOT THIS.
I GUESS I ALWAYS THOUGHT IT'D BE MORE...DRAMATIC.
DING DING
WAIT!
HDUW2DT?
YEAH, LIKE THAT.
KEVIN? WHAT ARE YOU--
I...I THOUGHT ABOUT WHAT YOU SAID.
YOU WERE RIGHT. I DON'T GET ANGRY. I'M NOT A FIGHTER. I'M AN ENGINEER.
SO, I DID SOME READING!
BEWARE YE WHO CHALLENGE THE BYLAWS.

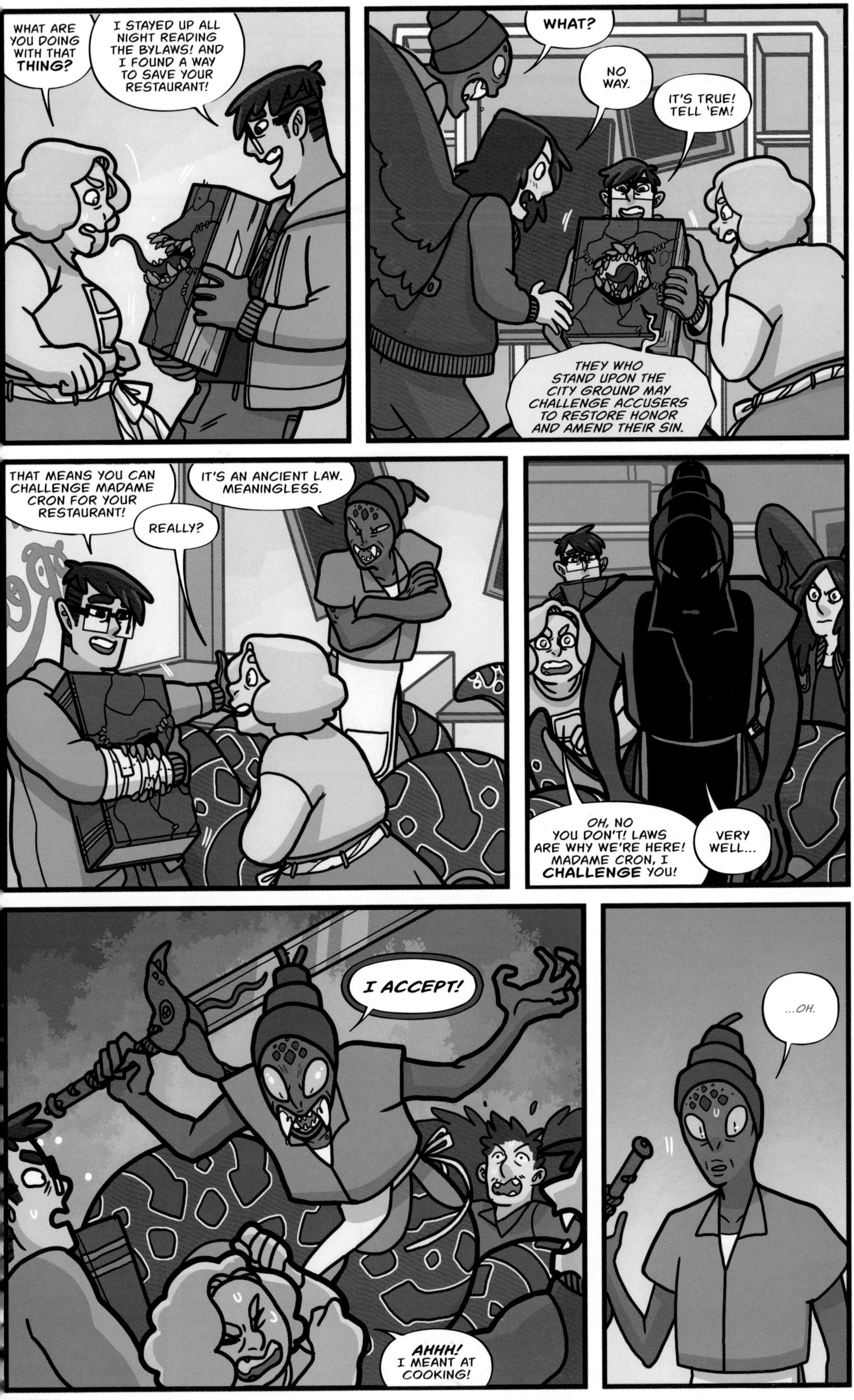
WHAT ARE YOU DOING WITH THAT THING?
I STAYED UP ALL NIGHT READING THE BYLAWS! AND I FOUND A WAY TO SAVE YOUR RESTAURANT!
WHAT?
NO WAY.
IT'S TRUE! TELL 'EM!
THEY WHO STAND UPON THE CITY GROUND MAY CHALLENGE ACCUSERS TO RESTORE HONOR AND AMEND THEIR SIN.
THAT MEANS YOU CAN CHALLENGE MADAME CRON FOR YOUR RESTAURANT!
IT'S AN ANCIENT LAW. MEANINGLESS.
REALLY?
OH, NO YOU DON'T! LAWS ARE WHY WE'RE HERE! MADAME CRON, I CHALLENGE YOU!
VERY WELL...
I ACCEPT!
AHHH! I MEANT AT COOKING!
...OH.

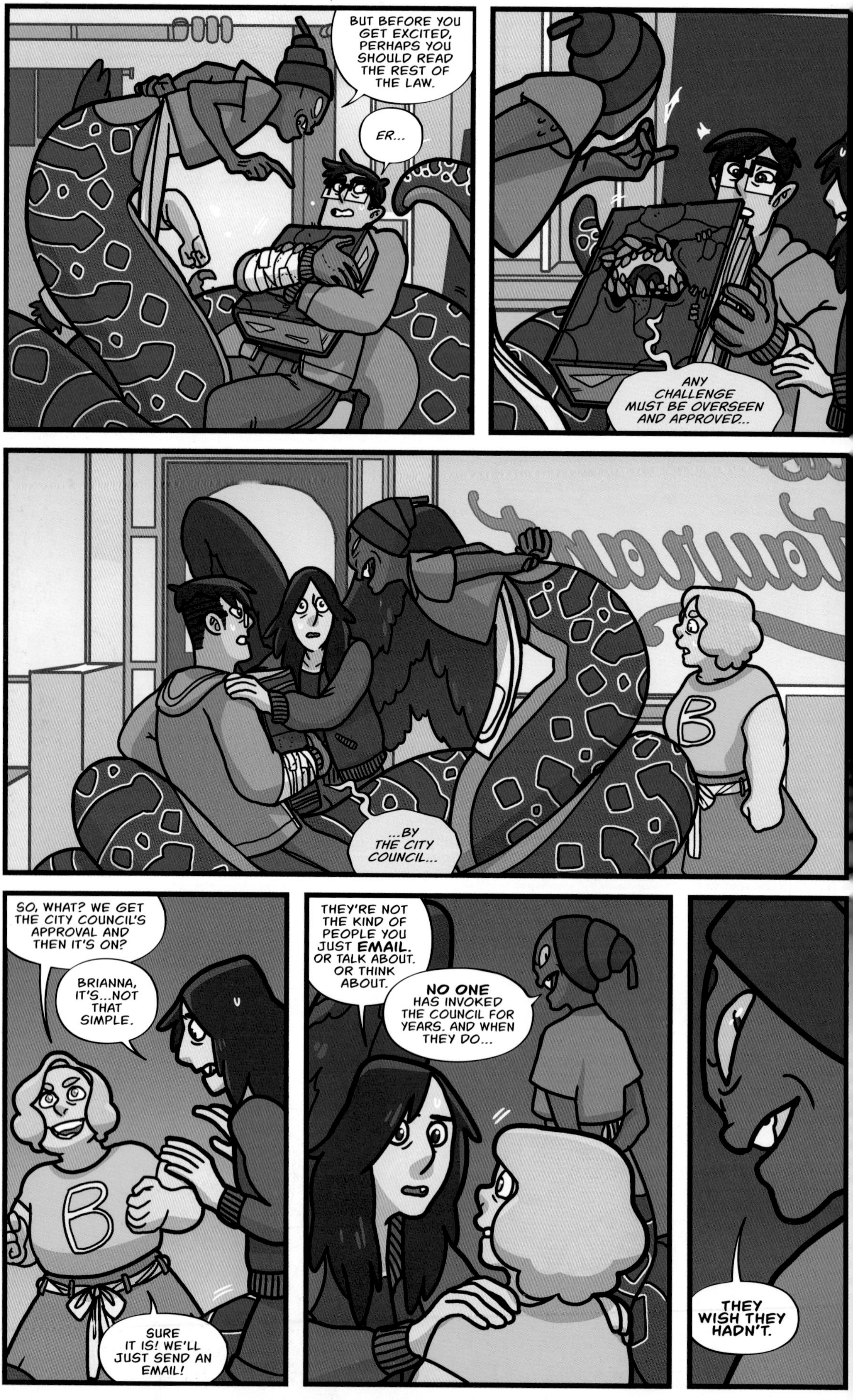
BUT BEFORE YOU GET EXCITED, PERHAPS YOU SHOULD READ THE REST OF THE LAW.
ER...
ANY CHALLENGE MUST BE OVERSEEN AND APPROVED...
...BY THE CITY COUNCIL...
SO, WHAT? WE GET THE CITY COUNCIL'S APPROVAL AND THEN IT'S ON?
BRIANNA, IT'S...NOT THAT SIMPLE.
SURE IT IS! WE'LL JUST SEND AN EMAIL!
THEY'RE NOT THE KIND OF PEOPLE YOU JUST **EMAIL.** OR TALK ABOUT. OR THINK ABOUT.
NO ONE HAS INVOKED THE COUNCIL FOR YEARS. AND WHEN THEY DO...
THEY WISH THEY HADN'T.

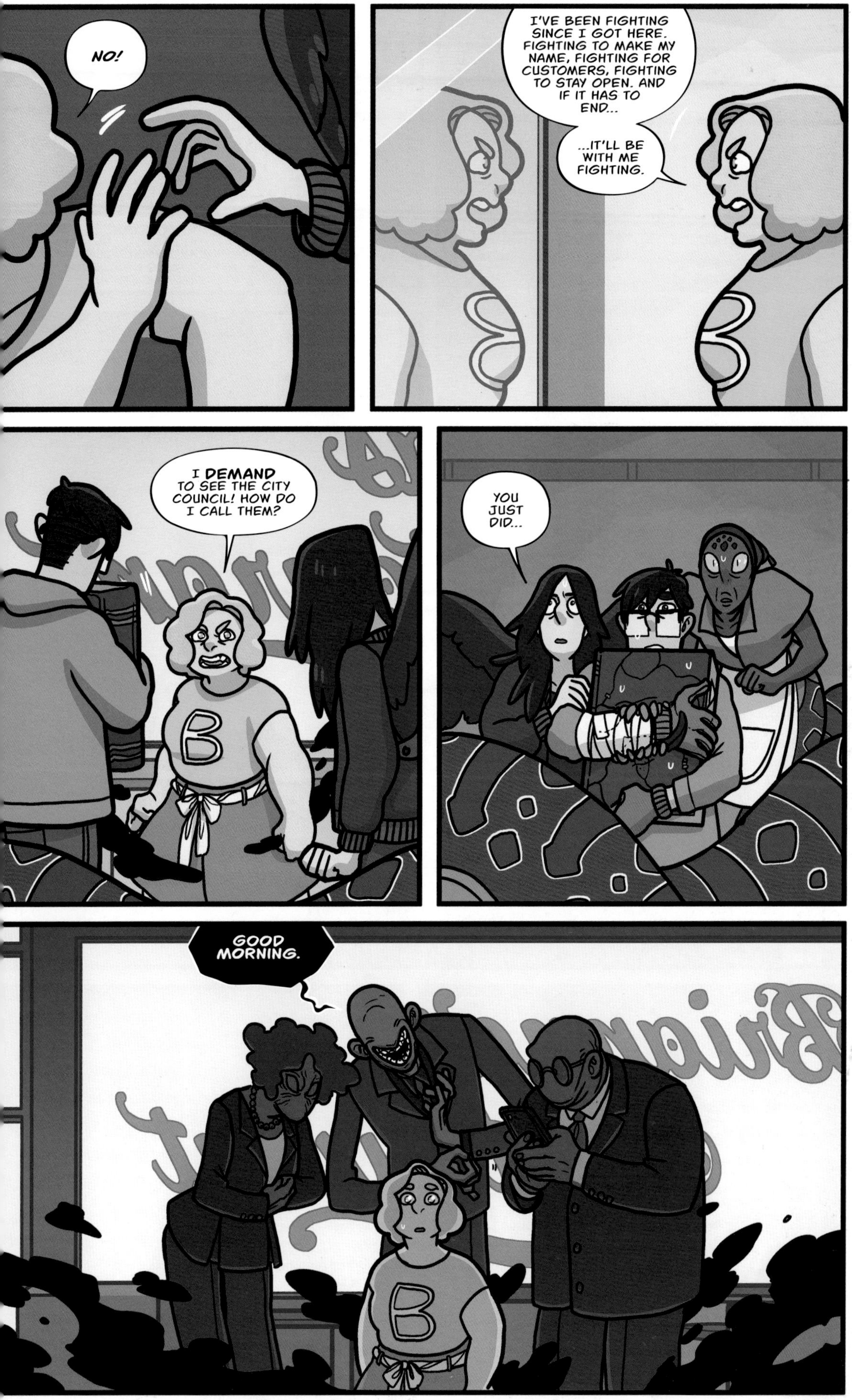
NO!
I'VE BEEN FIGHTING SINCE I GOT HERE. FIGHTING TO MAKE MY NAME, FIGHTING FOR CUSTOMERS, FIGHTING TO STAY OPEN. AND IF IT HAS TO END...
...IT'LL BE WITH ME FIGHTING.
I DEMAND TO SEE THE CITY COUNCIL! HOW DO I CALL THEM?
YOU JUST DID...
GOOD MORNING.

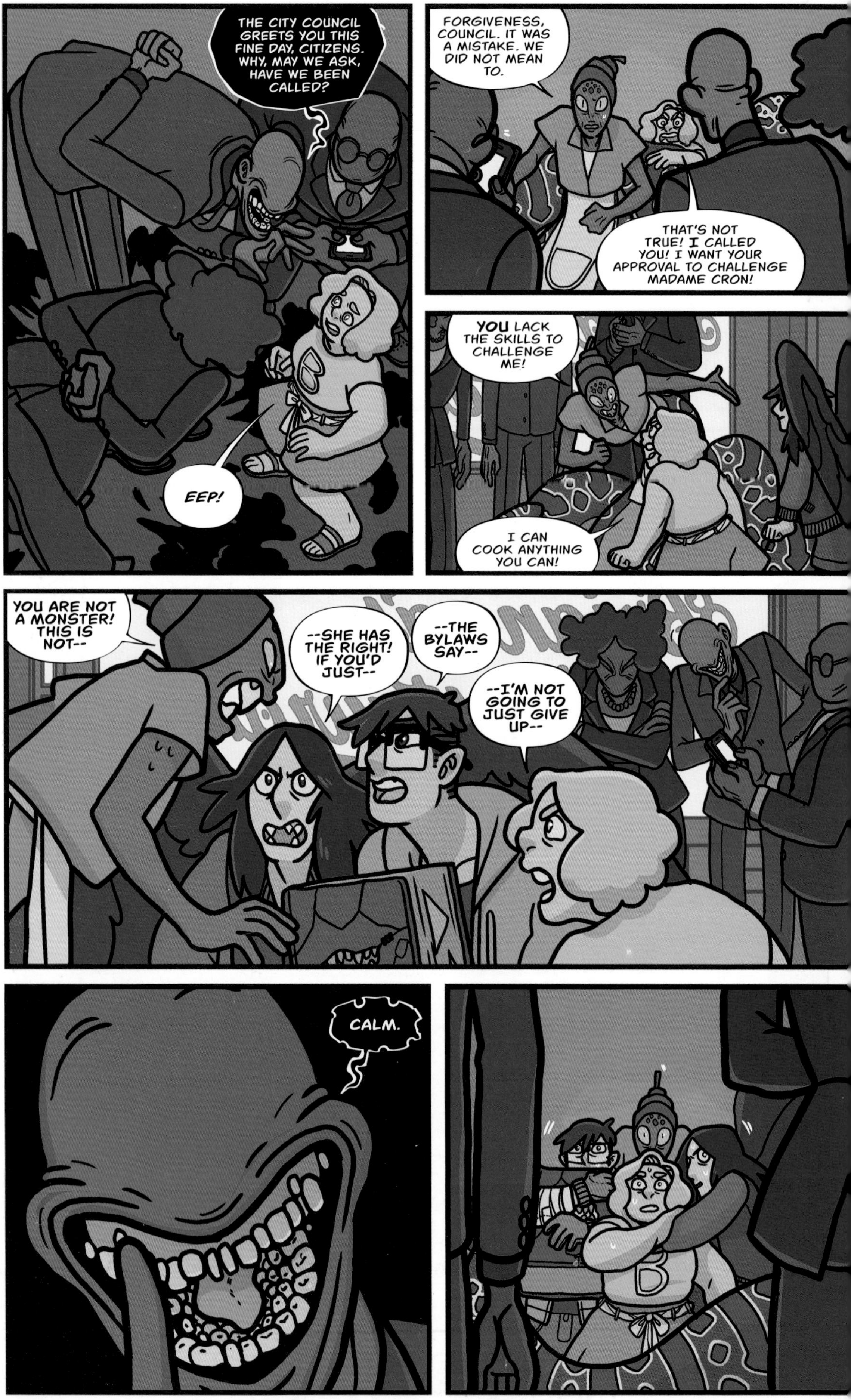
THE CITY COUNCIL GREETS YOU THIS FINE DAY, CITIZENS. WHY, MAY WE ASK, HAVE WE BEEN CALLED?
EEP!
FORGIVENESS, COUNCIL. IT WAS A MISTAKE. WE DID NOT MEAN TO.
THAT'S NOT TRUE! I CALLED YOU! I WANT YOUR APPROVAL TO CHALLENGE MADAME CRON!
YOU LACK THE SKILLS TO CHALLENGE ME!
I CAN COOK ANYTHING YOU CAN!
YOU ARE NOT A MONSTER! THIS IS NOT--
--SHE HAS THE RIGHT! IF YOU'D JUST--
--THE BYLAWS SAY--
--I'M NOT GOING TO JUST GIVE UP--
CALM.

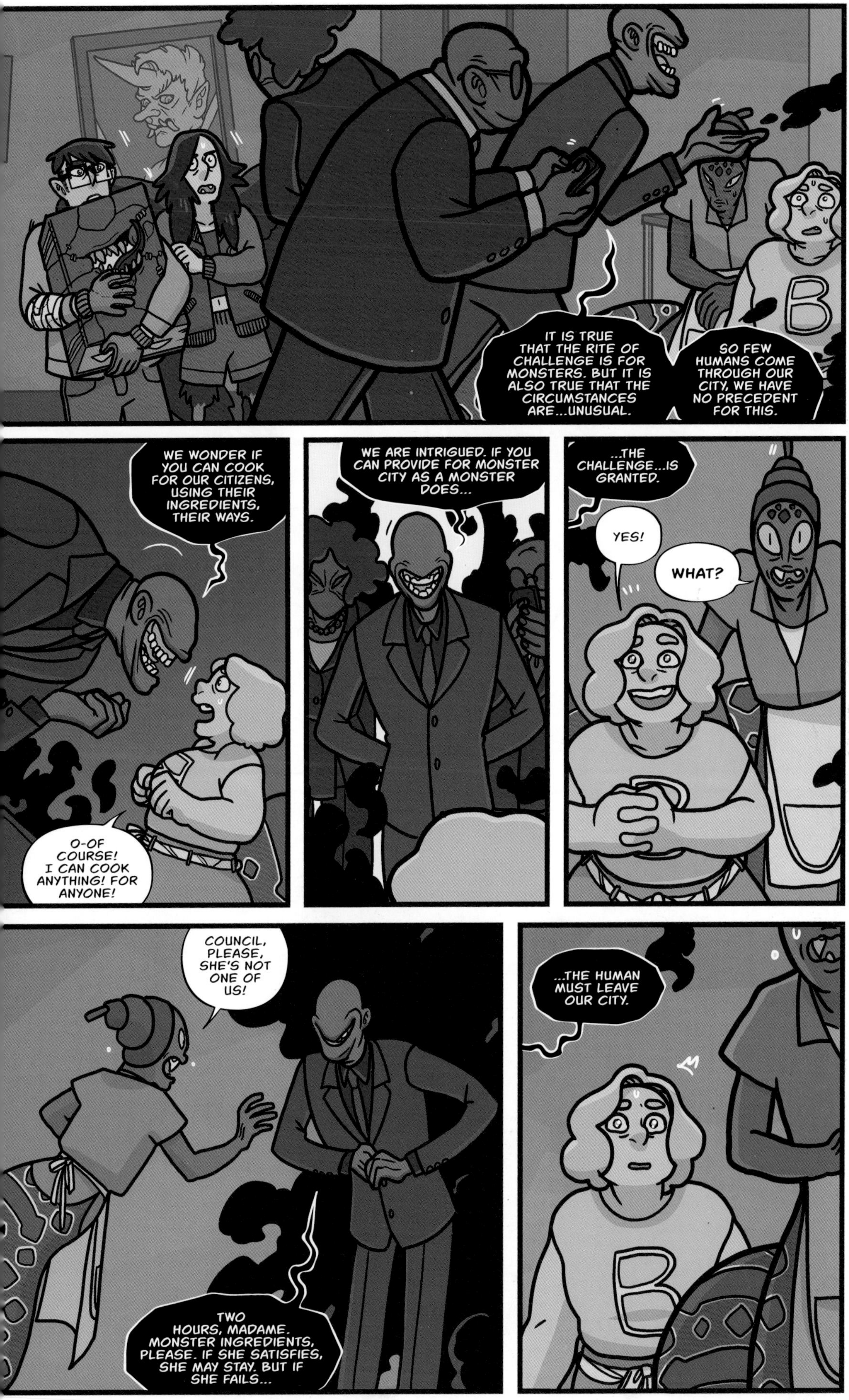
IT IS TRUE THAT THE RITE OF CHALLENGE IS FOR MONSTERS. BUT IT IS ALSO TRUE THAT THE CIRCUMSTANCES ARE...UNUSUAL.
SO FEW HUMANS COME THROUGH OUR CITY, WE HAVE NO PRECEDENT FOR THIS.
WE WONDER IF YOU CAN COOK FOR OUR CITIZENS, USING THEIR INGREDIENTS, THEIR WAYS.
O-OF COURSE! I CAN COOK ANYTHING! FOR ANYONE!
WE ARE INTRIGUED. IF YOU CAN PROVIDE FOR MONSTER CITY AS A MONSTER DOES...
...THE CHALLENGE...IS GRANTED.
YES!
WHAT?
COUNCIL, PLEASE, SHE'S NOT ONE OF US!
TWO HOURS, MADAME. MONSTER INGREDIENTS, PLEASE. IF SHE SATISFIES, SHE MAY STAY. BUT IF SHE FAILS...
...THE HUMAN MUST LEAVE OUR CITY.

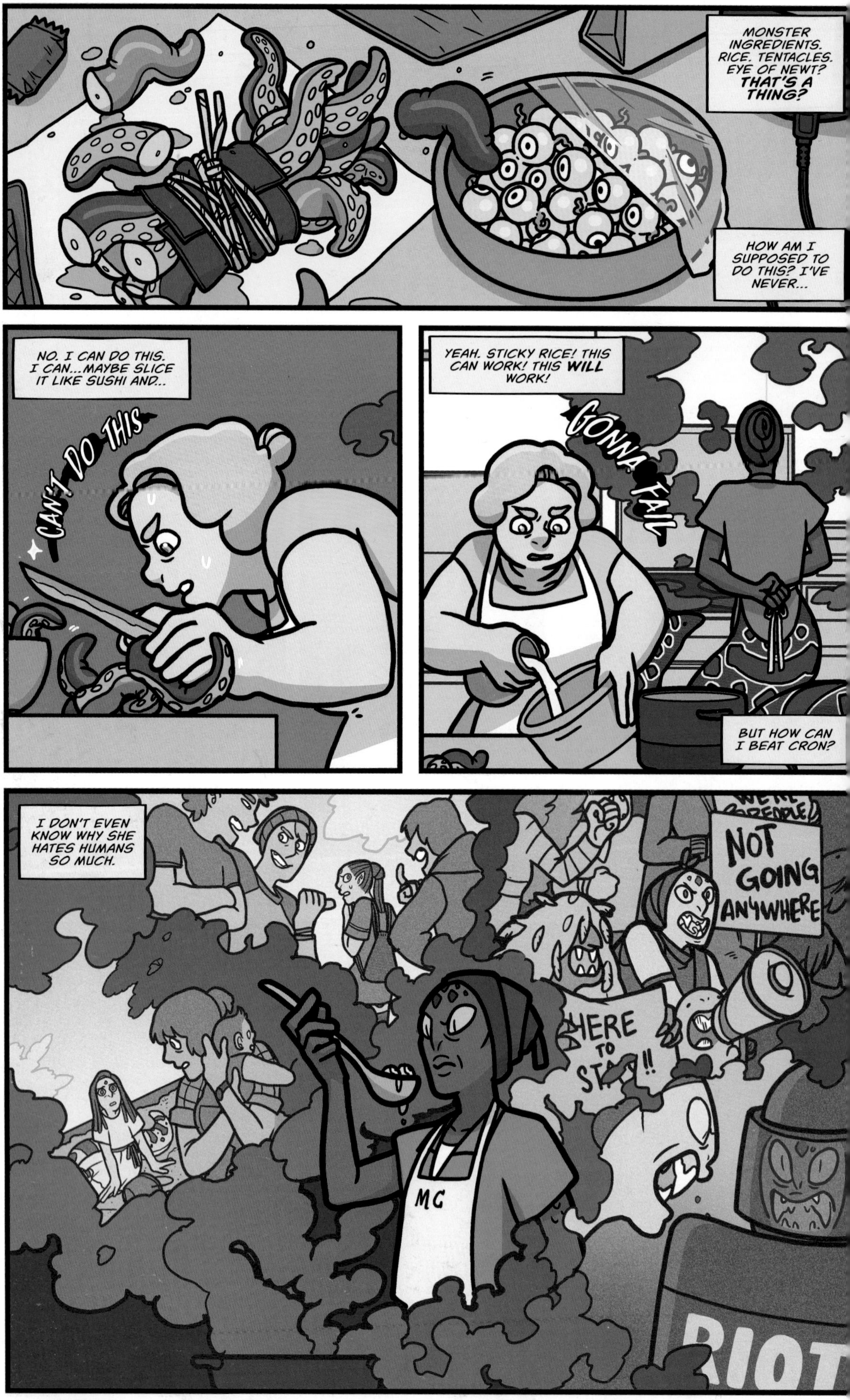
MONSTER INGREDIENTS. RICE. TENTACLES. EYE OF NEWT? THAT'S A THING?
HOW AM I SUPPOSED TO DO THIS? I'VE NEVER...
NO. I CAN DO THIS. I CAN...MAYBE SLICE IT LIKE SUSHI AND...
CAN'T DO THIS
YEAH. STICKY RICE! THIS CAN WORK! THIS WILL WORK!
GONNA FAIL
BUT HOW CAN I BEAT CRON?
I DON'T EVEN KNOW WHY SHE HATES HUMANS SO MUCH.
NOT GOING ANYWHERE
HERE TO STAY!!
MC
RIOT

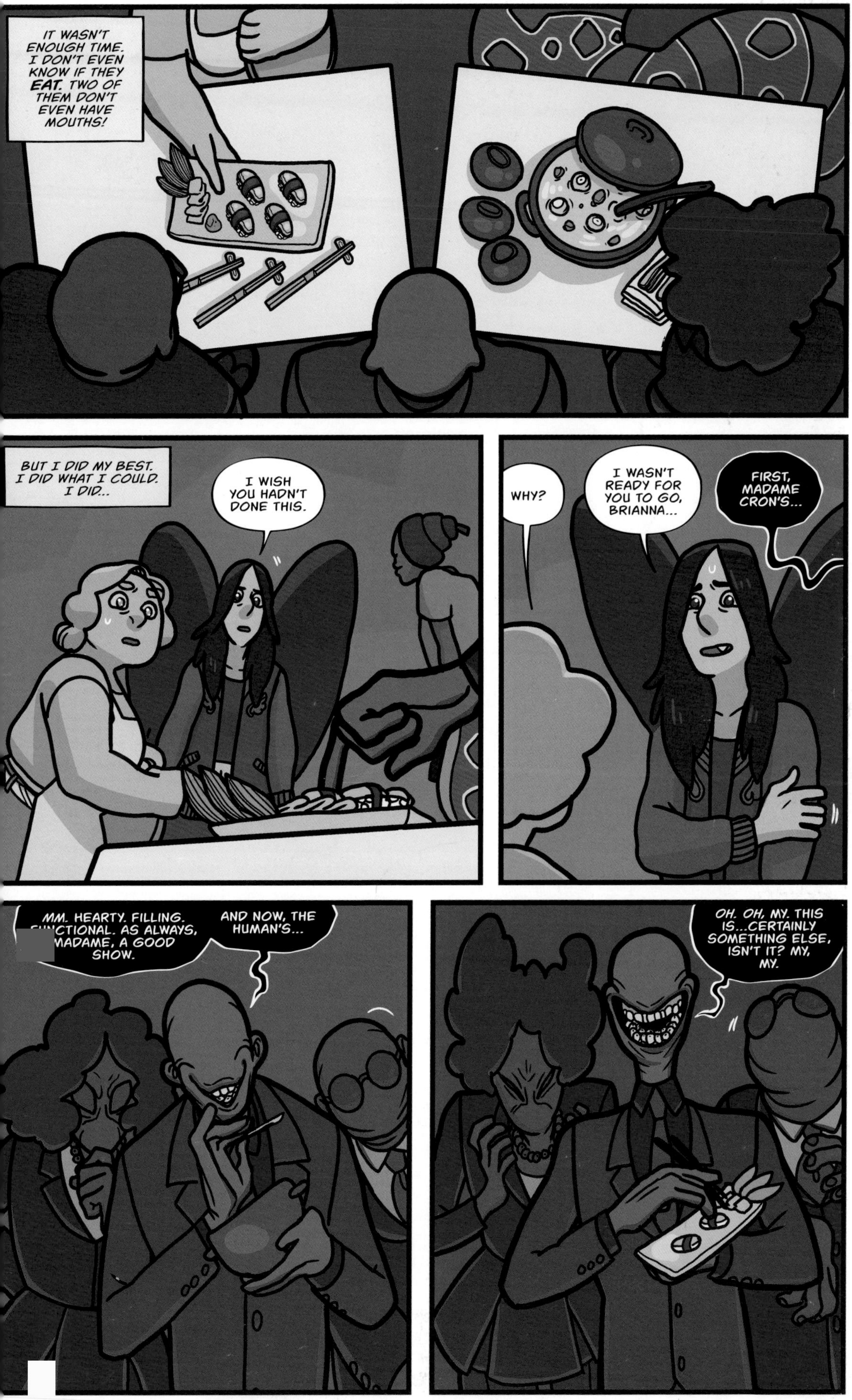
IT WASN'T ENOUGH TIME. I DON'T EVEN KNOW IF THEY EAT. TWO OF THEM DON'T EVEN HAVE MOUTHS!
BUT I DID MY BEST. I DID WHAT I COULD. I DID...
I WISH YOU HADN'T DONE THIS.
WHY?
I WASN'T READY FOR YOU TO GO, BRIANNA...
FIRST, MADAME CRON'S...
MM. HEARTY. FILLING. FUNCTIONAL. AS ALWAYS, MADAME, A GOOD SHOW.
AND NOW, THE HUMAN'S...
OH. OH, MY. THIS IS...CERTAINLY SOMETHING ELSE, ISN'T IT? MY, MY.

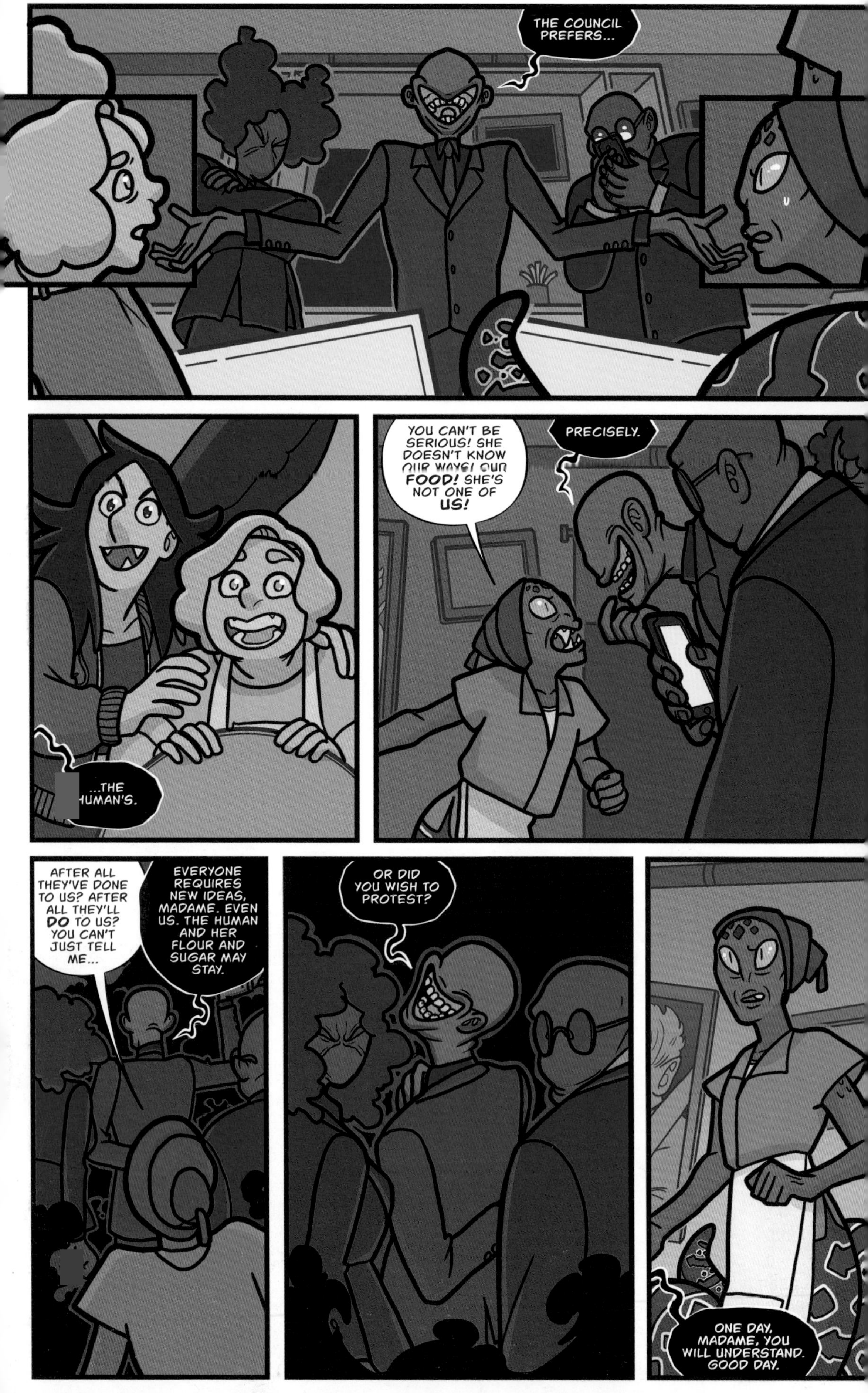
THE COUNCIL PREFERS...
...THE UMAN'S.
YOU CAN'T BE SERIOUS! SHE DOESN'T KNOW OUR WAYS! OUR FOOD! SHE'S NOT ONE OF US!
PRECISELY.
AFTER ALL THEY'VE DONE TO US? AFTER ALL THEY'LL DO TO US? YOU CAN'T JUST TELL ME...
EVERYONE REQUIRES NEW IDEAS, MADAME. EVEN US. THE HUMAN AND HER FLOUR AND SUGAR MAY STAY.
OR DID YOU WISH TO PROTEST?
ONE DAY, MADAME, YOU WILL UNDERSTAND. GOOD DAY.

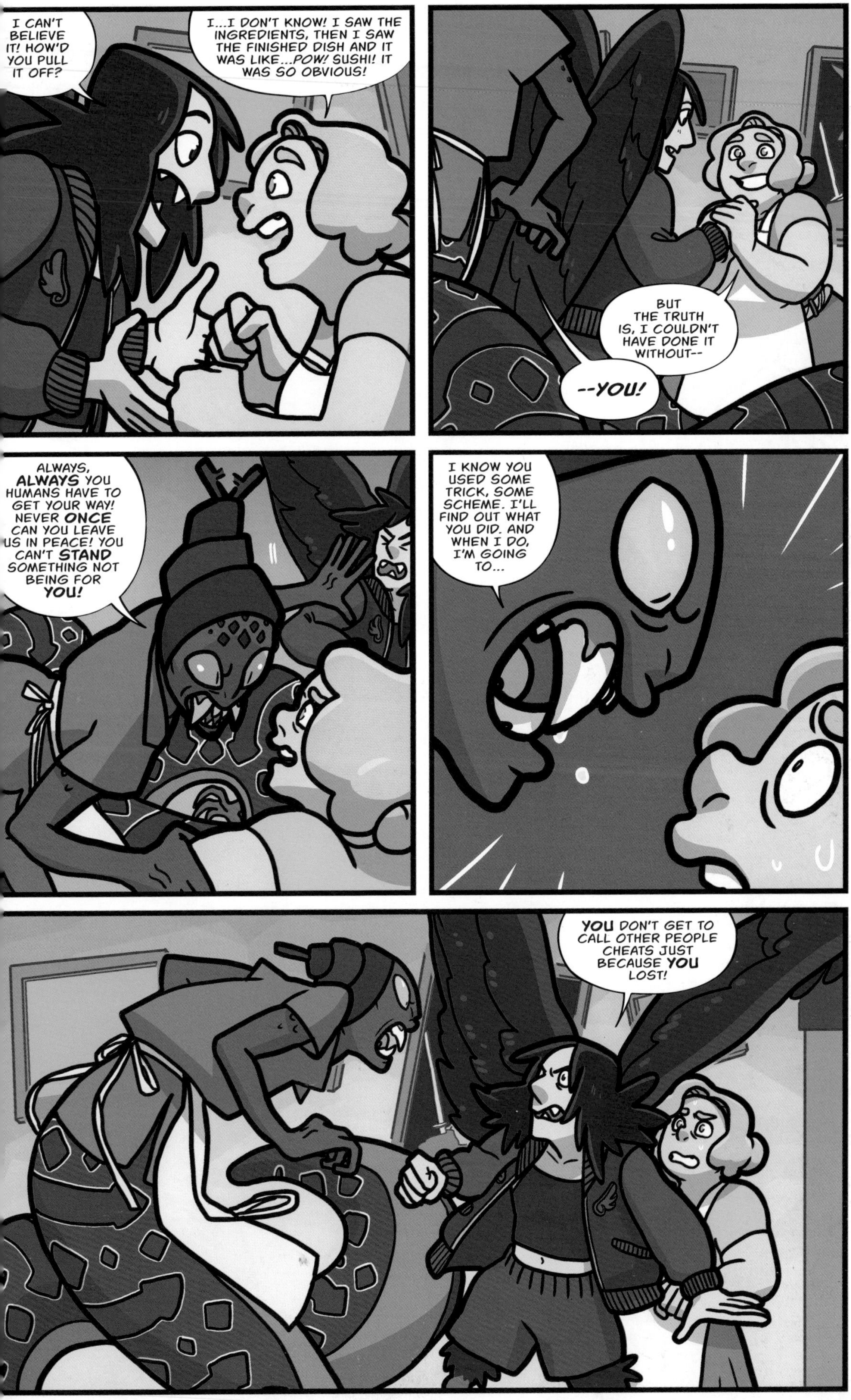
I CAN'T BELIEVE IT! HOW'D YOU PULL IT OFF?
I...I DON'T KNOW! I SAW THE INGREDIENTS, THEN I SAW THE FINISHED DISH AND IT WAS LIKE...POW! SUSHI! IT WAS SO OBVIOUS!
BUT THE TRUTH IS, I COULDN'T HAVE DONE IT WITHOUT--
--YOU!
ALWAYS, ALWAYS YOU HUMANS HAVE TO GET YOUR WAY! NEVER ONCE CAN YOU LEAVE US IN PEACE! YOU CAN'T STAND SOMETHING NOT BEING FOR YOU!
I KNOW YOU USED SOME TRICK, SOME SCHEME. I'LL FIND OUT WHAT YOU DID. AND WHEN I DO, I'M GOING TO...
YOU DON'T GET TO CALL OTHER PEOPLE CHEATS JUST BECAUSE YOU LOST!

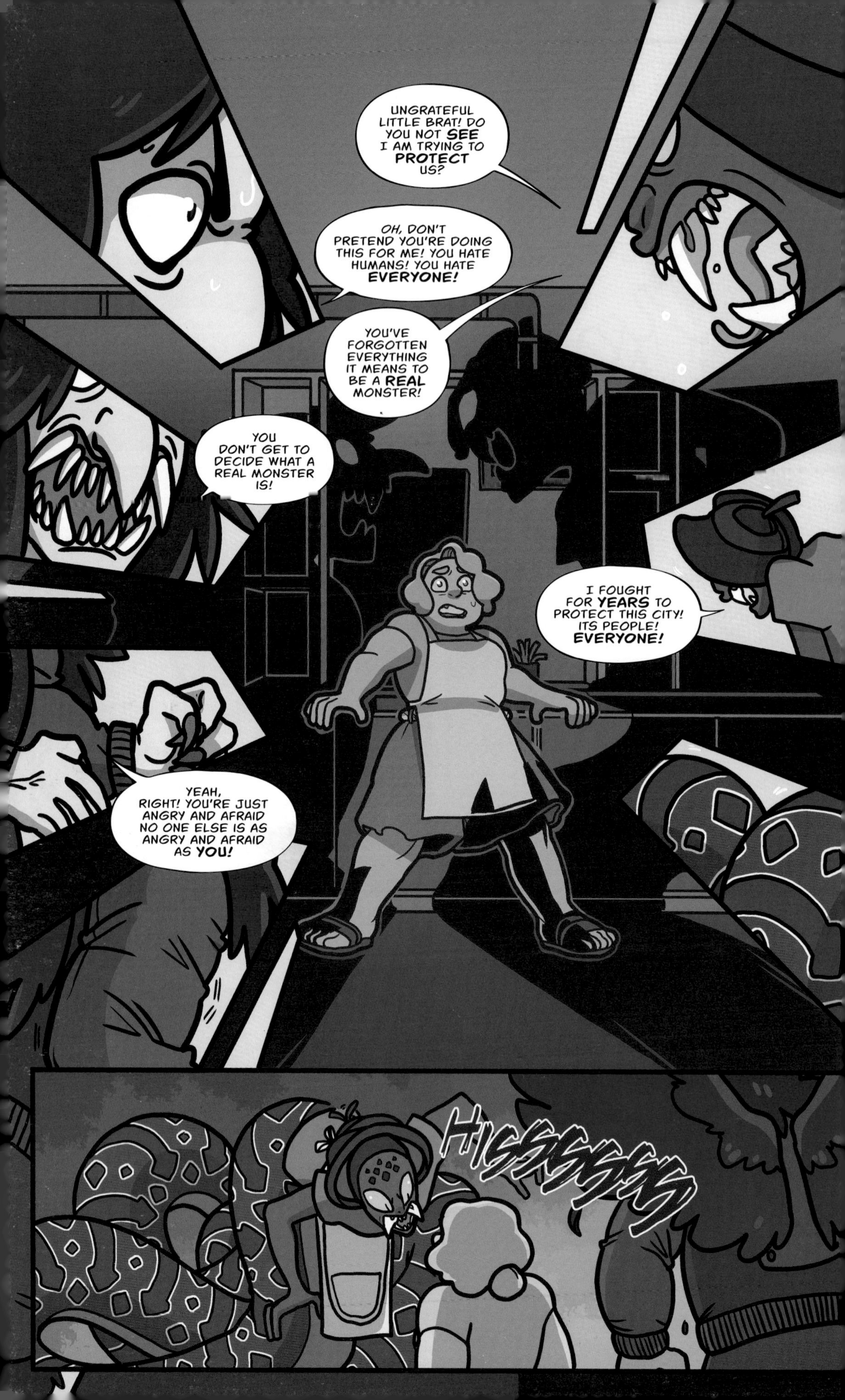
UNGRATEFUL LITTLE BRAT! DO YOU NOT SEE I AM TRYING TO PROTECT US?
OH, DON'T PRETEND YOU'RE DOING THIS FOR ME! YOU HATE HUMANS! YOU HATE EVERYONE!
YOU'VE FORGOTTEN EVERYTHING IT MEANS TO BE A REAL MONSTER!
YOU DON'T GET TO DECIDE WHAT A REAL MONSTER IS!
I FOUGHT FOR YEARS TO PROTECT THIS CITY! ITS PEOPLE! EVERYONE!
YEAH, RIGHT! YOU'RE JUST ANGRY AND AFRAID NO ONE ELSE IS AS ANGRY AND AFRAID AS YOU!
HISSSSSSS

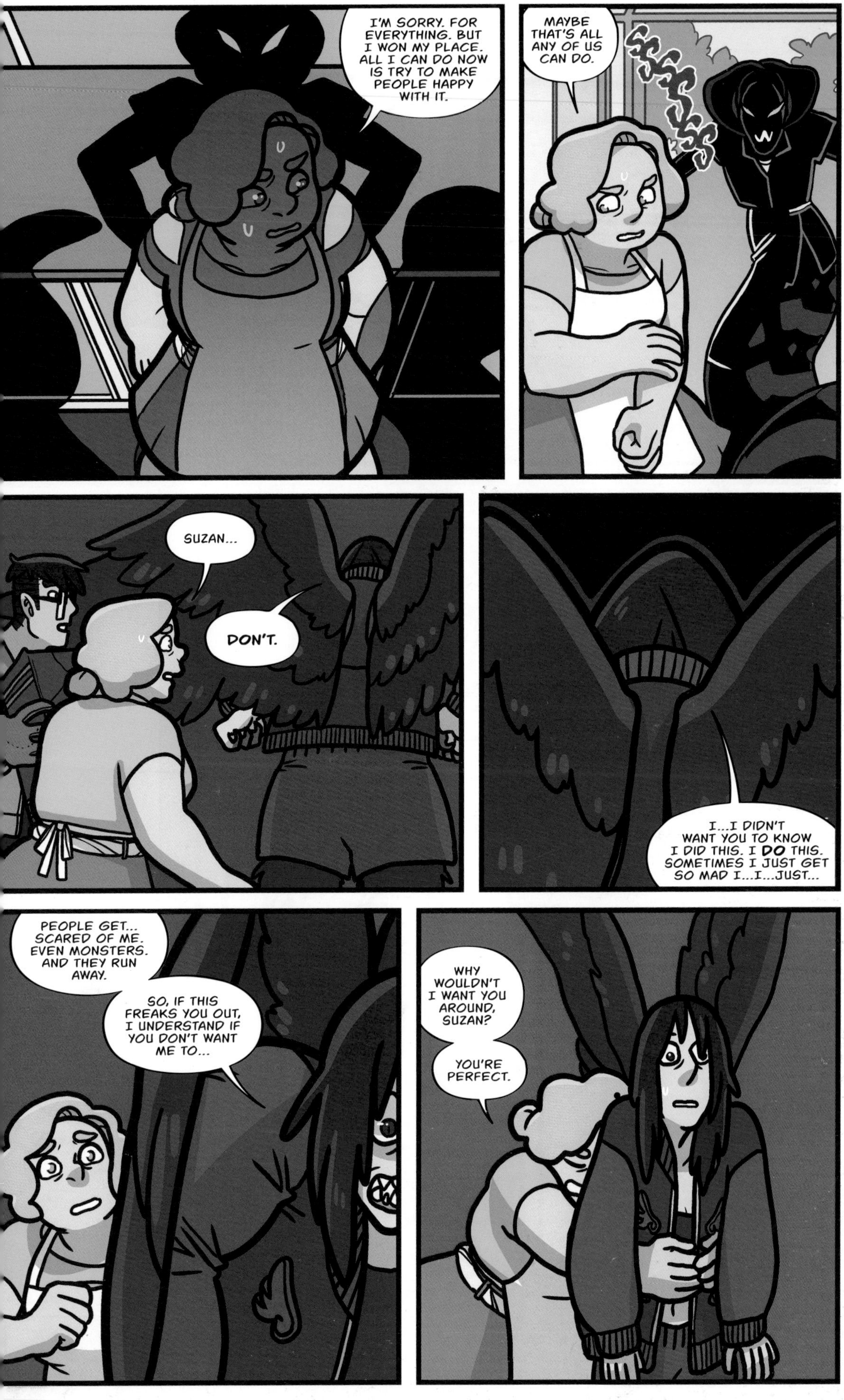
I'M SORRY. FOR EVERYTHING. BUT I WON MY PLACE. ALL I CAN DO NOW IS TRY TO MAKE PEOPLE HAPPY WITH IT.
MAYBE THAT'S ALL ANY OF US CAN DO.
SSSSSSSS
SUZAN...
DON'T.
I...I DIDN'T WANT YOU TO KNOW I DID THIS. I DO THIS. SOMETIMES I JUST GET SO MAD I...I...JUST...
PEOPLE GET... SCARED OF ME. EVEN MONSTERS. AND THEY RUN AWAY.
SO, IF THIS FREAKS YOU OUT, I UNDERSTAND IF YOU DON'T WANT ME TO...
WHY WOULDN'T I WANT YOU AROUND, SUZAN?
YOU'RE PERFECT.

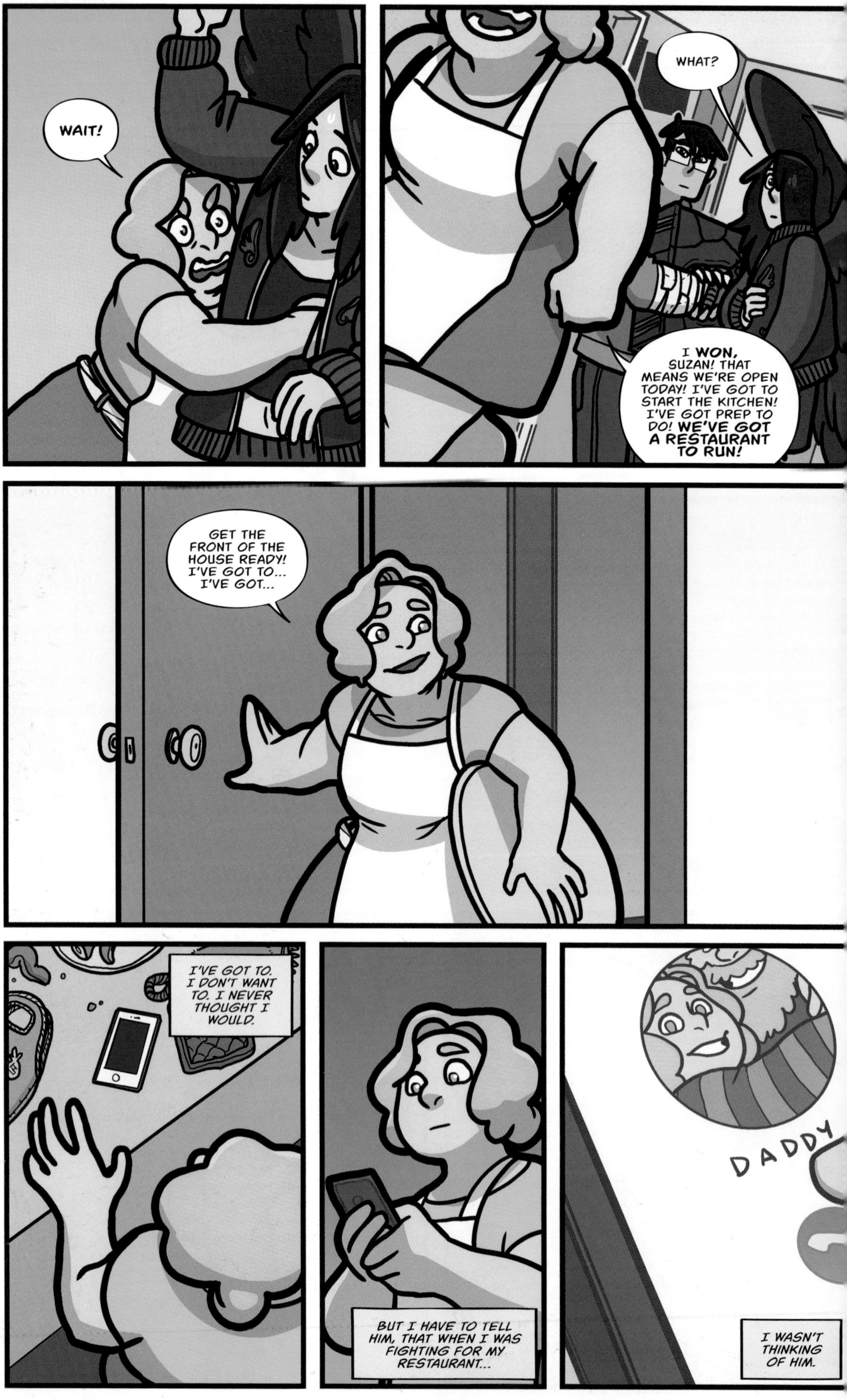
WAIT!
WHAT?
I WON, SUZAN! THAT MEANS WE'RE OPEN TODAY! I'VE GOT TO START THE KITCHEN! I'VE GOT PREP TO DO! WE'VE GOT A RESTAURANT TO RUN!
GET THE FRONT OF THE HOUSE READY! I'VE GOT TO... I'VE GOT...
I'VE GOT TO. I DON'T WANT TO. I NEVER THOUGHT I WOULD.
BUT I HAVE TO TELL HIM, THAT WHEN I WAS FIGHTING FOR MY RESTAURANT...
DADDY
I WASN'T THINKING OF HIM.

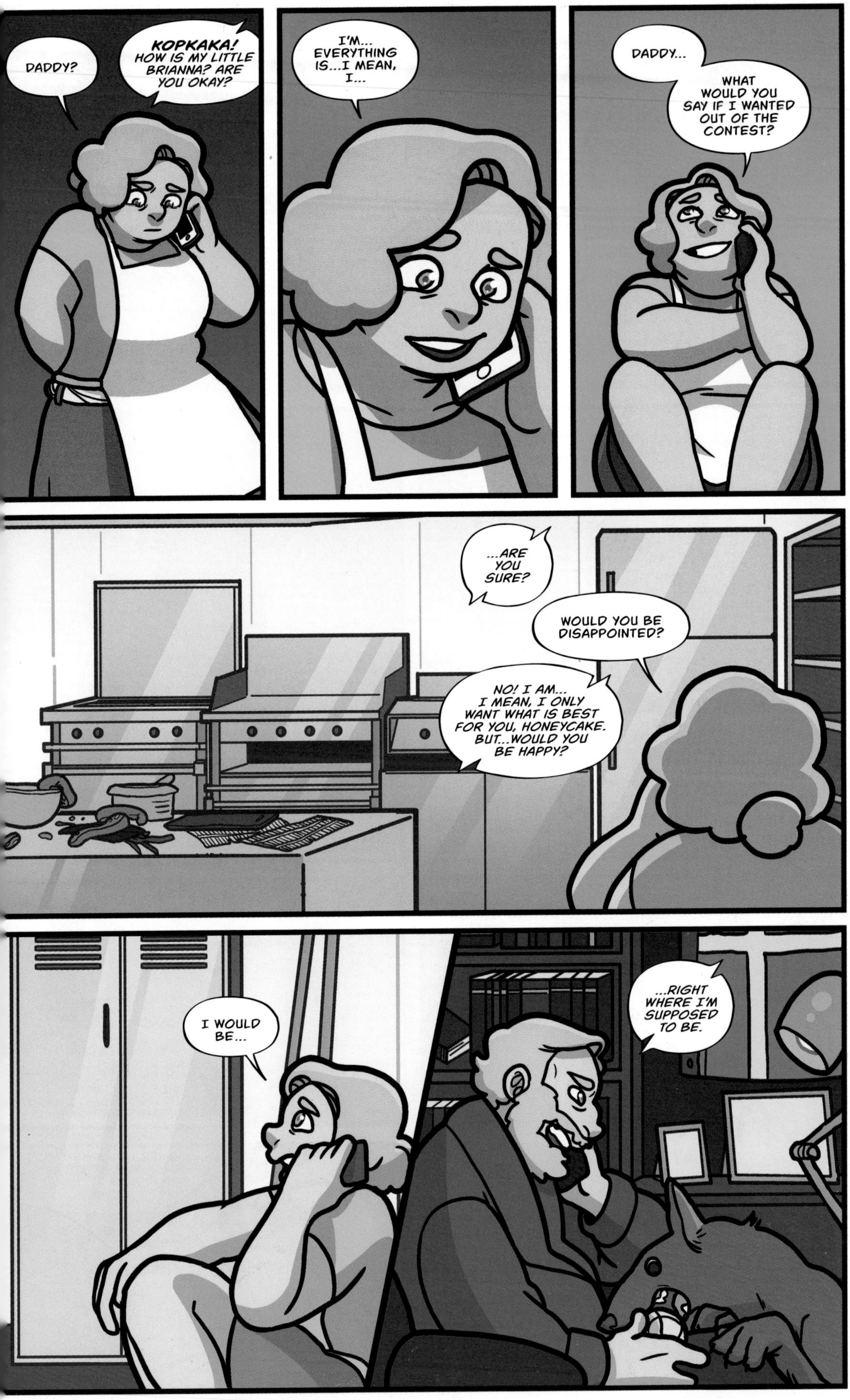
DADDY?
KOPKAKA! HOW IS MY LITTLE BRIANNA? ARE YOU OKAY?
I'M... EVERYTHING IS...I MEAN, I...
DADDY...
WHAT WOULD YOU SAY IF I WANTED OUT OF THE CONTEST?
...ARE YOU SURE?
WOULD YOU BE DISAPPOINTED?
NO! I AM... I MEAN, I ONLY WANT WHAT IS BEST FOR YOU, HONEYCAKE. BUT...WOULD YOU BE HAPPY?
I WOULD BE...
...RIGHT WHERE I'M SUPPOSED TO BE.

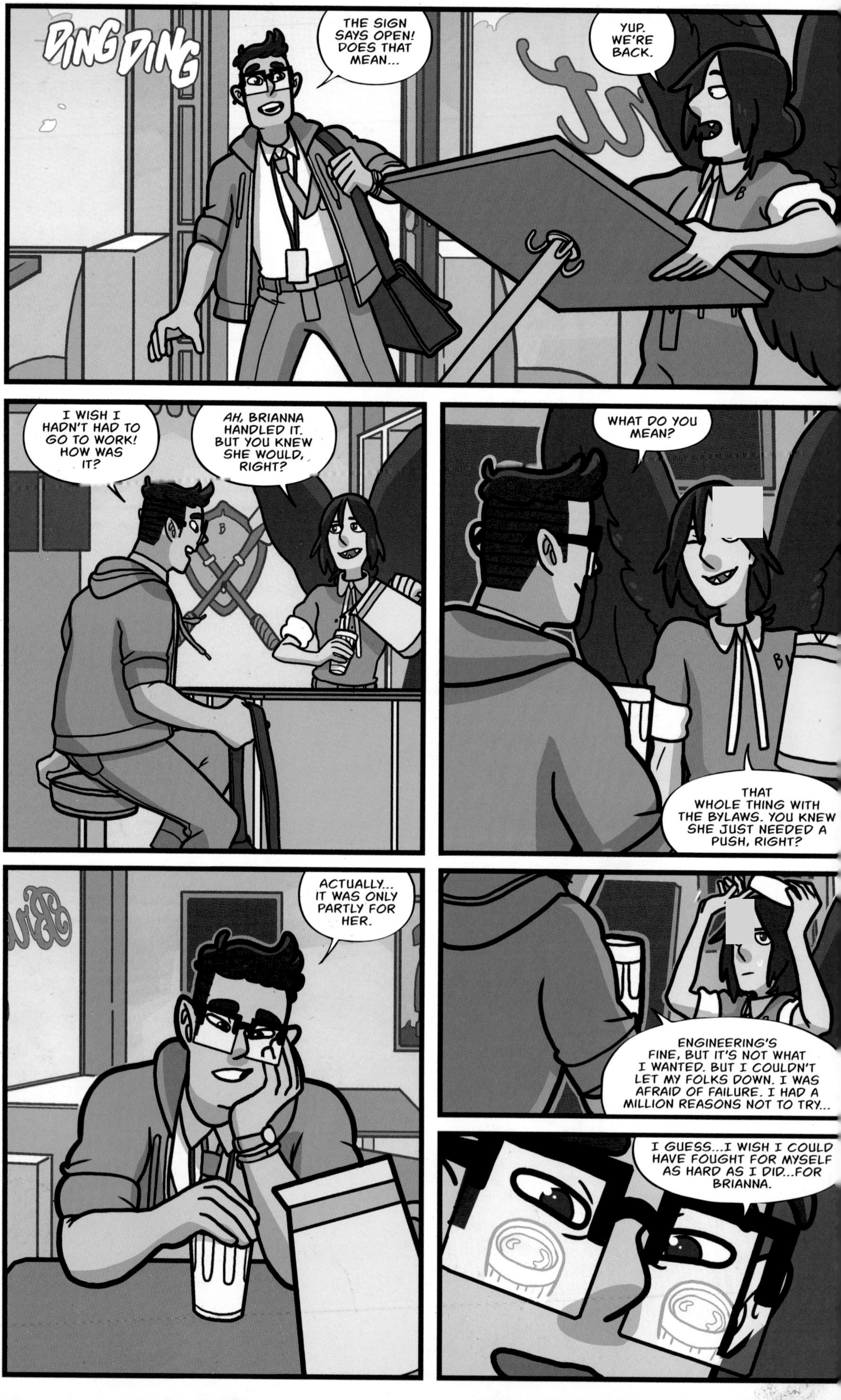
DING DING
THE SIGN SAYS OPEN! DOES THAT MEAN...
YUP. WE'RE BACK.
I WISH I HADN'T HAD TO GO TO WORK! HOW WAS IT?
AH, BRIANNA HANDLED IT. BUT YOU KNEW SHE WOULD, RIGHT?
WHAT DO YOU MEAN?
THAT WHOLE THING WITH THE BYLAWS. YOU KNEW SHE JUST NEEDED A PUSH, RIGHT?
ACTUALLY... IT WAS ONLY PARTLY FOR HER.
ENGINEERING'S FINE, BUT IT'S NOT WHAT I WANTED. BUT I COULDN'T LET MY FOLKS DOWN. I WAS AFRAID OF FAILURE. I HAD A MILLION REASONS NOT TO TRY...
I GUESS...I WISH I COULD HAVE FOUGHT FOR MYSELF AS HARD AS I DID...FOR BRIANNA.

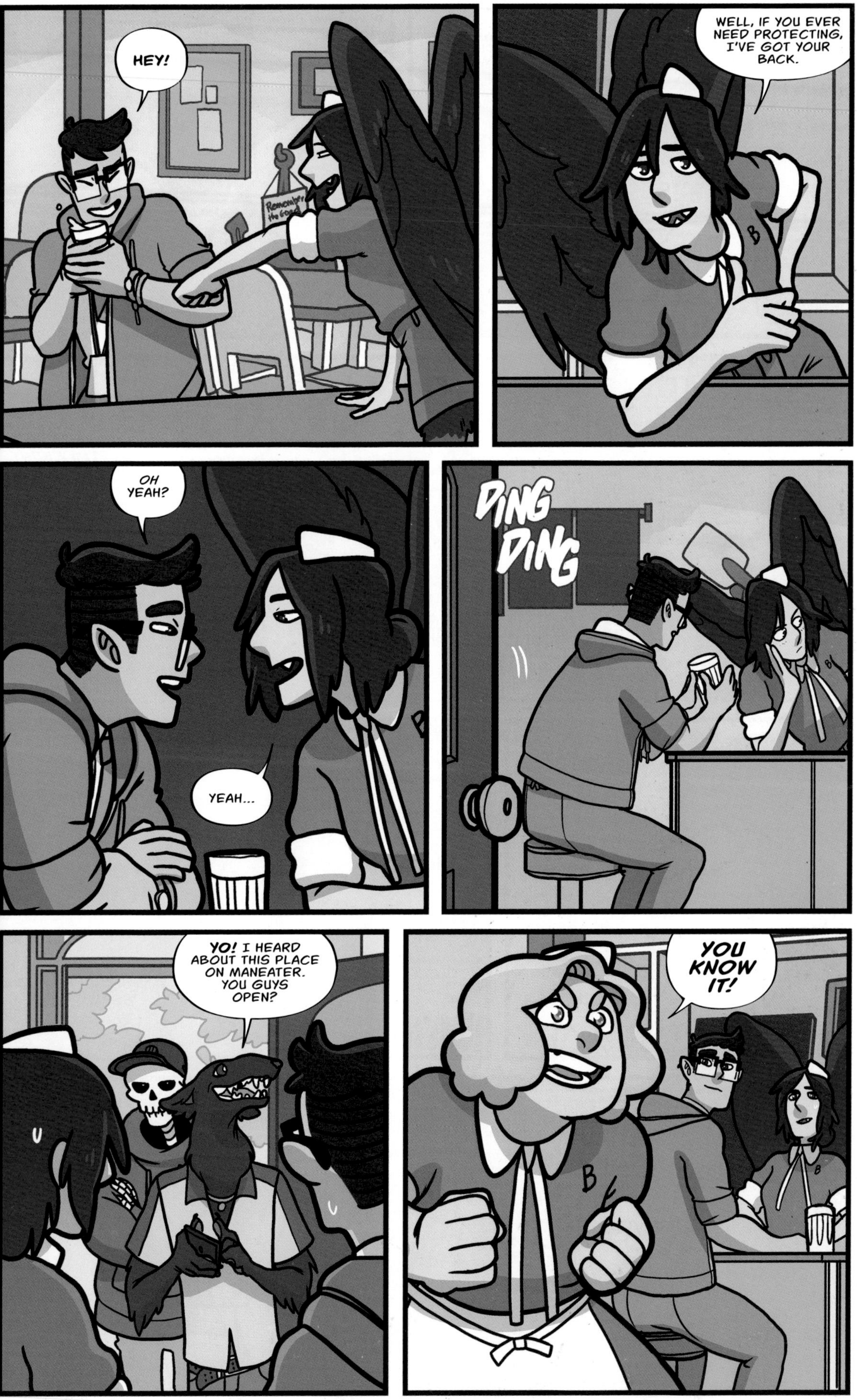
HEY!
WELL, IF YOU EVER NEED PROTECTING, I'VE GOT YOUR BACK.
OH YEAH?
YEAH...
DING DING
YO! I HEARD ABOUT THIS PLACE ON MANEATER. YOU GUYS OPEN?
YOU KNOW IT!

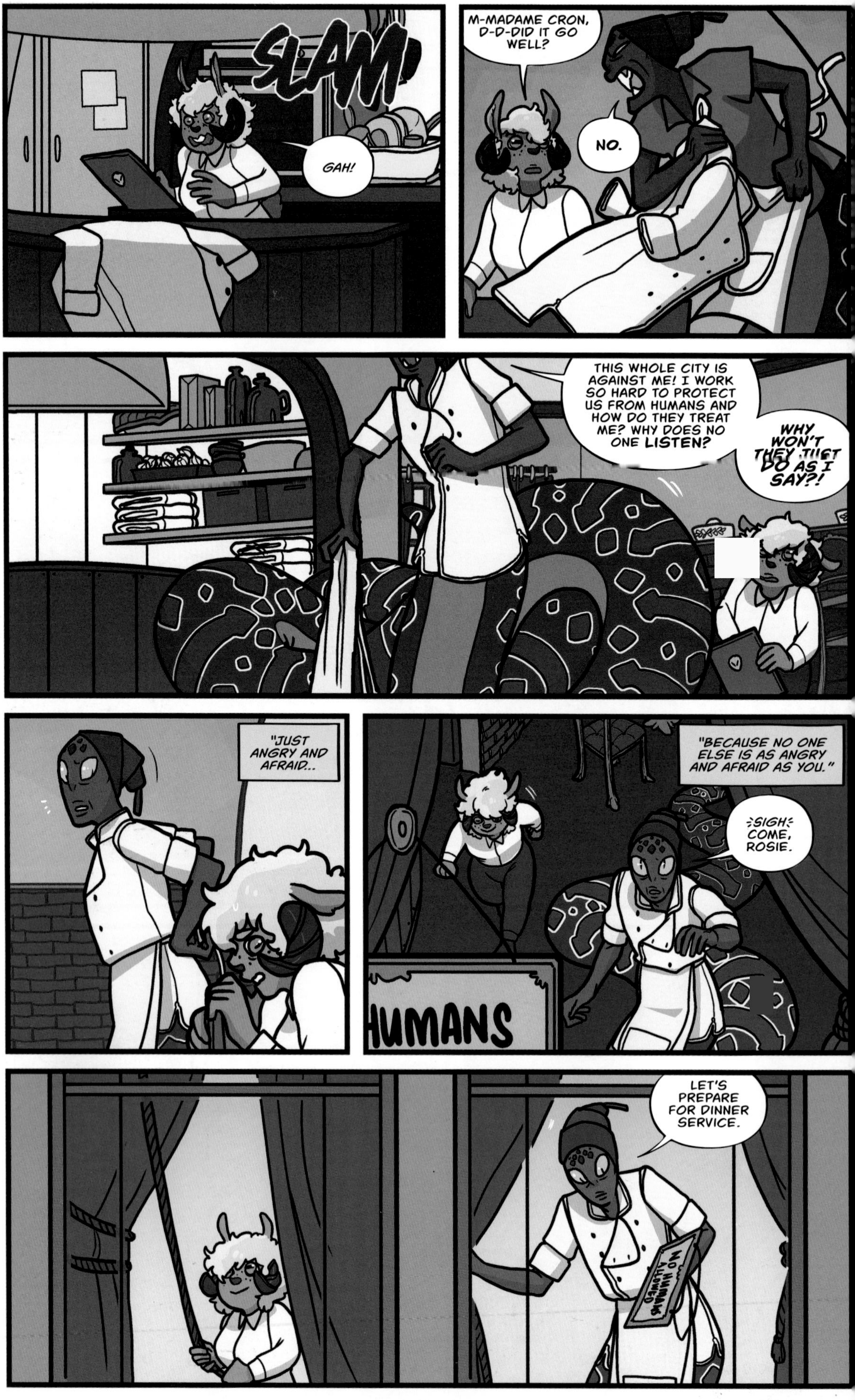
SLAM!
GAH!
M-MADAME CRON, D-D-DID IT GO WELL?
NO.
THIS WHOLE CITY IS AGAINST ME! I WORK SO HARD TO PROTECT US FROM HUMANS AND HOW DO THEY TREAT ME? WHY DOES NO ONE LISTEN?
WHY WON'T THEY JUST DO AS I SAY?!
"JUST ANGRY AND AFRAID...
"BECAUSE NO ONE ELSE IS AS ANGRY AND AFRAID AS YOU."
SIGH COME, ROSIE.
HUMANS
LET'S PREPARE FOR DINNER SERVICE.
NO HUMANS ALLOWED

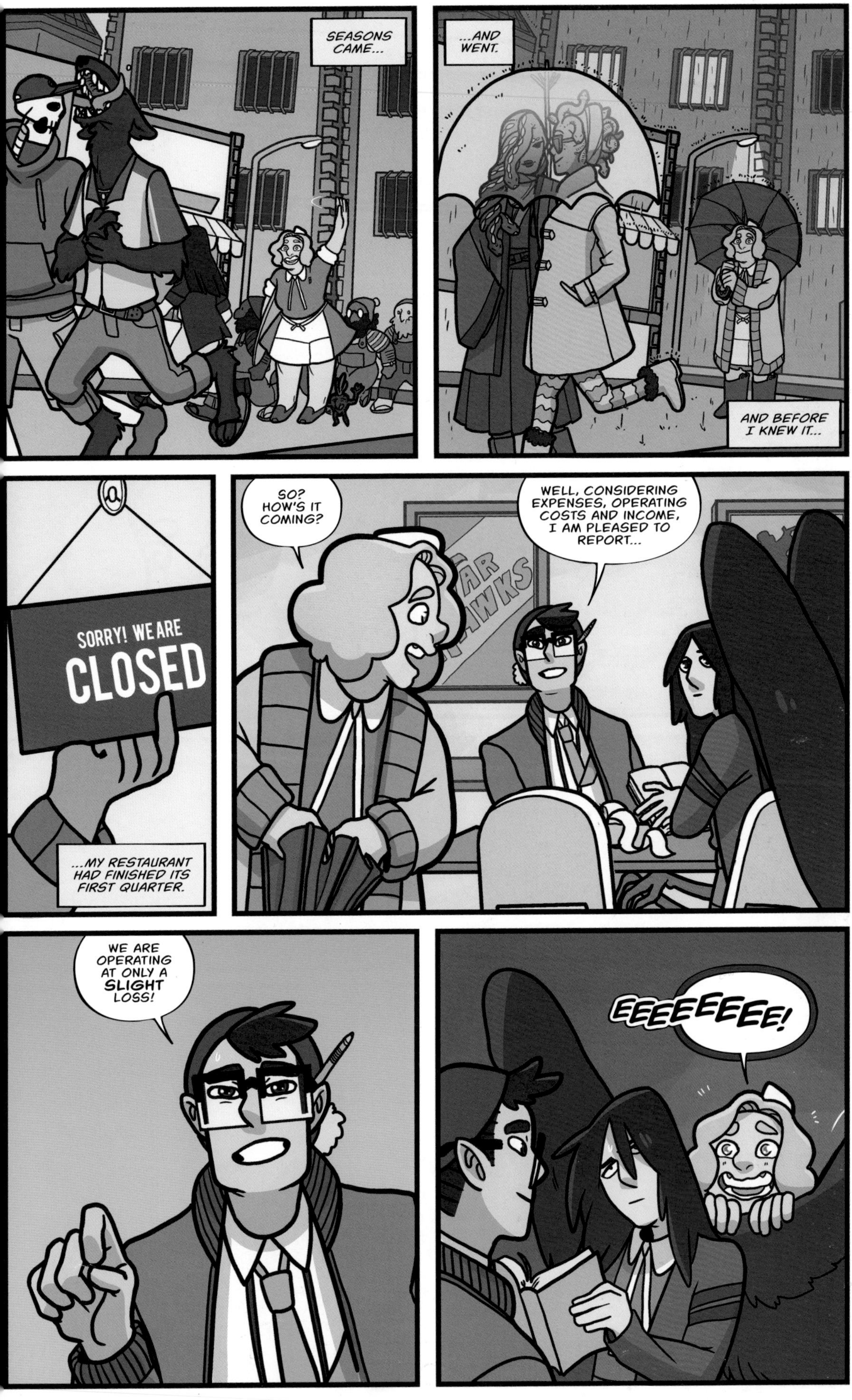

SEASONS CAME...
...AND WENT.
AND BEFORE I KNEW IT...
SORRY! WE ARE CLOSED
...MY RESTAURANT HAD FINISHED ITS FIRST QUARTER.
SO? HOW'S IT COMING?
WELL, CONSIDERING EXPENSES, OPERATING COSTS AND INCOME, I AM PLEASED TO REPORT...
WE ARE OPERATING AT ONLY A SLIGHT LOSS!
EEEEEEEEE!

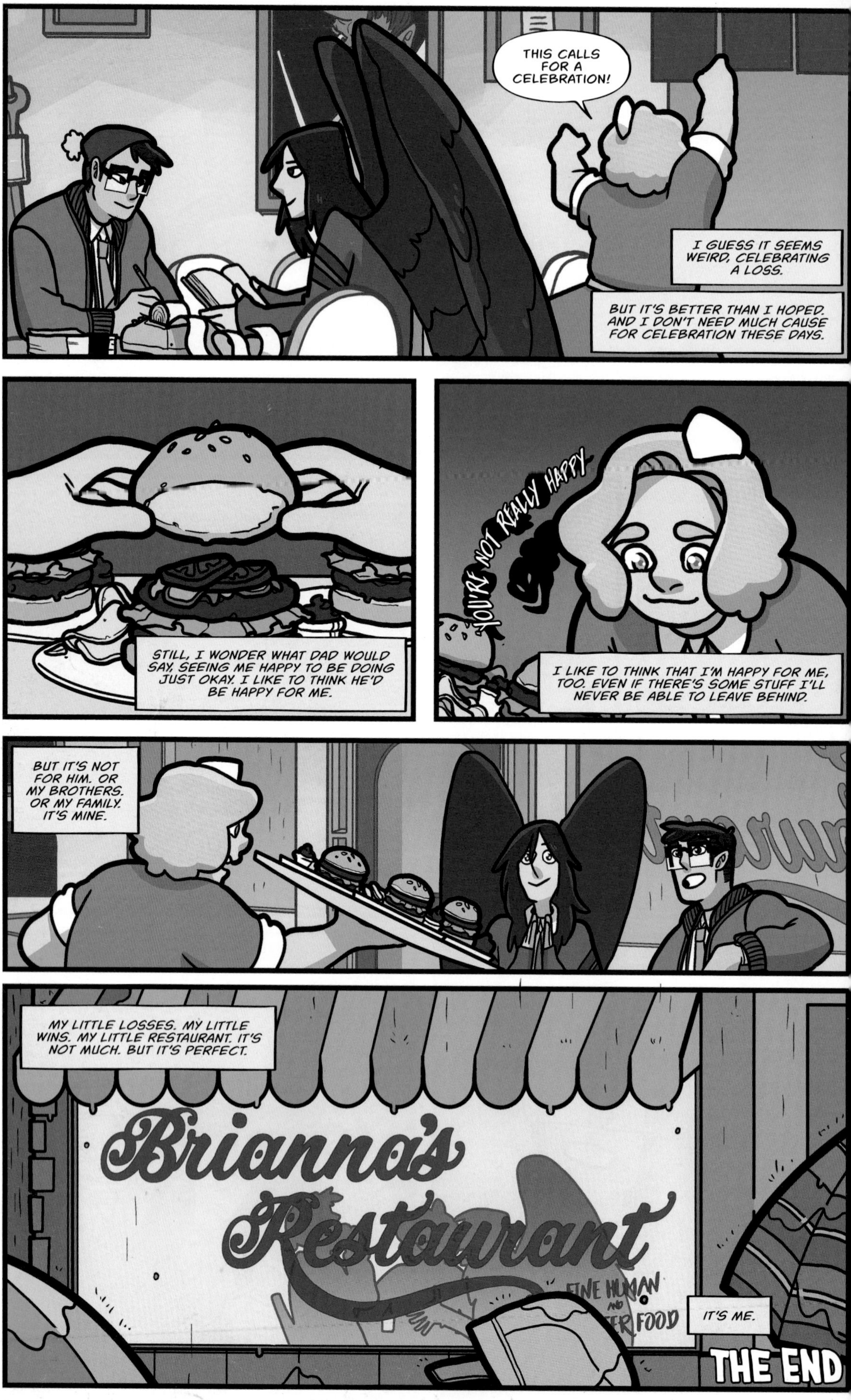
THIS CALLS FOR A CELEBRATION!
I GUESS IT SEEMS WEIRD, CELEBRATING A LOSS.
BUT IT'S BETTER THAN I HOPED. AND I DON'T NEED MUCH CAUSE FOR CELEBRATION THESE DAYS.
STILL, I WONDER WHAT DAD WOULD SAY, SEEING ME HAPPY TO BE DOING JUST OKAY. I LIKE TO THINK HE'D BE HAPPY FOR ME.
YOU'RE NOT REALLY HAPPY
I LIKE TO THINK THAT I'M HAPPY FOR ME, TOO. EVEN IF THERE'S SOME STUFF I'LL NEVER BE ABLE TO LEAVE BEHIND.
BUT IT'S NOT FOR HIM. OR MY BROTHERS. OR MY FAMILY. IT'S MINE.
MY LITTLE LOSSES. MY LITTLE WINS. MY LITTLE RESTAURANT. IT'S NOT MUCH. BUT IT'S PERFECT.
Brianna's Restaurant
IT'S ME.
THE END

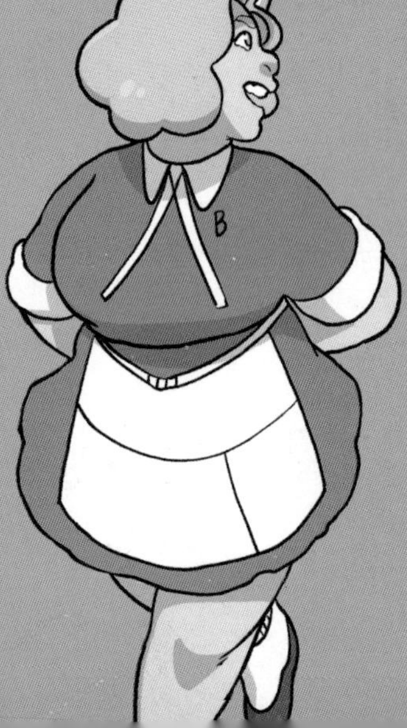
B

cover GALLERY

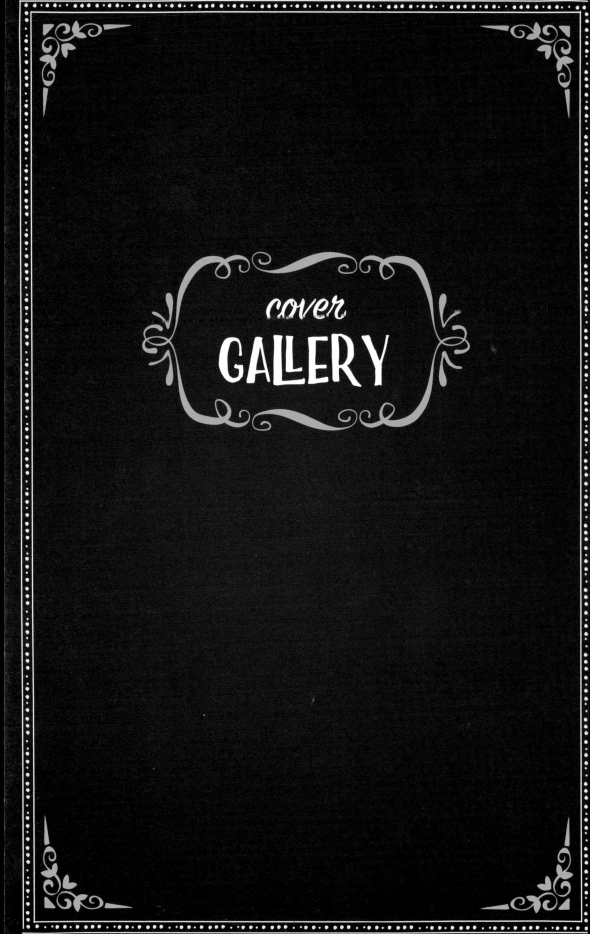

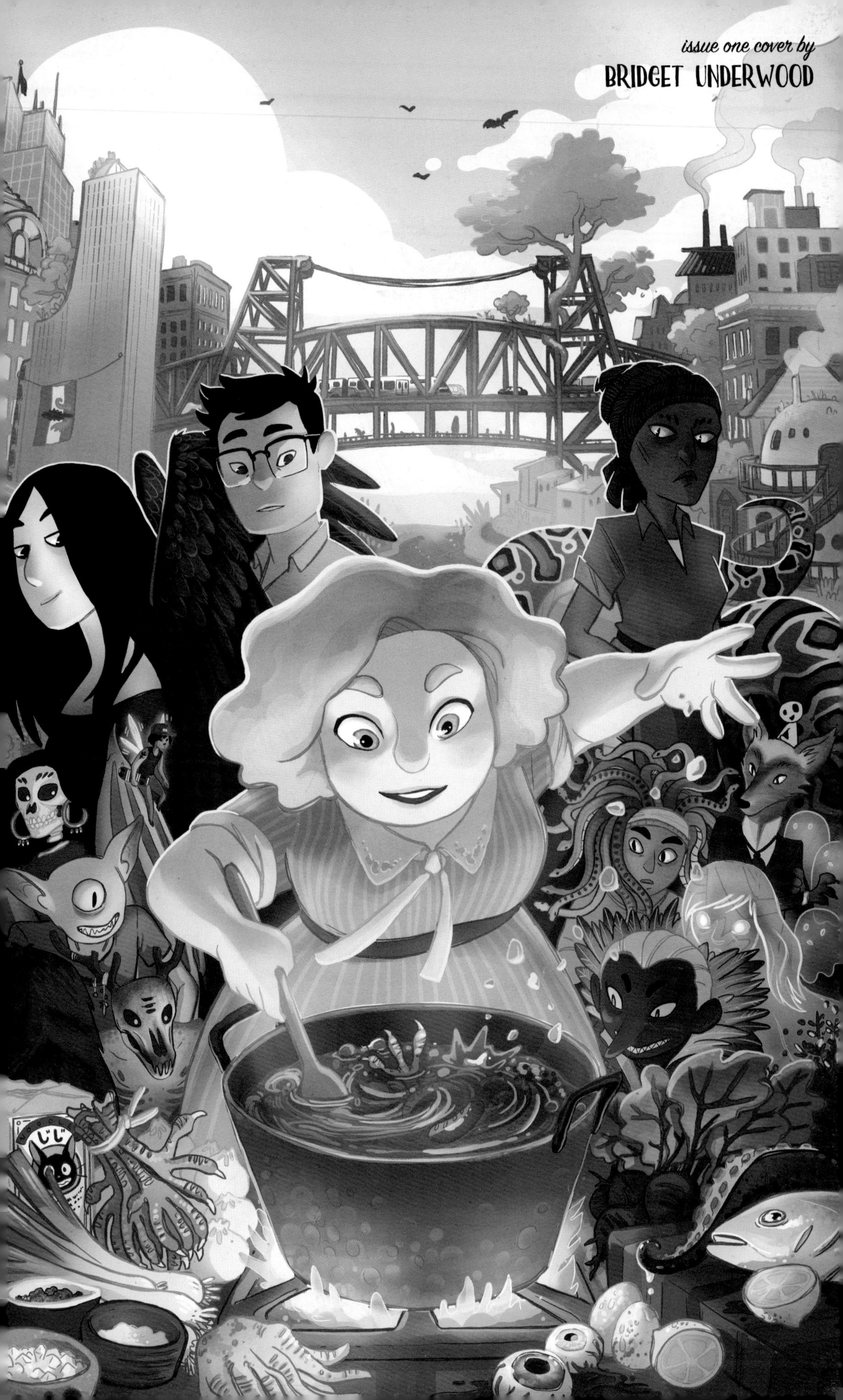
issue one cover by
BRIDGET UNDERWOOD

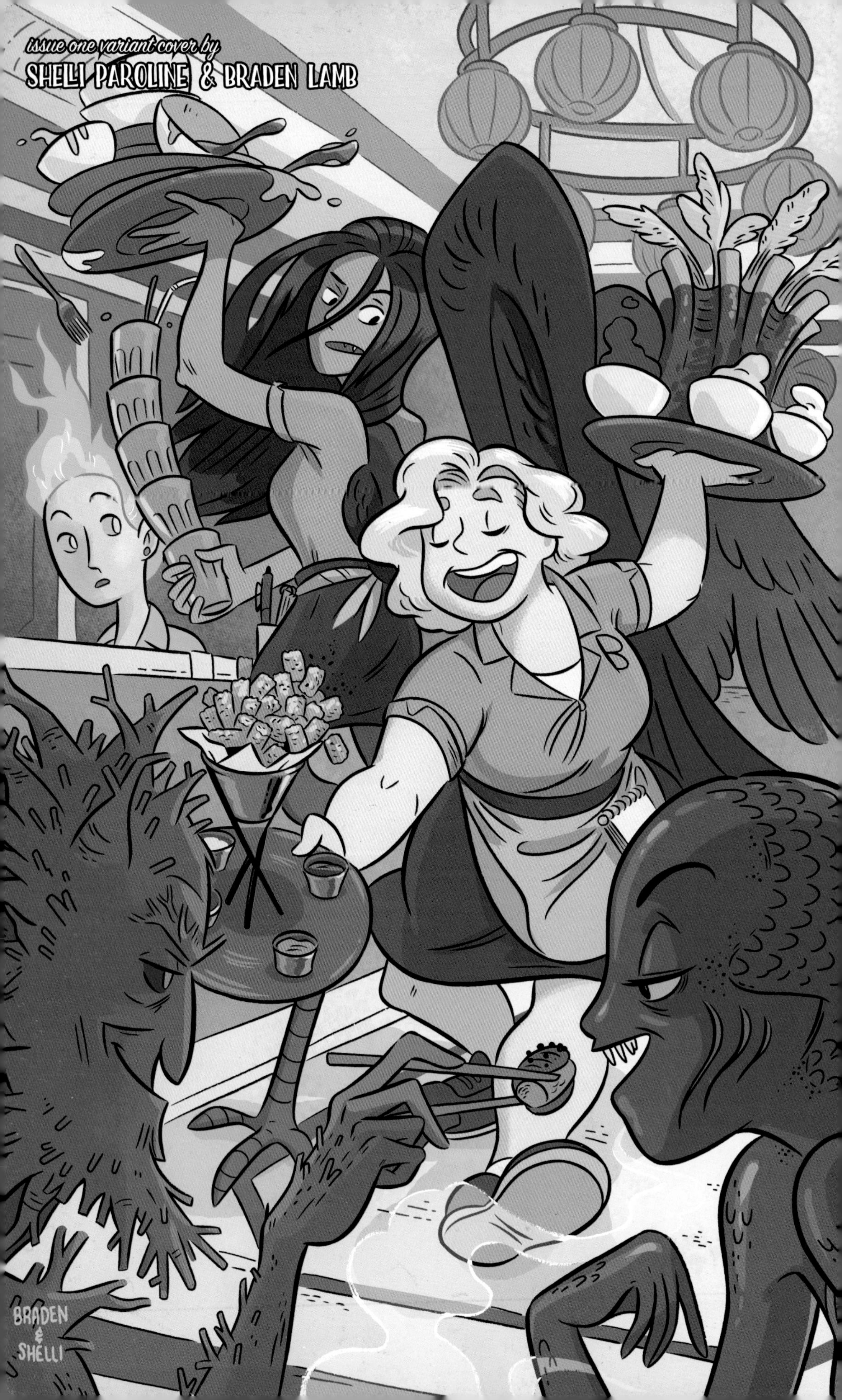
BRADEN
&
SHELLI

issue one variant cover by
SHELLI PAROLINE & BRADEN LAMB

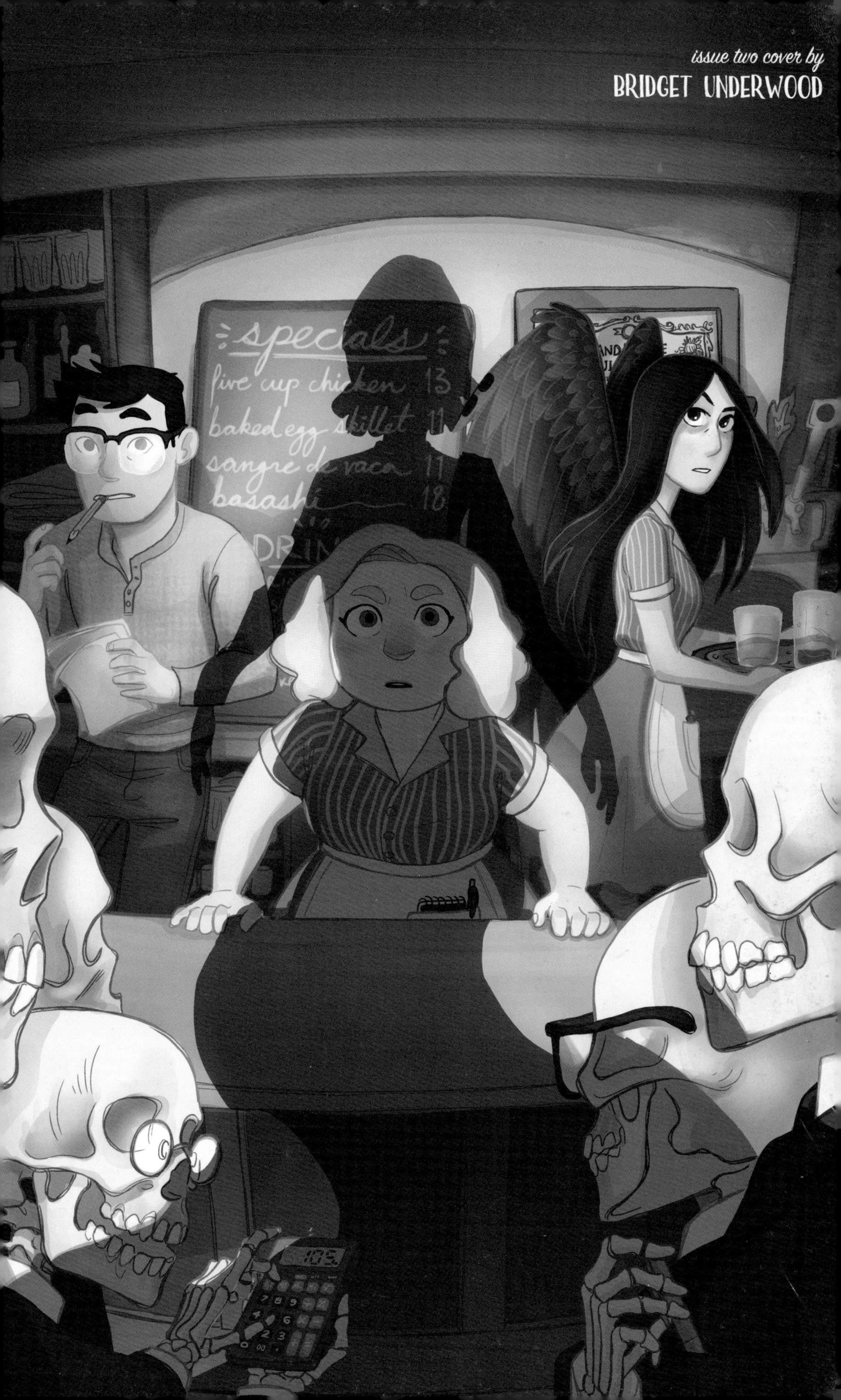
specials
five cup chicken 13
baked egg skillet 11
sangre de vaca 11
basashi 18

issue two cover by
BRIDGET UNDERWOOD

issue three cover by
BRIDGET UNDERWOOD

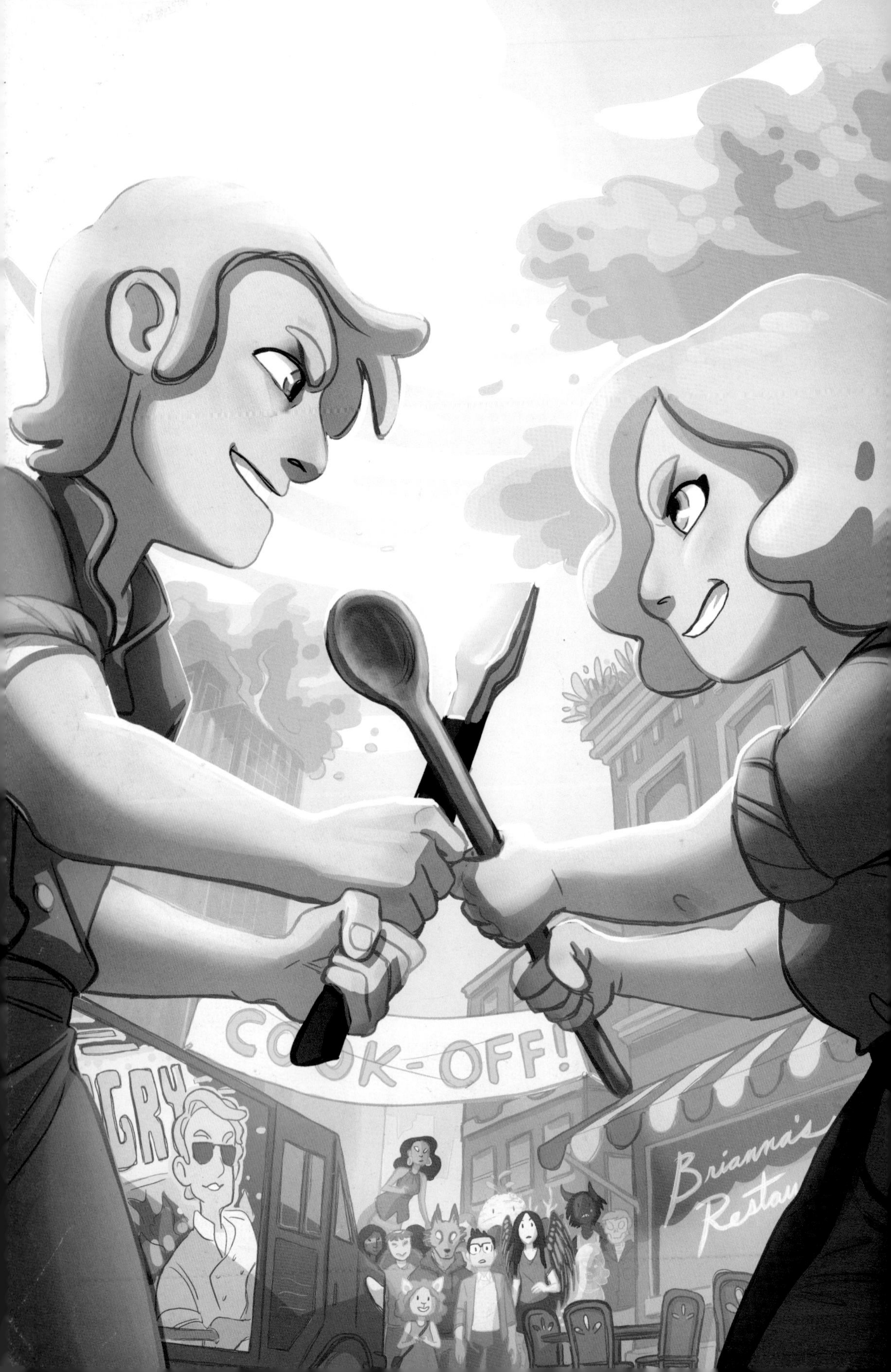
COOK-OFF!
Brianna's
Restau

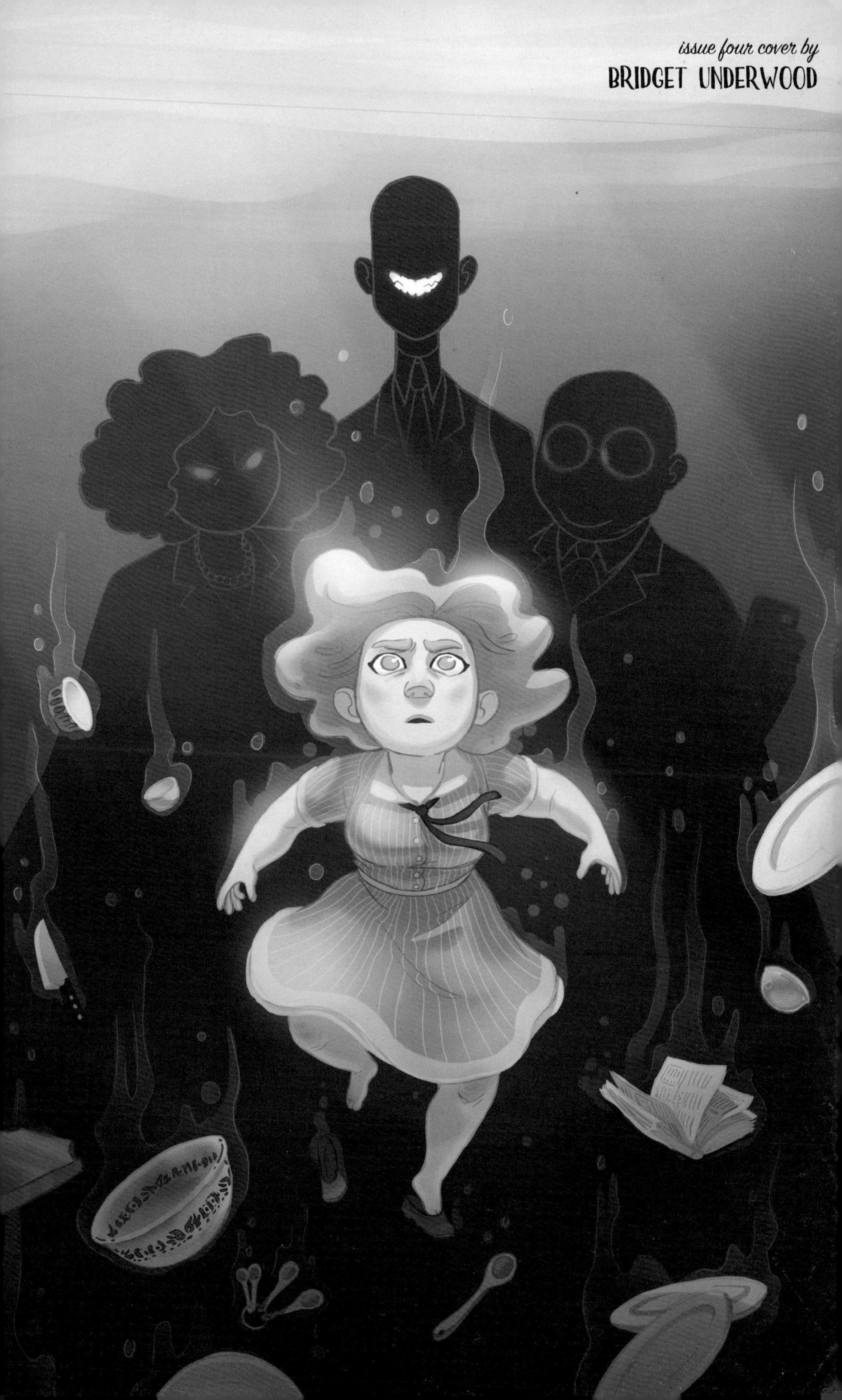

issue four cover by
BRIDGET UNDERWOOD

BRAZILIAN CHEESE WAFFLE BREAKFAST SANDWICHES

recipes provided by STEPHANIE GOLDFARB

Ingredients

For the Waffle Batter:
⅔ cup milk
½ cup butter, melted and cooled
1 egg
¼ teaspoon salt
1½ cups tapioca flour
¾ cup grated cheddar cheese

For the Breakfast Sandwich Fillings:
1 egg per serving
4 oz smoked salmon
1 cup arugula leaves, washed
1 avocado, sliced thin
Salt and pepper

Mix the milk, ¼ cup of the melted butter, egg and salt in a large bowl. Add the tapioca flour and cheddar cheese, and stir until the mixture is combined. Preheat a waffle iron. Use the extra melted butter to brush the inside of the iron. Ladle enough of the waffle mixture into the center of the iron to leave an inch of unfilled border. Close the waffle iron lid and cook the waffles for a few minutes, or until they are brown and crispy. Keep the cooked waffles warm in a 200 degree oven.

Fry the eggs until the whites are cooked, and the yolks still runny. Assemble the breakfast sandwiches by placing the egg, smoked salmon, and arugula leaves on top of one waffle. Top with slices of avocado, a pinch of salt, and another waffle. Cut the sandwich in half on the diagonal, and enjoy.

Stephanie Goldfarb is a Chicago-based cook specializing in seasonal, (mostly) vegetarian, and multi-regional cuisine. She appears regularly on *The Food Network* as a competitor representing home cooks everywhere. Stephanie also writes about food for Autostraddle.com and OyChicago.com.
http://www.sevenspecies.org/

Today's Special

BÁNH XÈO
SAVORY VIETNAMESE CRÊPES

Ingredients

For the Batter:
9 ounces rice flour
3 ounces all-purpose wheat flour
3 tsp dried turmeric
3 ½ cups water
1 14oz can full fat coconut milk
1 tsp salt
2 scallions, both white and
green parts sliced thin

For the Fillings:
3 tbs vegetable oil
½ lb ground chicken or pork (chef's choice)
1 onion, medium sized, thinly sliced
½ lb fresh shrimp without heads,
de-veined and de-shelled
1 lb pounds bean sprouts
½ cup fish sauce (clear brown)
½ cup soy sauce
2 tbs sugar
Juice of one lime

For the Garnish:
Fresh mint
Cilantro
Sliced fresh chile peppers
Fresh lime wedges
Romaine lettuce leaves

Combine all batter ingredients except scallions in a large bowl and let sit. Anywhere from 30 minutes to overnight is great. Add scallions only right before making the crêpes.

Heat a large skillet on medium-high heat with the vegetable oil. Add your chicken/pork and let brown for 5 minutes, or until the meat starts to caramelize. Add the onion and cook until soft. Add the shrimp and cook until they start to brown. Add a tablespoon of fish sauce and a tablespoon of soy sauce to the skillet to help release the delicious savory bits from the bottom of the pan.

Add 2 more tablespoons of oil to the pan. Pour in some batter and quickly tilt & rotate the pan so the batter is evenly spread. Add more batter if it wasn't enough to cover the pan. Add a handful of bean sprouts, and cover with a lid for 2-3 minutes, or until bean sprouts are slightly cooked. The batter should also be slightly cooked and transparent around the edges.

Meanwhile, make the dipping sauce. Combine the rest of the fish sauce, soy sauce, sugar, and lime juice in a small bowl and set aside.

Remove the lid, lower heat to medium and wait for the crêpe to become crisp. Fold in half, transfer to a plate and serve immediately with a plate of garnish and the dipping sauce. Use the romaine lettuce leaves to make a cup for pieces of the crepe and as much (or as little) garnish as you wish.

BUFFALO CHICKEN TATER TOT CASSEROLE

Ingredients

2 tsp canola oil
4 cooked chicken breasts, diced (about 2 pounds)
¾ cup butter
1 cup hot sauce (Frank's is a good option here, but any vinegar-based hot sauce works well too)

1 tsp garlic powder
1 tsp salt
1/2 cup crumbled blue cheese
1 package (1kg) frozen tater tots
1 cup grated cheddar cheese
¾ cup diced celery

Coat the chicken breasts in canola oil and season with a dash of salt and pepper. Sautee or grill the chicken until it is completely cooked, cut it into bite-sized pieces, and set aside.

Make the buffalo sauce by melting the butter in a saucepan on medium heat. Whisk in the hot sauce, garlic powder and salt. Let the sauce simmer for a few minutes and then remove from the heat and let cool to room temperature.

Preheat oven to 350F. Take ⅓ cup of buffalo sauce and set aside for later. Mix the remaining buffalo sauce with the cubed chicken and spread it in the bottom of a 13x9 casserole dish. Sprinkle the crumbled blue cheese on top of the buffalo chicken mixture.

Lay the tater tots lengthwise and in straight lines (rows), evenly on the buffalo chicken and blue cheese. Drizzle the reserved buffalo sauce on top of the tots and sprinkle with grated cheese.

Bake in the 350F oven for 30-45 minutes, or until the tots are crispy and the cheese is melted. Remove from the oven and let rest for 5 minutes. Sprinkle with diced celery before serving.

Today's Special

CALAMARI SUSHI

Ingredients

2 cups sushi rice
2 tbsp rice wine vinegar
1 tbsp sugar
1 tbsp salt
6-8 sheets nori
8-10 stalks asparagus

1 avocado
¾ lb calamari (bodies and tentacles, detached)
1 cup flour
¼ cup mayo, scooped into a Ziploc bag
Sriracha

Rinse calamari well. Cut the bodies in half lengthwise, then cut each half into skinny strips, and add them to the tentacles. Rinse them again until the water runs clear, then pat dry. Place them in a fine mesh strainer set over a bowl and leave in the fridge for a few hours (or overnight) to dry out a bit.

Meanwhile, prepare the rice: Rinse the rice well by soaking it in a large bowl with cold water for 5 minutes. Drain and repeat this process two or three times until the water is clear. Combine the 2 cups of rice with 2 cups of water and bring it to a boil over high heat. Once it's boiling, set it to low, cover, and let it simmer for 15 minutes. Then take it off the heat and let it sit for 10 minutes. Fluff with a fork.

Mix the vinegar, sugar and salt in a large bowl. Tumble the cooked sushi rice into the bowl with the mix and toss together until the rice is coated. Let it cool. Cut the avocado into skinny slices.

Meanwhile, dust the calamari in some flour and fry it in a few inches of oil (we used olive oil, but you can use vegetable oil, sunflower oil, etc.) You only need to fry it for a few minutes until the crust is a light golden brown — don't overcook! Set aside.

To assemble: Lay a sheet of nori on your cutting board in the landscape/hamburger bun position. Dip your fingers into a bit of water to keep the rice from sticking to your hands. A handful at a time, press the rice onto the sheet of nori, allowing for a small strip of bare nori to remain at the top. At the end closest to you, place a few slivers of avocado, a line of mayo (snip the corner off the bag and pipe out), a line of Sriracha, and a few pieces of calamari.

At the stuffed side, start carefully rolling away from you, tucking the edge underneath. When you're almost at the edge, use your finger to dab a little water on the naked edge of the nori to seal the end of the roll. Rock the roll lightly with your hand to make sure the edge sticks.

Cut the roll in half, then cut each half into halves, then those quarters into halves so that you get 8 perfect pieces of sushi. Enjoy!

DISCOVER
EXPLOSIVE NEW WORLDS

Adventure Time
Pendleton Ward and Others
Volume 1
ISBN: 978-1-60886-280-1 | $14.99 US
Volume 2
ISBN: 978-1-60886-323-5 | $14.99 US
Adventure Time: Islands
ISBN: 978-1-60886-972-5 | $9.99 US

The Amazing World of Gumball
Ben Bocquelet and Others
Volume 1
ISBN: 978-1-60886-488-1 | $14.99 US
Volume 2
ISBN: 978-1-60886-793-6 | $14.99 US

Brave Chef Brianna
Sam Sykes, Selina Espiritu
ISBN: 978-1-68415-050-2 | $14.99 US

Mega Princess
Kelly Thompson, Brianne Drouhard
ISBN: 978-1-68415-007-6 | $14.99 US

The Not-So Secret Society
Matthew Daley, Arlene Daley,
Wook Jin Clark
ISBN: 978-1-60886-997-8 | $9.99 US

Over the Garden Wall
Patrick McHale, Jim Campbell
and Others
Volume 1
ISBN: 978-1-60886-940-4 | $14.99 US
Volume 2
ISBN: 978-1-68415-006-9 | $14.99 US

Steven Universe
Rebecca Sugar and Others
Volume 1
ISBN: 978-1-60886-706-6 | $14.99 US
Volume 2
ISBN: 978-1-60886-796-7 | $14.99 US

Steven Universe & The Crystal Gems
ISBN: 978-1-60886-921-3 | $14.99 US

Steven Universe: Too Cool for School
ISBN: 978-1-60886-771-4 | $14.99 US

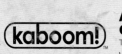

AVAILABLE AT YOUR LOCAL COMICS SHOP AND BOOKSTORE
To find a comics shop in your area, call 1-888-266-4226
WWW.BOOM-STUDIOS.COM

ADVENTURE TIME, OVER THE GARDEN WALL, STEVEN UNIVERSE, CARTOON NETWORK, the logos, and all related characters and elements are trademarks of and © Cartoon Network. (S17) THE AMAZING WORLD OF GUMBALL, CARTOON NETWORK, the logos and all related characters and elements are trademarks of and © Turner Broadcasting System Europe Limited, Cartoon Network. (S17) All works © their respective creators and licensors. KaBOOM!™ and the KaBOOM! logo are trademarks of Boom Entertainment, Inc. All rights reserved.